3.00

Nightmare Blue

Gardner Dozois & George Alec Effinger

A BERKLEY MEDALLION BOOK
published by
BERKLEY PUBLISHING CORPORATION

FOR:
DAVE HARTWELL, DAVE HARRIS,
AND DON KELLER

Published by arrangement with the authors.

Berkley Publishing Corporation
200 Madison Avenue
New York, New York 10016

SBN 425-02819-4

*BERKLEY MEDALLION BOOKS are published by
Berkley Publishing Corporation
200 Madison Avenue
New York, N.Y. 10016*

BERKLEY MEDALLION BOOKS ® TM 757,375

Printed in the United States of America

Berkley Medallion Edition, OCTOBER, 1975

Chapter One

Karl Jaeger was a dead man.

He knew it. The Aensalords, shouting and laughing inhumanly behind him, knew it very well indeed; they knew it as a certainty as irreversible as the rising of the sun. The grim-faced men and women who waited silently in the green-decked halls of Schwäbisch Gmünd knew it, while they waited for his corpse to be dragged back. They had known it all along, in fact, with the resignation that comes of long, painful experience.

The Dktar, the Aensahounds, which salivated in their greedy pursuit, following his track implacably across fen and brush, knew it best of all.

Only Karl Jaeger's body didn't know it.

His legs continued to carry him scrambling across the countryside. His body continued to stagger on with idiot energy, long after his mind, trapped within, had given up the fight and settled down blankly to wait for death.

Jaeger's foot tangled in a thick black root; he went down heavily amid a flurry and rustle of dead leaves. Grimly, mechanically, he raised himself to his feet and stumbled painfully on, hardly noticing or caring that he had fallen.

As he ran, most of his attention was directed to the rear, not forward. Behind him were no natural sounds at all: no owls or nighttime birds, no chirping insect songs, no quick animal scurries among the dead hedges. The landscape was peculiarly silent, black, extinct. The horrible quiet that surrounded him made him feel even more unreal, although the jagged outlines of barren trees leaned against the sky with lunatic clarity. Within the nightmarish prison of the blasted forest he was friendless, but he was not alone.

He strained eagerly, striving to hear the least sound, anything that would tell him that the Dktar were not already upon him, ready to make their silent, fatal leap. And yet he also dreaded hearing a sound, because a noise would mean that they were still behind him, still on his trail, as inescapable as death itself. Jaeger ran hopelessly, trying only to keep the distance between himself and the hunting monsters, knowing that the margin narrowed with every frantic breath.

The Aensahounds bayed. It was a loud note that carried over the dwindling distance between them and their pray: crystalline the sound was, ringing, intelligent—like a bell tolling, a funeral bell, but a chime of indefinite duration. It was a howling noise, wailing, wavering, moaning—unearthly and terrifying under the bright stars of a clear, moonlit autumn night.

As he fled through the skeleton of the forest, Jaeger discovered that he could still observe himself dispassionately. He wondered if that might be a sign of insanity, under the circumstances: the coolness with which he watched his panic build to a final, forlorn scream of surrender. He was muttering now, gasping and whimpering, mouthing strange, unintelligible phrases that only the deep animal core of his mind could interpret.

Yet even while he murmured these words, wrenched right from the basic soul-stuff of his personality, Jaeger, in a small, detached segment of his mind, wondered what the devil he was muttering about anyway; he realized that the scream had built up pressure, was straining against his tightly clenched teeth. It would surely give his position away and bring the Dktar down upon him twice as swiftly, but somehow it didn't seem to matter anymore . . .

A tremor shook his body; he quivered like a cornered animal and his lips drew back from his teeth in a silent snarl. The Aensahounds bayed again behind him, closer now. The scream was pressing against his teeth, leaking out hissing through the edges of his lips like a whistling teakettle just beginning to boil.

Any second now they would break from cover behind him, and he would see the horrible black shapes begin their deadly leap, and then he would go truly mad—

The trees spun dizzily around Jaeger. For a moment the night seemed to dance, and the cold stars above spiraled into tight, pale coils of light; then he hit the water with a stinging splash and sank down and down. For many seconds he did not understand what had happened. He cried out, choking in the dark water of the stream.

Jaeger floundered, thrashing desperately until his feet found solid bottom, and then he stood, panting.

The water was cold; it stung him like a thousand tiny ice-needles jabbed into his naked flesh, and the sudden shock of it was like a quick, bright light flashed into his eyes. The scream died in his throat and settled reluctantly back into his chest, grumbling.

Like a man waking from a bad dream, Jaeger shook his head. In his panicky flight, he had stumbled over the edge of a weed-choked embankment and fallen perhaps four feet into a small stream. The water ran fairly deep at that point, deep enough that he avoided a serious injury.

Jaeger wondered how much noise he had made, tumbling and splashing into the water. Had he shouted in fear? He could not remember. He had regained his self-control, but had he also invited his hunters to the capture?

The Dktar bayed one more time, even closer than before. Jaeger felt a brief resurgence of panic, and fought it down grimly. He had gone that way before, and had nearly lost all hope for survival because of it. If anything could get him out of this, it would be a coolly logical brain, not one fogged and muddled with terror.

Jaeger stirred; he ought to be moving. He sloshed his way through the chest-deep stream to the opposite bank. Mere flight wouldn't help; he had proven to himself that it was impossible to outrun the Aensahounds even when he was urged along by the whips of deepest primal fear. He had been absurdly ill-prepared for this job; in retrospect, his mission in the sector of the Aensa seemed vague and trivial. What real information did he or anyone have about the secretive traders from space? Now his assignment—no, damn it, his *life*—appeared lost because of the little and useless data that he had.

He had to find a weakness in the Aensa, something that he could exploit. He had to come up with some clever stunt; there might be something easy enough to devise at the worn oak desk in his office, but it was frantically improbable as he ran for his life. If only they hadn't come upon him so quickly. If only he had known that his blindcoat would fail to deceive the alien eyes of the Dktar. If only his casual habit of traveling light hadn't persuaded him to leave behind the rifles and grenades he had first considered; not, he reminded himself, that rifles and grenades would have any effect against the electronic defenses of the Aensa or their monstrous servants.

Jaeger scrambled up the muddy bank. He tore his way through the thorny bushes at the top, ignoring the bloody scratches they made. He needed something that he could do *here.* Something he could do *now.* Swiftly he evaluated everything that he had brought with him, everything that he was wearing upon his body, everything in the dark forest around him, searching for a weapon.

If the Dktar or their masters, the Aensalords, had no weaknesses that he knew about, perhaps he could use one of their strengths against them. The basic theory of oriental combat; certainly that was a smug enough, glib enough solution. Now find one! Everything so far had failed: the blindcoat had not worked, the white noise generators had not masked the racket of Jaeger's flight. It was obvious that the Aensa's senses were either much more efficient or different altogether. It was possible that the Aensa had senses that he could not even imagine.

But it was also possible that some of their senses were like those of Terran creatures. Maybe enough like them, maybe not.

Jaeger had the glimmer of an idea.

He hunkered down on the forest path—taking the chance that the Aensahounds were far enough behind to give him a couple of minutes grace—and unslung the bulky camera bag from his shoulders. How he had cursed the heavy awkwardness of the thing as he ran! If he'd had even one free second to do it in, he would have tossed the bag away as an encumbrance. He had not had that one free second. Now perhaps, the lack of that second would prove to be the thing that saved him, because he still had the camera bag, ready to hand when inspiration struck and required it as its single and indispensable prop.

The camera within the bag was one of the newest models available, able to take hundreds of three-dimensional pictures before it was necessary to reload. It didn't use film. Instead, the images were etched directly into a tiny, complex crystal filament. When the filament had reached its practical limit of information storage, the photographer removed the filament and dropped it into a small vial of powerful chemical fixative that would freeze the molecular structure of the crystal into the already registered configurations, forever.

Eventually, in twenty years or so, someone would get around to designing a newer model of the same camera that would do all this automatically within the camera casing, at the touch of a button. At present, though, the changing of the filament had to be done by hand, which required the photographer to carry with him a number of screw-top vials of sloppy, strong-smelling fixative.

Jaeger held a vial of fixative up to the wan starlight.

He remembered how overpowering and dizzying the fixative was to even his numbed, city-dweller senses in confined quarters, how its strong chemical reek had bitten painfully into his nose . . .

The Aensahounds bayed behind, the screaming howl of their voices shrill with unspeakable yearning and fierce triumph. Jaeger clutched the small vial even tighter. Its contents grew in importance as he listened to the monsters' hideous calls. The fixative was his only chance. It was all that stood between him and an unimaginably horrible death. He dared not think about that. He wiped the entire possibility from his mind with an effort of will and concentrated on honing the details of his plan. Nothing else existed for him, not the forest of dead trees, not his cold, wet clothing, certainly not his pursuers.

Unnaturally calm, Jaeger reflected carefully for a few

more seconds, then made up his mind. He spun on his heel, stalking hurriedly away into the brush at a right angle to the trail he had been following.

The howl of the Dktar slashed at his ears, the sound now edged with a terrifying undertone of lustful gibbering and moaning. They were just across the stream. This was it.

Jaeger wrenched the stopper from the vial and dashed its contents on the ground around him. Then in one great leap he jumped far to the side and circled widely to take a concealed position near his original trail. His footsteps had been muffled as well as he could hope for by the needles of the forest's pine trees. By human standards, he had made no noise. By the standards of the Aensa, it made no difference.

He could run no more. His mind was as exhausted as his body; he could only wait, lying flat on his belly in the tall weeds, watching the trail from behind the gnarled roots of a great old tree. His thoughts drifted in his weariness, and his fatigue smothered even the grotesquely excited cries of the hunting Aensahounds. He remembered what Dark Lightning had shown him the morning before he left on this mission.

The Dark Lightning that Jaeger owned was a Kurasu model, about three years old. It had none of the newer features that had been introduced by Ford, but Jaeger was satisfied with it. He had been more apprehensive about this mission than usual. Dark Lightning had sensed his fear, had measured his heartbeat and respiration as he leaned back in the padded chair, had read his blood constituents through his earlobes, had decided which program would be the most beneficial and therapeutic. In less than five seconds after sitting in Dark Lightning's comfortable reclining chair, Jaeger was unconscious.

He was walking along a narrow dirt path. The sun was shining, warm and bright in a cloudless blue sky. The air smelled of moist earth and flowers, a smell he remembered instantly from his childhood. The smell and the warm sunshine made him feel filled to the brim with happiness. He was dressed in a loose robe, an old garment, and he was barefoot. His hair was long and unbound, and his beard was in need of a trim. He began climbing a small grass-covered hill, and he leaned on his wooden staff. After a moment, he saw a tall, strong warrior coming toward him on the path. The other man was dressed in the uniform of the Emperor's guards, and carried a huge, gleaming-bright sword. "Hullo, old man," cried the soldier, acknowledging Jaeger's acquired character of age and wisdom.

"Good day, warrior," said Jaeger. He wanted to continue his walk after the initial greeting, but the man would not step out of Jaeger's way.

"I would ask you a question," said the soldier. "It is rare that I meet venerable sages in my occupation."

"So?" said Jaeger with a brief smile. "I find that it is the same with me."

"Then tell me, is there really a heaven after death? And a hell? I must be prepared for a sudden and violent departure from this world, but I cannot accept that fact as I should."

Jaeger laughed derisively. "That is because you are so stupid," he said. "You are much too brainless even to attempt serious thought. I would wager that you wouldn't know which end of that sword to use."

The soldier was enraged. He tore the sword from its place and raised it above his head. Before he began the deadly downward stroke, Jaeger raised a hand and smiled. "There," he said, "you have opened the gate of Hell."

The warrior stared, comprehension growing in his expression. He bowed and put his sword back in his sash. "There," said Jaeger, "you have opened the gate of Heaven."

Its program completed, Dark Lightning brought Jaeger back to full consciousness, theoretically filling the man with inner peace and confidence. Now, as Jaeger waited fearfully in the damp coolness of the autumn night, he could only frown ruefully at the memory of the vision. "The gate of Hell, all right," he murmured. "But these bastards will be damned if they're going to yield to my superior wisdom. I'll see the gate of Heaven soon enough, but only because I'll be bouncing off it with my head in my hands."

The baying of the Aensahounds rose to a deafening pitch, seeming to set Jaeger's brain echoing painfully. Even if the chemical didn't work, he could still fight. He would have no chance at all against the Aensahounds, of course, but perhaps he could get his hands on one of the Aensalords themselves. Then at least the odds might be fairly even. Jaeger told himself this, over and over, trying to believe it. He wanted to believe that he could have a chance, at least to take someone with him.

Something huge and incredibly evil brushed closely by in the dark.

A second later, Jaeger tasted blood and realized that he had bitten his lip. He didn't remember doing it; all that he could recall was something tall and black, with a sickly blue glimmer from long fangs. The pale light flickered, disembodied, where a head should have been. The thing padded silently past, multiple rows of legs ending in foot-long claws clicking slightly as they bit firmly into the forest turf.

Jaeger forced himself into calmness and fought to remain motionless. The taste of his own blood was salty in his mouth; he wondered if the Dktar could smell it. His plan depended on their unearthly senses being too engrossed in their task, so aroused that they might overlook him just long enough to reach his trap.

Close on the pack of Dktar came something else.

It was tall and black and silent, and moved through the dreadful landscape like a solidified shadow. Only a slight golden glow that played flickeringly about its brow served to mark its presence as it slipped by. The aura that surrounded it was chilling, numbing, almost a physical cold. The Aensalord did not rustle the leaves of the forest in passing.

Another Aensalord separated from the midnight background and spoke to its companion in a rasping buzz. They disappeared in the direction that the Dktar had taken, seeming to glide rather than walk through the night.

After a moment, Jaeger noticed that he was suffocating. He released his involuntarily pent-up breath in an audible sigh.

There was silence.

Jaeger's fingers curled into tightly clenched fists. He drew his legs under him slowly. The Aensahounds were too close to their prey now for baying; the forest was hushed and still under a brooding cloak of fear.

Soon now the Dktar would be hitting the chemical, and if that failed to stop them, they would break from cover to his right a few seconds later. They would sweep hugely down upon him—

So far, thought Jaeger, the plan was working. So far, the plan meant nothing in the way of his survival. He had no way of guessing what results his action might have; he could not watch the Dktar, he could not listen to them to judge how much longer he might have to live. There was only waiting.

The silence of the hunting beasts was more frightening than their grotesque baying had been. Jaeger chewed his lower lip. He would not have believed, only a few short minutes ago, that he would have been grateful to hear those creatures crying aloud. Jaeger strained his eyes. He thought that he saw pale blue glimmers through the massive black limbs of the dead trees. He told himself that the golden flickers were circling toward him, getting closer. He could not be certain. He squeezed his eyes closed and rubbed the lids. His fingers were stiff. His skin prickled.

There was no movement. There was no sound. A tune ran through Jaeger's mind, over and over. He smiled coldly; even in this situation, his mind could still find trivial things to occupy itself with. Then, of course, it was possible that replaying the tune was a kind of defense, a distraction to prevent irreparable emotional damage. The tune was simple but elusive; it was the kind of melody that Jaeger could rehearse in his mind easily enough, but which he could never successfully hum or whistle. He heard the tune played on a piano. Jaeger sighed. The fingers on the keyboard were long and slender. The girl was as joyful as the tune, with the same lurking hint of unmeasurable sorrow. The music was "The Maple Leaf Rag" by Scott Joplin, an American composer who had lived a little over two centuries before. The girl was Nati. If Jaeger lived through this, he promised himself, the first thing he would do would be to have Nati play the tune for him. Then he'd tell her that he loved her.

He thought he heard a twig snap.

He decided that if he got back to Nürnberg, he could let the piano music wait. Nati seemed very far away.

Never before in his life had Jaeger wanted a drink so badly. He shook his head at that thought, too. He wondered, while he waited helplessly, how much longer his body could go on operating on a full panic-alert. He had been in more than his share of difficult situations before; after all, that was what he was paid for. He had been sure on several different occasions that he would never get out of the dilemma alive; why, then, was he so horribly afraid now? Death was death, and he had never been particularly reluctant before. Why were his legs so weak, his hands so unsteady, his stomach so cold and empty? Was it only that the Aensa were more than human enemies, the monster-shapes of bad dreams? Jaeger couldn't make that kind of decision, not under those circumstances. He only knew that he was more afraid than he ought to be, and that he would happily trade his entire interest in the Aensa territory for three fingers of Jack Daniels.

The forest seemed to explode.

Dead trunks of trees geysered from the forest ahead, uprooted by the scrambling multiple legs of the Dktar, as the Aensahounds went mad. A howl hacked its way through Jaeger's head like a dull axe, so much louder than any of the others that it seemed to kill all his own thoughts. The leafy top of a small tree some twenty yards to the side quivered, swayed violently, and then toppled with slow-motion grace, tearing a gaping hole in the skyline; one of the Aensahounds must have thrown its full, ponderous weight against it in a blind effort to escape from agony.

Jaeger showed his teeth in a satisfied grimace; the chemical must have had some serious unforeseen effect on the Dktar's metabolism. All the better. Jaeger was a mouse, an easy prey that had turned a searchlight into the staring eyes of a night-hunting owl. The chemical was unpleasant enough to the dull senses of a human being. For the Dktar, who knew what pain it had caused? Perhaps the fixative was more than an annoyance; perhaps the stuff was as lethal to the Aensa as chlorine gas was to Jaeger. He could not hang around long enough to experiment. The Dktar would be in poor shape to track him now, but they might soon recover. With luck,

Jaeger might manage to survive until dawn, after all.

The noise of the Aensahounds and the confused shouts of their masters reached a pain-filled climax; Jaeger slipped quietly through the tangled underbrush until the clamor had dwindled behind. He was fairly confident that his passage could no longer be heard. Then he turned his face to the north and began to run in an easy, loping stride toward the distant edge of Aensa territory—and safety.

When Corcail Sendijen had been younger, his parents had tried to frighten him into obedience with stories of the Aensa. Corcail Sendijen had been frightened, surely enough, just as most of the immature beings on countless worlds were frightened. The Aensa were no fanciful dream-bogey; they were real, they walked the dirt-packed streets or rode the vast highway networks of most of the civilized planets in the galaxy. Of course, the terrible Aensalords had little interest in the behavior patterns of the individual offspring of their host cultures. Corcail Sendijen never thought of that, though. He was always afraid that some moonless night, a tall, black Aensalord would climb through the round ventilator of the nursery and take Corcail Sendijen off to some Aensa fortress, there to spend the rest of his life as a slave of malevolent enchantment. Corcail Sendijen was frightened by his parents, like most of the immature beings in the surrounding segment of the galaxy. And, like his distant cousins, that was not really enough to make him obey.

At the age of forty, when Corcail Sendijen was approaching his sexual maturity, he entered the physical paralysis that characterized the adolescence of his species. It grew on him gradually; he had been warned, of course, of what to expect, by his teachers, by his parents, and by the priests at the temple. But their language had always been vague and evasive. They spoke of a kind of nervousness which he might expect, a not-altogether unpleasant tension. Corcail Sendijen was apprehensive. What did they mean? He wanted to be prepared, if this thing were really inevitable. It was no use. The teachers and the priests all said that further details might be indelicate and referred him to his parents. His parents were disturbed by his questions. They suggested that it was the duty of the teachers and priests to answer them. His father insisted that he did not want to be responsible for providing inexact or misleading answers. Finally, Corcail Sendijen gave up asking.

Over the period of several months the paralysis grew. He was virtually helpless; he remained on his sleeping platform, which was moved from the communal nursery. He was fed by his mother, given water by his father, but otherwise left alone during the long days and quiet nights. Soon his mother and father stopped feeding him completely. They came in at the regular hour, but left the bowls close to Corcail Sendijen's side, as though he were able simply to roll over and feed himself. He begged his parents to give him food and water; they would not answer. They did not speak to him again for many days.

At last, the hunger and thirst becoming unbearable, Corcail Sendijen struggled to reach the tempting bowls. His tentacles, which for the most part had hung flacid and useless during his infancy and childhood, waggled in the direction of the bowls. Corcail Sendijen realized that if he could coordinate his movements, he could bring the food and water close enough to eat and drink. He worked for hours on end; soon his tentacles had developed a suppleness and strength he had never known before. He easily reached the bowls which his parents replaced each day. He felt a fulfilling sense of pride and well-being; the paralysis ceased to be a trial. He passed the hours in serious thought; his parents spoke with him during their visits, and answered his many questions.

He learned that the paralysis had been drug-induced, that the development of his tentacles would have occurred in due time, as the result of normal activity and exercise. The adults of Corcail Sendijen's world had agreed that the drugged procedure was warranted by the threat of the Aensa. Now the young were encouraged to mature at an earlier age, and with the added effect of increased self-reliance and courage. The best of them were sent off for special training against the Aensa. Those who lacked the will and determination to live were sadly but easily weeded out. Corcail Sendijen understood his parents' explanations, and he was grateful for the training they had given him as a child, which enabled him to pass the barrier into adulthood.

"Then the bedtime stories of the Aensa weren't completely untrue?" he asked.

"No," said Corcail Sendijen's father. "The Aensa have moved from world to world, stealing the best from each, leaving nothing but dust and ruins behind. Their method is slow. There is little violence—there are more kinds of warfare than mere armed combat. The Aensa prefer psychological and economic destruction. And the Central Council has become weak and divided—they will not interfere with the Aensa without open proof of aggression. They fear to risk war with the Aensa Empire, except as a last resort. So the civilized worlds fall slowly one by one, and our galactic civilization gradually disintegrates. One day the Central Council will no longer be strong enough to make war on the Aensa, even as a threat held in potential. On that day all civilization will end, even as ours is about to be ended. The Aensa have won themselves a beachhead on our world, and it is only a matter of years before we, too, will be mindless beasts whose only purpose is in serving those dark lords."

"Don't frighten the boy," Corcail Sendijen's mother had said quietly.

"Don't frighten the boy?" cried his father. "For years that's all we did. We told him the Aensa would crawl through the drains to snatch him away to their stronghold. We told him they'd sneak up in the night if he wasn't a good boy, and cut off all his tentacles. We scared him witless, for no good reason. Now we have to scare him again, for the best reason in the world." Corcail Sendijen's mother looked like she was about to cry. She turned away. His father touched his two longest tentacles to his son's, in a gesture of tenderness. "You understand what I'm saying, don't you?" he asked. "There isn't much time left for us. The Aensa never give their 'hosts' time to prepare a defense. But I want you to remember. Remember your mother." Corcail Sendijen stared at his mother, who had slumped onto a long divan. He had never seen his mother so weak, so emotional. He didn't exactly understand what his father was trying to say, but Corcail Sendijen knew that he would never forget that it was the Aensa that had made his mother act so terrified.

Years later, under the strange stars of a strange planet, Corcail Sendijen remembered that scene clearly. "I wish the Aensa had only come to punish bad children and gone away," he thought. It would have made his life a great deal simpler. He would have gladly exchanged his tentacles to be home with his parents. If they were still alive, still sane.

The noise of the hunt for Jaeger faded gradually away. Corcail Sendijen left his hiding place and scurried across the shadowed courtyard to another shelter in a pool of blackness formed by the angle of two massive walls.

The baying of the Dktar was thin now and far away, but it still caused Corcail Sendijen to shudder; he crouched motionless for a second and stared up thoughtfully toward the cold night stars. The gold-flecked irises of his eyes dilated slowly. He ought to be grateful, he supposed. Some unfortunate creature was buying with its life this precious chance to reconnoiter. The thought of what the Dktar would do with their prey once they caught up with it sent a cold chill rippling along Corcail Sendijen's scaled spine. He touched one of his tentacles briefly to the short chitinous horn on his forehead (this was the Thirty-First Gesture of the Rites: Sympathy for Those about to Die). Then he turned briskly away. Enough of sentiment. He had a job to do.

This sudden hunt was unexpected luck. Not only were the sleepless Aensahounds gone for once, but those Aensalords—a god shrivel them—that still remained in the citadel all crowded the southern wall, trying to keep track of the chase with infrared scopes and night glasses.

Corcail Sendijen touched the tiny breathing filter concealed beneath his throat membrane with the sensitive tip of a tentacle, making sure that it was still firmly in place; without a device to filter the sulphur compounds from the air on this planet, he would soon lie dead, poisoned. Assured that the filter was still secure, he scrambled across the courtyard, running on his two main locomotive legs, balancing himself with his four large and four small upper tentacles.

About halfway to the broad wall he heard and smelled the approach of an Aensalord. Corcail Sendijen hid himself as best he could in a patch of deep shadow.

There were two Aensa. They glided past slowly, talking in voices that sounded like mixtures of buzzes, crackles, and soft bell-chimes. To Corcail Sendijen's sensitive ears, their voices were quite audible, though pitched very high and rasping unpleasantly. They were without the defensive devices and offensive weapons that their fellows employed while hunting; thus, they remained ignorant of Corcail Sendijen's presence. And also, of course, the Dktar were gone. Corcail Sendijen would have been dead hours before if a single one of the hellish Aensahounds had been loose in the area.

The Aensalords talked of death and the dark thrill of the hunt. Corcail Sendijen never heard the Aensa speak without a feeling of revulsion running through him. Now these two Aensalords remarked that it would be best if the trespasser were brought back still half-alive at least. The Aensa Board of Science had developed some ingenious new schedule of torment. Of course, said one of the brutes, even if the subject were dead, there were certain things that could be done to the nerve centers of the body which would provide an effective punishment for the dissociating ego trapped within. This process had to be utilized within an hour of death—

The Aensa chatted of the kill soon to be made as joyously as children discussing a new toy. The other Aensalord hoped that if the trespasser were human, they would vote to keep him this time, instead of sending his body back as a warning. Each Aensa hoped that it would get the heart as its portion when they served the victim; human flesh was one of the more interesting delicacies this world had to offer.

Corcail Sendijen's body stiffened in the shadows. He wasn't afraid that they would spot him—his vision in the darkness was much better than even the nocturnal Aensalords. He was only worried that his hatred might make itself too loudly evident. He had been suddenly filled with an almost unbearable loathing for the Aensa, for the castle, and for everything around them.

He knew it was foolish and very primitive to condemn an entire race, or to despise an intelligent species because of its peculiar moral standards. That sort of thinking was prejudicial, less than rational. But yet—Corcail Sendijen narrowed his eyes, listened to the mutter of blood as it coursed through his ears, and thought how very nice it would be to kill these two Aensalords. Very slowly. His strong tentacles curled and uncurled, and the fighting claws at the ends of his outside upper tentacles opened in tense anticipation. And it would be so easy; merely reach out for the slender black figures as they drifted past and then—

Corcail Sendijen shrugged and relaxed. It was a natural enough reaction, he supposed. Disguised as an ignorant laborer, he had worked in the black gang that tended the intricate environment-control machinery buried in the depths of the castle. He had toiled on the planet of the human beings for over three months now. In that time, his hatred for the Aensa had been reinforced a hundred times.

The Aensalords floated silently away and were gone. Corcail Sendijen waved a tentacle in a wide circle (the Sixteenth Gesture of the Rites: Obscene) and scuttled after them like a large, scaled spider. He gained the shadow of the inner keep wall, glanced up along it, and muttered a brief invective. He'd been to the ramparts on top of the wall several times during the daytime on black gang business, but it seemed that there was no way that he could make it now without crossing territory where he would be sure to be seen.

Corcail Sendijen touched the rough stone of the wall with a tentacle tip, briefly considered climbing, then decided against it; a large black blotch against a pale stone background would be too easy a target.

At any rate, he knew that the ramparts only overlooked an extensive lake that lapped peacefully against the ancient walls, surrounding the castle on three sides. The drug that Corcail Sendijen was searching for couldn't be produced or stored out there, so it had to be manufactured and hidden somewhere within the keep itself.

But where?

It was impossible to produce the stuff in large amounts without leaving some traces here somewhere. Corcail Sendijen made a slow circuit of the inner wall, moving only when flying black clouds shrouded the sky and his scurrying black form might look more like a shifting shadow.

There was a roughness underfoot, an uneven area that did not seem natural. He crouched, looking like a frantic octopus, whipping his probe tentacles back and forth over the ground, "seeing" by touch.

Yes, he thought, ah, yes. There—two ruts. Corcail Sendijen traced the ruts back toward the outer wall. They were deep; only something heavy could have made them, and they were pronounced enough so that probably more than one trip had been made over the same route. He scooped up some dirt with a tentacle and held it close to the sensitive olfactory organ near the top of his skull. Yes, the dirt was freshly turned; something ponderously heavy had been along this way within the hour. But what? And which way had it been going, toward the outer wall or away from it?

And what had it been carrying?

It was likely that the tracks were perfectly innocent, as innocent as anything could be that was marked by the Aensa. The ruts could easily have been made by produce wagons or farm machinery, or even by some sort of armored guard robot, though Corcail Sendijen had seen no precautions of this type in use. But, perversely, he hoped that the tracks *weren't* innocent, he hoped it fiercely, even though he knew what an unfair and unprofessional attitude it was. Damn it, he hated the Aensalords so intensely, and they were such an ugly, amoral race that they just had to be guilty of something. If only he could find the concrete proof.

Corcail Sendijen froze. He smelled something unusual, too unusual. It was a smell at once acrid and sickeningly sweet, cloying and sharply biting. It was a smell he had known before, one that did not belong at all in the slumbering courtyard. It was very, very near. Corcail Sendijen's eyes narrowed into hard golden slits, as he probed cautiously with his tentacles. One of his four larger tentacles touched something warm and wet and stinging; he recoiled involuntarily.

A hunter's moon above had been wrapped in the arms of an approaching storm, but now it peered through a jagged hole ripped in the clouds by wind. Soft light wavered across the castle courtyard. Corcail Sendijen bent forward intently to study what he had touched.

It was a small pool of bright blue liquid; to Corcail Sendijen's eyes it appeared to be a deep, luminous black.

He knew what it was.

And he knew what it could do.

Corcail Sendijen was slowly filled with a sense of cold, passionless satisfaction; his fighting claws clicked softly together in an automatic reflex. It was true, then, it was all true, and the organization to which he belonged had not been misled. Corcail Sendijen had not wasted months of his life toiling in the black gang for nothing, after all. His job was just beginning, he knew, and the most dangerous part of the game was still ahead. But at least he had proven that there was a job here . . .

Baying. Loud and getting louder; the baying of the Dktar, unusually strident. They were returning.

Corcail Sendijen jerked himself into spring-taut alertness. They shouldn't be returning this early; they never did. He spat angrily. Maybe they didn't, but somehow they *were*. He would have to act. Now.

Abandoning caution, Corcail Sendijen ran straight back across the courtyard; any one at the walls in a position to observe him would most likely be staring in the direction of the racket that marked the returning hunters. But if by chance they weren't—he rippled his tentacles in his equivalent of a shrug.

As he ran, Corcail Sendijen wondered briefly what could have gone wrong with the Aensalords' hunt. Perhaps it had all been a false alarm, or perhaps the Aensahounds had missed their prey, though that was a thing unheard of.

The criss-cross grating of a ventilator shaft appeared in the ground ahead. Taking his time, Corcail Sendijen worked with the catch-release and swung the grating open. He was relatively safe now. This was his escape tunnel, a secret route from the depths of black gang territory to the courtyard of the

Aensalords' keep. It was a sheer, vertical shaft falling a great distance into the depths of the castle, and it was as grim and black as the mouth of the Hell Pit itself.

Corcail Sendijen was amused by the thought as he lowered himself over the edge and into the ventilator shaft; luckily he had never been a very superstitious person. Not since childhood, anyway, he added, remembering the old fears of the Aensa.

But before he pulled the grating shut after him, he stared back toward the Aensalords' keep and remembered the tiny pool of dark liquid. His eyes grew very narrow.

He would be back.

Chapter Two

There was a line of demarcation between the Aensa lands and the neighboring German countryside, as distinct as though some gigantic hand had scratched a furrow in the soil. The Aensa had not thought to put up physical barriers; there were no fences of barbed wire or electrified cable, no signs warning in multiple languages of mine fields or brain guns. These things were simply not necessary. Everyone in the world knew who the Aensa were, and where they were. Everyone knew what might happen to a spy or an idiot who crossed the boundary. And the boundary was so plainly visible.

On one side there were autumn gold leaves on tall, ancient trees, fields dotted with bundled hay, dried husks of the season's corn. Gray hills looked down on white and red farm buildings. It was a lovely area, the kind of scene that had graced commercial calendars for scores of years. It was an agricultural area, devoted to the raising of hogs, cattle, corn, and wheat. A few large cities, whose urban sprawl had been checked by the urgent need for farming land, had grown up many centuries before and still served the same functions: manufacturing centers and trading outlets for the farmers. Stuttgart to the west, Munich to the south, Nürnberg to the north all prospered, all mixtures of the ancient glorious days and the frantic modern ones.

In the middle of this triangle, like a bullet lodged next to the heart, was the Aensa lands.

From what Karl Jaeger had seen, every square yard of the creatures' territory looked like every other square yard: black, misshapen, dead, very dead. The smell of the air across the line had been almost more than he could bear. The sights of the blasted landscape had been chilling enough, too. He admitted that he had been unnerved. He had never before taken an assignment that had so overcome his natural talents and his acquired skills. He had an idea that the intense fear that he had experienced was not altogether natural. That would be something to investigate in the office.

Jaeger ran. The smell of the place was still in his nostrils, and the charred, crippled vegetation spread before him, perhaps another hundred yards. He concentrated on sprinting those last fifteen seconds. He did not think about the smell or the trees. They would only remind him of worse things, beasts that carried a more awful threat. It would be many hours before Karl Jaeger could think rationally about the Aensa, and longer still before he could call to mind his memories of the Dktar. Now was not the time.

He crossed the line and stumbled. He fell down gratefully in the damp, green, living grass. Only a few inches away the grass was a black, ominous parody of life. But here, across the boundary, Jaeger was safe. He felt tears on his cheeks, and he wondered when they had fallen from his eyes. He breathed deeply and slowly. After a while his heartbeat slowed to normal. He stared back into the Aensa land and cursed. Then he stood up; the sun was rising, and the scene before him was more beautiful than anything he had ever seen.

Jaeger took another deep breath and resumed his journey, walking now rather than running in terror. The countryside was peaceful and gave him a kind of therapeutic spiritual bath. The horrors of the previous hours did not diminish in his memory, but he was once again able to realize that there was something else in the world, after all, besides the golden flicker of the Aensalords and the pale blue glimmer of their hounds. The sun climbed steadily in the sky; the morning haze melted, and the last remaining clouds blew silently over the horizon. For a while Jaeger delayed going back to his office; he wanted to stay where he was, rambling over the low hills of what had been, in more nationalistic times, southern Germany.

He did not turn around again. He did not look back toward the province of the Aensa.

The sounds of grazing cattle came to him on the warm breeze. The contented mooing brought a smile to Jaeger's lips. He had never realized before how wonderful cows were. He wondered briefly what effect the Aensa lands might have on the people who dwelt so near. Jaeger shuddered. He knew that, even never having seen the Dktar or their masters, he would not want to live so near the blasted blackness. Still, he thought, shrugging, the survivors of the eruption of Pompeii had settled right back on the volcano's slopes afterward. Most people gave little thought to the future.

The future. All it represented to Jaeger was the chance to take a long, hot shower and settle down in his worn black swivel chair with more Jack Daniels than a person might be expected to consume. That was the order of the day, if he had anything to say about it. He wondered if he would have anything to say about it.

After the long, slow walk, Jaeger arrived at the depot some five miles outside the town of Schwäbisch Gmünd. He caught the train at the tiny hamlet that was the first stop on the way back to Nürnberg, rather than continue on into Schwäbisch Gmünd, where he would have a better chance of finding a good breakfast and a head start on the drunken bout he had promised himself. It was better that way; to the townsfolk of Schwäbisch Gmünd he had been merely mad Herr Schultz, another unfortunate who had strayed into Aensa territory for some unfathomable reason of his own. The local people would assume that he had been casually destroyed by the Aensa, like a bug beneath a huge and impersonal thumb. Rest in peace, Herr Schultz. Surely the residents of Schwäbisch Gmünd would pity him, but not for very long. Next time—if there was a next time, unlikely as it seemed—Jaeger would have to think up another disguise.

The train pulled into the Nürnberg station over half an hour late. Jaeger didn't care; the combination of utter weariness and a few strong drinks had pushed everything else back to a comfortable distance. He stepped from the terminal's liftshaft at street level and limped tiredly through the swirling morning crowds of downtown Nürnberg.

Karl Jaeger reached his office on Koenigstrasse without further incident. The ancient street was as hot and dusty under the brilliant autumn sun as his aching head felt; he gave a small sigh of relief as the coolness of his building's lobby washed over him. The elevator lifted him silently to the fourth floor. He walked along the carpeted corridor and pushed through a big frosted-glass door. The black letters on the glass made him smile. They made him smile often. They said: JAEGER, INC.

The building that housed Jaeger's office was located in the finest, oldest section of Nürnberg. The city had been growing since prehistoric times; the first recorded mention of the city was in 1050, and it was likely that the court assembly of Emperor Henry III was held not far from Jaeger's Koenigstrasse address. It made for an impressive business card. It let the rich old women and the divorce-seeking husbands know that Jaeger had better things to do than attend to their problems. Of course, JAEGER, INC. had not always been situated in such imposing quarters. And it was possible, thought Jaeger, that if too many people saw him running in and out of the building in his present condition, JAEGER, INC. might have to move back into more recently built yet shabbier offices. Or, simply, office. Or, if things really fell apart with this assignment, some desk space in the apartment of a close friend.

No, this business with the Aensa wasn't going to bother Karl Jaeger. He shook his head ruefully. Karl Jaeger was much too tough, too smart, and too competent. It would take more than one staring Aensalord to rattle him. But not much more.

Inside the frosted-glass door was a small waiting room; it was richly paneled in dark wood and gave the operation its only real touch of sophisticated taste. The paneling had been in the room before Jaeger had rented the place. A thick carpet in muted colors, a few comfortable chairs, a small couch, and a table all presented an image of solidity, reliability, and culture. A desk at the far side of the waiting room indicated an immediate link to the mysterious and somewhat less-than-legitimate enterprise that potential clients imagined JAEGER, INC. to be.

Behind the desk was the only genuine beauty in the room, Jaeger's secretary, Marga Geier. She guarded the door to

Jaeger's inner office like some mythological heavenly sentinel. Marga was tall and fair, her hair as pale as moonlight on snow. Her eyes always surprised Jaeger; he always expected them to be light, light blue, and they always turned out to be shiny black. Jaeger hoped they had the same effect on the clients.

He nodded to Marga and closed the front door behind him. The secretary was astonished by Jaeger's ragged and filthy condition, and half rose from her chair. "It's all right, Marga," he said, waving a hand at her. "I'm all right. I'll tell you about it later."

"Do you want anything?" she asked. Jaeger wondered if there was anything beyond simple concern in her expression.

"No," he said. "Hell, yes, there is. No, never mind. I'll call you later." Marga said nothing. Jaeger waited until she pressed a button hidden on her desk that unlocked the inner door. He went through without looking at her again.

Beyond the inner door was a short hallway, too narrow for more than one person to walk comfortably. On the left were three doors. On the right were two windows, commanding a lovely view over rooftops toward the very old twin spires of the St.-Lorenz-Kirche. The doors led into small offices; the first belonged to Herr Stahl, Jaeger's scientific consultant. The second door was the office of Hans Weissmann, Jaeger's business manager and closest friend. The last door was Jaeger's own private office. He passed the door to Herr Stahl's workshop and knocked on Weissmann's door. A bright blond rectangle of wood shone in the light from the windows. Jaeger waited a brief time and opened the door. Inside, both Herr Stahl and Hans Weissmann were waiting. They had evidently been having a loud and emotional argument, but they both fell silent and stared as Jaeger entered.

Herr Stahl was waving a thick scientific journal in one hand. The waving ceased, and the hand holding the magazine fell slowly to his lap. He looked at Jaeger sourly. Stahl was a stubby, balding, taciturn little man who very seldom thought of anything except his work and an occasional bottle of wine. He had worked for Jaeger for several years, reluctantly at first, drawn chiefly by the opportunity to do lab work more interesting than the routine forensic techniques of the large police combines. When JAEGER, INC. became a financial success, there had been even more incentive. Nevertheless, Stahl remained outwardly unpleasant, cynical, and unsocial; he seemed always to be instigating arguments with Weissmann or Jaeger or even Marga Geier. No one paid much attention to his pessimistic attitude; he had rarely failed Jaeger in his technical projects, and he was almost as good as Fräulein Geier at playing bridge, which is what occupied the time of the employees of JAEGER, INC. between clients.

Stahl's slow little eyes flicked over Jaeger, silently taking in his dilapidated condition. Carefully he inserted a bookmark into his scientific journal, closed the magazine, placed it on Weissmann's desk, and arranged its edges to parallel the edges of the desk. "Guten Tag, Herr Jaeger," he said.

Jaeger just looked at the man. For once, there was no hint of sardonicism or repressed curiosity in the clipped, neutral voice. But after a moment's reflection, Jaeger understood that it wasn't that Stahl was too polite to ask what had happened. Instead, it was likely that Stahl didn't care; after all, Jaeger had returned safely. Beyond that, the details would only bore Stahl. Jaeger could have entered naked, or with a bloody corpse slung over his shoulder, and not the least glimmer of interest would have shown in Herr Stahl's opaque, muddy brown eyes.

Jaeger sighed. "Guten Tag, Herr Stahl," he said. He took out a crumpled piece of paper scribbled over with penciled notations made on the train ride to Nürnberg. "I'd like to see if it's possible to make a blindcoat that will function according to these specifications. The present model proved unsatisfactory, and I think the band of wavelengths we're blocking is too narrow. I'd like your estimate as soon as possible. It's urgent."

Jaeger released the paper; it fluttered down past Stahl's blank face and drifted to a stop on the technician's knee. Stahl's hand scuttled sideways like a sluggish spider to catch it; he flattened the paper out, and his eyes began to crawl back and forth, examining Jaeger's barely legible instructions. A gleam appeared in his eyes as he read, like a lantern shining dimly through a thick bank of fog. Hurriedly, Stahl got to his feet and brushed by Jaeger without speaking, the piece of paper clutched tightly in one hand. Weissmann's door slammed; a moment later, Jaeger heard the slam of Stahl's own door. Stahl had a technical problem to solve now, and for that man the world of humanity had ceased to exist.

Jaeger stared at Weissmann's motionless door for an instant, a slight trace of envy in his face.

Slowly, he eased himself out of his jacket, wincing at bruises. He threw the jacket across the chair Stahl had vacated. He inspected his tattered, stained shirt, shook his head ruefully, and gently lowered himself into the chair. The office contained a bank of phones, some file cabinets arranged in a row along the wall opposite the door, Weissmann's desk, and a small table with a portable computation machine. Everything seemed in order to Jaeger, as he made a weary, wistful inspection. Judging from this room, JAEGER, INC. might be almost any kind of operation: insurance, securities investments, at worst, illegal gambling. Nothing to indicate the kind of activity Jaeger endured the night before. He shook his head again; Jaeger realized that the only unharmonious note in the entire suite of offices was himself.

Hans Weissmann had still not spoken. Jaeger smiled at his friend, then yawned. "Karl!" said Weissmann softly, "Was ist los?"

"Euro, Hans," said Jaeger, chiding his friend mildly. "Speak Euro. You need the practice."

"Yes, yes, Karl," said Weissmann impatiently. "But, my God! What happened to you? You are battered and bloody—" A spasm of bewilderment twisted his face. "And you're not due back for days yet. Did something go wrong with the mission?"

"No, nothing went wrong except that the whole assignment was a disaster. *Everything* went wrong. Merciful Lord, I've never been involved in such a complete and utter fiasco. I managed to escape with my life, but even that was little more than luck, pure and simple. Not any credit to me, that's for sure. Luck! That's a hell of a thing for somebody in my job to have to rely on." He fell silent, and from Jaeger's expression Weissmann could guess that there were bitter things still left unsaid.

Weissmann leaned forward across his desk. His florid face, somewhat older in appearance than Jaeger's, reflected his anxiety. "What happened? I would have sworn that we had it all figured out perfectly. Was it—"

Jaeger cut him off with a chopping motion of his hand. He swayed unsteadily as he stood, fighting waves of fatigue. "It's too complicated to go into now. I've got to tackle this thing while it's still fresh in my mind—and sometime before I agree to collapse from exhaustion." He waved away Weissmann's unvoiced objections.

"I've got a job for you, Hans, immediate rush. Check our files and then call Central Data downtown. I want a copy of everything that's ever been reported on the Aensalords on my desk within an hour. This is urgent. I've got to find out why I fumbled this job, and the answer has to be there somewhere." His battered face distorted momentarily into a wry smile. "It's not quite as impractical as it seems. My self-confidence needs salving badly, yes, but it will also be good business. The data fiche will run to a little money, I suppose. But, remember, Herr Schiller won't be too pleased with the way his retainer's been spent. We have to show him that we have a way to correct our failures, eh? Ja. Sure."

By the time Jaeger emerged from the company washroom, shaved, showered, and feeling alive again, new clothes were waiting for him in a neatly folded pile. A shaft of sunlight squeezed through a crack in the curtain covering the big bay window behind his desk and set all the dust motes in the air to dancing. Jaeger watched the sunbeam as he toweled himself off, admiring the way it glimmered from the polished desk and bleached the cloth and upholstery of the furniture.

He picked up a shirt and pulled it over his head in one ragged motion. He was a huge man, cat-muscled, deeply tanned, dark blond, with a grim weather-beaten face; his expression was dominated by a strong, almost unpleasantly massive jaw line and large, canny gray eyes, which were recessed beneath bushy eyebrows.

Jaeger slipped on the rest of his clothes, then stepped to the window and threw the curtain wide with a vehement jerk; he'd had enough of darkness for a while.

Shadows scurried insectlike from the sudden flood of sunshine, taking refuge in the constant pools of darkness that remained beneath desks and heavy furniture and in far corners. Jaeger stood looking out over his city for a few moments, then turned and walked stiffly to his desk. Rather absently, he thumbed through his memorandum book, riffled the pages of his desk calendar, and checked the desk drawers again. It was sheer habit, something he did several times a day, always sadly hoping to discover some tiny but precious item that he had overlooked. Anyway, there was nothing he could do until the files on the Aensa arrived.

Memories awoke, against Jaeger's will, and the very strangeness of some of them served to trigger other thoughts in his mind, conflicting ones. First, the fresh tang of the earth after a rain, and the salt and pepper smell of newly mown hay. Then an afternoon filled only with animal noises and the long, ecstatic whisper of wind through tall grass. Nothing in sight but the high blue vault of sky and rustling rows of crops.

A pencil broke in Jaeger's hand with a staccato snap. Here was a touchy, painful memory; he decided to stay away from it. He couldn't. He had been brought up on a small farm south of the city, and probably would have remained there for the rest of his life except that his parents had decided to send him to the University.

There had been several universities, as a matter of fact. First the one at Nürnberg, then at Bonn, then at the capital of the Anglo-European League, London, where he finally ended his scholastic sampling and settled down to serious work. Not that his parents could ever have afforded the University of London; he had made the last two transfers on the strength of government scholarships, after his parents died with thousands of others in the Thirty-Day Riots. After the University had come a little post-graduate work, and then the army.

His job in the Intelligence Section of the League's armed forces had been interesting, though demanding. His tour had been cut short by a half year, thanks to a minor brush with the Slavic Confederacy's border guards and a hand grenade that netted Jaeger a load of shrapnel in the leg and an honorable discharge.

After a brief stay in a service hospital, it had been back to the University for more post-graduate work, enough to earn him his Master's, and then a series—actually, the correct word might be something like "multitude"—of jobs, none entirely satisfactory. He had flirted with and rejected positions as a teacher, a research scientist, musician, engineer, lab man with the Southern European Police Group, journalist, and commercial artist when it occurred to him that he was searching for a job that didn't exist.

He enjoyed the intellectually stimulating life in the academic world. The clean complexities of the sciences delighted him, and at the same time the subjective pleasure of painting in oils was his favorite pastime. Still, he missed the vital, dangerous life of the Intelligence Section, and his glimpse of criminology while he had been employed by the SEPG had fascinated him. That science had come to intrigue him more and more, and the almost inevitable result had been JAEGER, INC., a corporation with only one thing to sell: himself.

Sherlock Holmes, that old fiddler, had delighted often in informing people that he was the world's first consulting detective. Jaeger was its last, and the only one at all in many years. The political and economic situations in the world had made such quasi-autonomous combines as the SEPG more efficient than the innumerable local and national police forces; at the same time, the huge networks drove the individual investigators out of business. Now, though, Jaeger believed the combines had grown too large, too ponderous to handle delicate inquiries. The SEPG and its like were leviathans; Jaeger was the single shark.

This was the age of the Big Institutions. Even criminology had been geared to a mass-consumption principle; the SEPG and its other counterparts around the world were motivated by financial profit, rather than any tarnishable ideals of justice. Thanks to the commerical aspect, the police combines often developed new techniques that seemed to increase their efficiency, techniques that governmental organizations might be too red-tape bound to care about. Of course, as Jaeger well understood, that increase in efficiency was always more apparent than real. The effects of progress were divided and shared through the entire police group, until the actual result was too small to measure.

As the only individual private investigator on Earth, as the last of an otherwise vanished breed, Jaeger caught the public's fancy. The use of very unorthodox techniques, sound business methods, and even sounder principles of criminology held that interest. At first he had been a joke—any criminologist who would try to go it on his own, instead of staying with the SEPG or some similar group, was obviously crazy. Gradually he had won respect. Good fortune had brought him his first client, an apparently unsolvable case his second, and his success in both matters and his rapidly spreading reputation had lured the rest. In his first two years he had cracked five relatively big assignments and a host of minor ones. His exploits had been reported by the press with growing interest and enthusiasm. A failure now would damage his image.

The coffee and the files on the Aensalords arrived simultaneously.

Jaeger thumbed through the files intently at first, but then with increasing disappointment. There was nothing new there; an ocean of ink had been spilled over the Aensalords, but somehow the articles were ali curiously similar. He sipped the scalding coffee wearily, hardly noticing its warmth as the numbness of fatigue once again spread through his body.

He slipped a new microfiche into the small fiche reader and projector on his desk. He turned the control knob, idly searching the microfilm card for something, anything, that might develop into an avenue of investigation. He scowled; there was something missing, something big. Although they went on at length, the articles managed to avoid saying anything. It seemed to Jaeger that it was more than the usual journalistic agility. Something was *missing.*

Oh, all the well-known facts were there, of course: the first tentative contact with the Aensa ships just within the orbit of Mars, ten years ago; the frightening rumors of alien invasion that had panicked the world; the inevitable military clash when two of our ships and one of theirs had vaporized in a blinding flash, one hundred miles up, turning night into day for half of Earth; a world in prayer, a world of fear and crazy hate; and then, unbelievably, the first hesitant, almost shy peace feelers; the truce; the hasty devising of an artificial language; the first face-to-face meeting in a pre-fab dome on the moon; the summit meetings with the Aensa representatives in Denver, in London, in Capetown, in Rio de Janeiro, in Moscow; the final agreement—

And so it had turned out that the hostilities had all been a mistake. The Aensalords were really friendly interstellar traders, not invaders at all, and their only thought was the making of a mutual profit for both worlds and both races. They only wanted to open up Earth to interstellar trade, as Perry had opened Japan to the rest of the world hundreds of years before. Mankind heaved a collective sigh of relief. If the Aensalords were human enough to want to exchange goods, if their society was enough like ours to make them greedy for a profit, then we could understand each other and we could get along.

The Aensalords had been given a ten-mile-square area of land in southern Germany for use as a local base of operations, in return for certain mineral and trading rights, left unspecified. Everyone had proceed to live happily ever after.

Jaeger grunted. He slapped the switch and turned off the fiche reader. He flipped a few paper pages in the Aensa file, barely seeing the printed words on them. Happily ever after. Nowhere did it say that the Aensa hunted men by night for sport.

Nor did it mention that the poor unfortunates were dragged by the heels across the boundary, staked out naked on the ground, and left for scavengers to feed on. Nor did the articles mention the Dktar, even in passing, which Jaeger thought suspicious; the Aensahounds were a singularly large and colorful detail. Too large and colorful for copy-hungry journalists to have missed.

He had made a mistake. If the information given in these articles and books was correct, he ought to have succeeded. That he had failed was proof enough for him that the information had been false. He had based his entire plan of action on the file before him because it was all the data that was available. If the information was false, then the books were false, and if the books were false—

Then, very simply, somebody had clamped a lid on the entire matter of the Aensa. There were a lot of people who might be motivated to do just that.

Jaeger didn't look up again until Herr Stahl entered with the news that making a blindcoat work in accordance with the new specifications was not feasible.

"Impossible?" Jaeger snapped.

"Aber nein, Herr Jaeger. Infeasible." A slow humor flickered lazily in Stahl's eyes. "Give me a few million dollars, a well-equipped research laboratory, my own staff, and then, perhaps, perhaps yes. But here? In that workshop, with that equipment? Never." Stahl said nothing more, turned abruptly, and left.

Jaeger sighed. There went his present hope of regaining the offensive. It appeared that he was stymied. There was nothing he could do now but refund the retainer to Herr Schiller and accept his losses; Schiller would just have to find someone else. Jaeger didn't enjoy thinking about that. It was much more serious than a simple failure. JAEGER, INC. enjoyed a certain success because of its growing reputation for offering services unavailable elsewhere. If Schiller publicized Jaeger's shortcomings, it would be more than a black eye for the firm. And publicizing shortcomings was what had made Schiller's fortune. The secret photos of the aliens' outpost would have to be taken by someone else, if at all. Schiller's magazines would have to deal with the SEPG, after all, as distasteful as that evidently was to the millionaire publisher. Jaeger certainly wasn't going back into the Aensa territory as unprotected as he had been the first time, to be hunted again through the dark by slavering beasts from a Hieronymus Bosch nightmare. There wasn't enough money in the world to make him do that.

Still, the puzzle of the lying data fiche was a tantalizing itch in the back of his mind. He shrugged. A failure was a failure, and it was better to face up to it honestly than delude himself with false hopes. If he was lucky, he might be able to hush up the whole business and keep it out of the papers. Anyway, Jaeger was too much of a professional to let mere personal curiosity lure him into a situation where he didn't stand even a fifty-fifty chance of getting out alive.

Hans Weissmann entered softly as Jaeger swirled the black dregs of coffee in his cup. Jaeger wondered if he should finish the rest of the oily liquid or succumb to the waves of weariness that lapped with increasing frequency at his mind.

"Karl," said Weissmann, "there has been a call for you."

"Ja, so?"

"From the International Congress. I think they want to hire you."

Jaeger arched an eyebrow. He was incredulous; this was unheard of. Besides, the IC had a security force of its own and an army of agents. What did they need of him? "Hans," said Jaeger, "are you certain of this?"

"Yes. Three IC attachés are coming here tomorrow to see you. An appointment at two o'clock."

"Who?"

"I don't know their names, but two are representatives from the North American Urban League, and one a representative from the Slavic Confederacy."

"Which part of NAUL are they from, according to the old system?"

Weissmann shook his head. "Karl, the old system has been obsolete for years. It couldn't make any difference now. One is from the Northeastern Monocity, and one is from the—"

"That doesn't satisfy me. What section of their respective city-states are they from?"

Weissmann muttered to himself and consulted his notebook. "One is from New York, one is from Houston. Satisfied now? Or do I have to look up their street addresses, too?"

Jaeger smiled wryly. "No, but now I'd like you to tell me what part of the Slavic Confederacy the other representative calls home."

"All right, Karl, all right. He's from Warsaw. But honestly, how can it be of any importance? The old world is dead, buried, and gone."

Jaeger took a deep breath and sat back in his chair. He stared above his friend's head, at the dusty wood paneling of the walls. "Dead and buried, perhaps," he said, "but not gone. Old ethnic patterns make stubborn ghosts. My God, Hans, in many respects a man is what his home makes of him, his entire psychological framework is shaped by the atmosphere and traditions of the place where he has grown up and lived. If you don't know a man's background, how can you know the man? How can you deal with him?"

Weissmann chuckled softly. "Poor Karl. Always a perfectionist." He rapped his knuckles on Jaeger's desk and stretched. "Time to go, Karl. Get some sleep. You look too much like a dead man. I will watch the office as usual, like an angry hawk with little hawklings to guard."

"Chicks," said Jaeger tonelessly. Then he added hesitantly, "I think."

"Hawklings, chicks, it makes no difference," said Weissmann. He gave an airy wave of his hand and chuckled. "Get some sleep, Karl. Even you are not made of iron, although you would like to think that you are. You are just flesh and blood like the rest of us."

"Blood," said Jaeger. "Thanks for reminding me, Hans. Send Stahl back in. I want a sample of my blood analyzed."

Weissmann shook his head but said nothing. He turned and left the office.

Jaeger swayed unsteadily to his feet and blinked at the wall clock. It was still early afternoon. Lunch would have to wait until some day when he could manage to keep his eyes open long enough to eat. He made it to the couch, sat down, started to take off his shirt. Then sleep washed over him like a physical thing and he did a long clean dive into soothing blackness.

Corcail Sendijen was returning from another futile night of searching when he walked right into an armed Aensa patrol.

He had just emerged from the bottom of his ventilator shaft, laboriously replaced the grating, and was preparing to follow the bend in the narrow corridor that led down to the black gang quarters, when he heard footsteps approaching rapidly up the corridor toward him, boots ringing loudly against stone. He froze. He could smell them now as well and, as they moved closer, hear the distinctive beating of their hearts. Aensa. Closing down on him fast.

Corcail Sendijen stared about wildly. This corridor was normally deserted at this hour; that alone had made his nightly forays possible. There was no cover on this stretch, no branch corridors to duck into, no furniture or machinery to hide behind. Only naked rock: floor, walls, ceiling. He had gambled that he would never encounter anyone here. Now it appeared that he had lost the bet, and the unexpected Aensa patrol would collect on it. What could he do? He had only seconds. It would take much too long to open up the ventilator shaft again, and even if he could get it open he'd never be able to get the grating back in place in time: The Aensa would see that it had been removed, investigate, and catch him in the shaft. Corcail Sendijen could cover ground very rapidly when he wished, but from here on the corridor was long and straight and empty—run as he might, he'd never be able to get out of sight before they turned the bend in the corridor and spotted him. And there was no hope of slipping by them unseen.

These and a dozen other thoughts flickered frantically through Corcail Sendijen's mind in a fraction of a second. It was hopeless. They'd probably shoot him down as soon as they turned the bend and saw him, and they would turn the bend in a heartbeat, were turning it now—

As the first Aensa turned the bend, Corcail Sendijen leaped straight up in the air.

He spread his tentacles wide as he rose, and so powerful was the leap that he splatted hard against the smooth rock ceiling and stuck fast, like a child's suction-cup arrow, held by the adhesive disks on his four main tentacles. He could sense the Aensa passing directly underneath him, although he dared not move to look. He was barely six feet above their heads, and would have been spotted instantly if one of them had looked up. But they did not. They weren't expecting anyone to be there, for one thing, and even if they had been actively searching for him, beings evolved from ground-hunting animals rarely think to look up during a chase; almost instinctively, they will scan no higher than eye level, ninety-nine out of a hundred times. Corcail Sendijen had gambled that they wouldn't, and it seemed that this gamble too had paid off.

The Aensa marched several yards further on and then stopped. At first Corcail Sendijen feared that they had spotted him after all, but they sent up no alarm. Instead, they began to speak together in conversational tones, but Corcail Sendijen was momentarily too preoccupied with his own situation to eavesdrop. His grip was slipping; already one of his tentacles had worked free of the ceiling, adhesion broken, as gravity relentlessly tried to pull him back down. Ayai! the Aensa would have to stop here for their chat! How long could he keep himself up here? Another tentacle was peeling away from the stone. If he fell, it would be practically at their feet.

Frantically, he whipped his four lesser tentacles back and forth across the smooth ceiling, searching for purchase. One of them touched a grilled light-fixture, set into the ceiling, and Corcail Sendijen gave a shudder, his equivalent of a sigh of relief. Quickly he wrapped his lesser tentacles around the grillwork, braced himself against it, and so was able to renew the adhesive grip of his four main tentacles. Now secure, he could turn his attention to spying on the Aensa. By twisting himself almost in half, he was able to get a look at them.

There were six of them: three Aensamen, two proud Aensalords, and—Corcail Sendijen's eyes narrowed. The sixth member of the party was a bovine triped named Malmo, one of the black gang. Malmo was standing a little apart from the Aensa, his back to the corridor wall, his massive, shaggy head sunk dejectedly on his breast. The Aensalords had pistols in their hands, and they kept them loosely pointed in Malmo's direction, with deceptive nonchalance.

One of the Aensalords was saying: "—far enough. None of the black gang will hear us now. By the morning, they will probably have forgotten that we came for this one. Or that he ever existed at all."

"Truth," the other Aensalord said. "Still, it is better to do it away from their sight. The death of one of their own unsettles them when it is not a part of proper work routine. Their minds are low-grade, and they are easily panicked.

And they would remember a death. No creature is so low-grade that he does not remember death."

"Death," said the first Aensalord in a soft, caressing tone, as though he savored the word. "Ah, the Dark One is coming for Malmo with his sack! Can you not sense him, Malmo, getting nearer? Can you not feel him approach?" To the other Aensalord: "A shame to waste a slave of moderate intelligence, compared to the rest. How unfortunate that he has coincidentally seen what he has seen."

"This is so," the second Aensalord replied. "But it must be done. The secret is there in his mind for any competent spy to read, and why waste psychoediting on such a one? There are cheapter, more efficient ways."

At this point, Corcail Sendijen stirred. Fighting down a distracting wave of compassion for his fellow black-ganger, he tried to probe Malmo's mind for the information that had doomed him, information that could be the key to unlock this whole investigation. But he found, to his dismay, that it couldn't be done. Outwardly, Malmo seemed resigned, even placid, but inside he was roaring wide open with white-hot emotion—death-fear, hate, rage, perverse sexual excitement—and this howling cacophony was enough to keep Corcail Sendijen from reading him clearly. And besides, ironically enough, Malmo's fear had disturbed him so greatly, taken up so much of his limited mental capacity, that he had almost entirely forgottten the information he was about to be killed to protect.

"The Man with the Sack is here, Malmo!" The first Aensalord called mockingly. "Can you not smell him? Can you not smell the blood that coats the inside of his sack, wherein you soon shall be? Can you not smell the blood, Malmo, and the old brittle bones?"

Malmo said nothing, but he raised his shaggy head and looked at the Aensalords. A shudder went through his huge frame, and he shuffled his three feet nevously, but he did not move. His massive shoulders were slumped, his arms limp, the long-fingered hands hanging straight down and nearly brushing the floor. His eyes were sad and mild.

"Will you not speak, Malmo?" the first Aensalord cried.

"Will you not plead? Will you not rage?"

"Lords," Malmo said. His voice was very deep, slow and thick and patient. His eyes smoldered now, like embers. He slowly raised his arms and spread them wide apart. "Lords, I am your creature," he said.

The first Aensalord shot him in the stomach.

There was no noise or muzzle flash, but the impact of the shot punched Malmo back against the wall. He rocked drunkenly for a moment but did not go down. Thick mahogany-colored blood was welling from the wound, and he placed one of his big hands over it. His eyes did not leave the Aensalords. He had not moved.

"Attack!" screamed the first Aensalord. "Charge us, Malmo! Gore us! Crush us! Kill us!"

"Lords," Malmo said in a bloody, bubbling voice.

The first Aensalord shot him three more times in rapid succession. Malmo bounced off the wall, reeled, and then pitched headlong, falling with a crash that shook the corridor.

"No style," the second Aensalord said disapprovingly. "No technique. He didn't manage to fulfill even one of the Fifteen Stations of Death. Such a poor showing."

"He was low-grade," the first Aensalord agreed. He gestured to one of the Aensamen, who walked over to the spot where Malmo had fallen and, producing a squat black box with a nozzle, used it to pump out a cloud of dry silver powder. The powder settled down onto Malmo's body. There was a brilliant flash of flame, a gout of oily black smoke that soon dissipated, and all trace of Malmo was gone.

The Aensa patrol continued on down the corridor, the two Aensalords still discussing Malmo's deficiencies as a participant in the Noblest Game.

As soon as they were out of sight, Corcail Sendijen let himself drop lightly to the floor. He was feeling queasy in his second stomach, and guilty, and he sternly repressed both emotions. Poor stupid Malmo. Corcail Sendijen felt his fighting claws click in reflexive rage. This emotion he could not entirely repress. He had killed Aensalords in the past, and he looked forward to killing more in the future . . .

No, it was useless to lose himself in bloody daydreams. His mission was far from over. He had learned nothing from his search of the castle grounds, and he had been unable to take advantage of a unique and precious opportunity to gain the secret information he sought. He also sensed, uneasily, that he was missing something about the death of Malmo, overlooking something—that somehow he should be able to use that death against the Aensalords and to his own advantage. He couldn't see how, but the feeling persisted.

One thing was definite: He had been given a graphic demonstration of what would happen to him if he was caught. It was a lesson, however, that he already knew too well. Too damn well.

He whirled around and scuttled for black-gang territory.

Chapter Three

Jaeger awoke to darkness and dusty silence. For a moment he lay still, letting consciousness trickle slowly back into his mind, letting the pool of awareness grow within him. He stretched. Despite the pains in his overworked body, he felt good. Exhaustion had burned itself out, and a reaction to his earlier fit of depression had set in. He felt calm and assured, with the vitality of an animal with no laws to govern it but its own. Jaeger found his desk clock and bumped his nose against its plastic crystal to puzzle out the position of its hands. Eleven p.m. He had slept through the rest of the day and into the warm autumn night.

Jaeger realized that he was monstrously hungry. He pawed his way along the wall until he found his coat. Then he let himself out of his office. The narrow hallway beyond was lit by pale yellow trapezoids of moonlight, beaming in through the two windows. Jaeger paused to look outside. The night was clear and bright; it brought thoughts of the previous evening. Already that adventure seemed to belong to a different time, a different life, to someone who didn't exist in Jaeger's real world. It belonged in a place of dreams. Jaeger was willing to consign the entire Aensa matter to the realm of his darker fantasies, but with a sigh he realized that he couldn't solve the thing as easily as that.

There were eight taxis waiting at the cab stand in the Marktplatz, near the ancient fountain. Jaeger raised a hand and the cab driver started his engine. Jaeger climbed into the rear seat and gave the driver his address. They drove without conversation for ten minutes, through the dim streets lit by peach-colored lamps on high aluminum poles. There were few pedestrians, few other automobiles. Jaeger heard only the muffled hum of the taxi and the regular click of the meter. He slouched in the seat, his hands buried deep in the pockets of his overcoat. His mind strayed to the subject of the Aensalords, to the scene he would have to have with Herr Schiller eventually. With a sour frown he shook those thoughts from his head. They returned. They would not let him rest.

He paid the driver when they arrived at Jaeger's apartment house. He stood on the sidewalk, staring blankly up the street, watching the taxi drive away. Windows were lit in a random pattern in the buildings across the street; behind those windows, unknown families lived their narrow but happy lives. What did those citizens know or care about the Aensa? Only what they heard on television or read in the newsfiche, which Jaeger now realized was more than merely censored. With a shrug, he turned and climbed the stoop outside his building and unlocked the outer door. He looked in his mailbox; nothing but a bill from *Gegenwart* magazine—one of Schiller's magazines—and an offer to enroll in a mail-order correspondence course in real estate brokerage. He threw the latter away, stuffed the bill in one of his pockets, and unlocked the inner door. He climbed the two flights up to his apartment and unlocked his own front door. Inside, the room was dark. He had forgotten to leave a light on; no, he hadn't actually forgotten. He just hadn't expected to return home after dark. Events had made that unavoidable. Events . . .

As he walked through the door, he heard a small sound. Too late, he spun away. A hand holding a gun swung down and smashed Jaeger's head. The pain was intense, blinding. Jaeger grabbed his head.

"All right," said the man who had attacked him. "Put your hands up."

"God damn it," said Jaeger, ignoring the man. He walked around the living room, rubbing the back of his head. "Oh, hell. What was that for? You got a gun. If you want to rob me, go ahead. What the hell you want to smear my brains for?"

"You were supposed to fall down unconscious," said the

man, his voice sounding amused and confident.

"It doesn't always work," said Jaeger. "You have to have the right touch." He stopped rubbing his head and looked at the stranger. The other man was shorter than Jaeger, very thin, with long hair and a beard covering much of his face. In the dim light from the hallway, Jaeger couldn't see the man well enough to be able to identify him later, if the opportunity ever arose.

"I don't have the right touch," said the man.

"No, you don't. You'll either kill your mark or give him a nasty headache. I already had mine, thank you. Are you one of Schiller's men?"

"Schiller?" said the stranger. "The *Monatliche* man? Never met him."

"Excuse me for a minute," said Jaeger. "Hold the gun on me and I'll just get me something to ease the pain. Do you have anything you want eased?" Casually, Jaeger flipped on the light switch.

"Thanks," said the man. "Whatever you're having."

"If you're going to be any kind of success at this," said Jaeger with a slight smile, "I'd suggest that you close the door. The old lady across the hall likes watching me more than the old movies on stereop."

"Thanks again, said the man, moving backward to the door and slamming it shut.

Jaeger had poured a stiff jolt of scotch into two glasses. Before he brought the drinks to the coffee table, he pulled out a handkerchief and dabbed at his head. The handkerchief came away streaked with blood. "Wonderful," said Jaeger. "Another thing. You should never have let me go for this. I might have had something else in the pocket. Or in a holster on my back."

"You live and learn. I won't let you do that again."

Jaeger put the two drinks on a small tray and carried them to the couch. He sat down and put the tray on the table. "The best thing for you to do now, I think, is pull a chair up on the other side of this table. I wouldn't sit on the other end of this couch, if I were you." He took his glass and swallowed half of the liquor in it.

The man with the gun said nothing for a moment, but took

Jaeger's suggestion. When he sat down, Jaeger started to hand the man the other glass. "Hold it," said the man. "I'll get it myself."

"Whatever you want," said Jaeger quietly. The man reached for the glass. Jaeger swung his arm in a short arc, hurling his own glass at the man's head. At the same time, he leaned forward and chopped down hard on the man's wrist. The stranger dropped the gun and Jaeger grabbed it.

"I haven't been at this very long," said the man.

"You won't be at it much longer, either," said Jaeger. "Stand up and put your hands on your head." The other man obeyed. Jaeger stared at him for a few seconds, then slowly reached out and took the man's glass. He drank the scotch gratefully, never letting the muzzle of the gun waver from the man's chest. When he finished the drink, Jaeger smiled. "All right," he said, "who are you?"

"My name is Connor Coffey," said the man. "My arms are getting tired."

"That's a good sign. They're supposed to. I don't want to know what you name is. I don't care about that. I want to know who you are. Who sent you?"

Coffey smiled. "Couldn't this just be a simple burglary?"

"Not with the magnelocks I have on my door and the windows. You had help getting in here. Whose help?"

Coffey smiled some more, but he said nothing.

"Oh, hell," said Jaeger. "I have a gun on you, remember? You do understand that much about the business, don't you? When I have the gun, you're supposed to give me the information. You have heard about that, haven't you?"

Coffey sighed. "You can shoot me dead, right here," he said. "That wouldn't get you anything. You could beat me, pistol whip me, torture me a little. I don't know if you'll believe me, but I promise you I won't give you the information you want. I don't know it. I don't know who sent me."

"And you were supposed to do what?"

"I was supposed to lay you out, turn your apartment upside down as if I was searching for something, and not steal anything. Make you worry."

"You don't have to bother," said Jaeger. "I'm worried."

"Can I put my hands down now?"

"Yeah," said Jaeger. "Here." He gave the man back the gun. Coffey looked at Jaeger in surprise. He took the gun and put it in a pocket. Then he backed slowly to Jaeger's door, opened it without turning around, and started to sidle through it. "Wait," said Jaeger. "I want to know how you got hired."

Coffey laughed. "You don't have the gun anymore," he said.

"It didn't make so much difference when I did."

"I got this letter in the mail" said Coffey. "Special delivery. A hundred dollars to do what I told you. The money would be in the mail tomorrow. With the letter was fifty dollars, for 'expenses,' they said. I figured it wasn't a joke. Not a fifty-dollar joke. They said your door would be unlocked. It was."

"And you don't know who 'they' are?"

"Not the faintest idea."

Jaeger frowned. "Another piece of advice, and from here you're on your own. I wouldn't go home tonight. I might not go back home for a very, very long time. 'They' might not be too happy about how you loused up."

Coffey looked stricken. "Would they know?"

"I don't know," said Jaeger, grinning. "Would they?"

Coffey didn't answer. His eyes got large. He bit his upper lip for a moment while he thought. Then he closed Jaeger's door loudly. Jaeger stared at the door and listened to Coffey's hurried steps fade away down the corridor. He sat on the couch for a minute, then he got up and made himself another drink.

He went into his small bathroom and looked at his reflection in the shaving mirror. He sighed; then he tossed some cold water on his face, made a few half-hearted swipes at his hair with a brush, and hurried out of the apartment. He felt too isolated. He felt almost exiled. He wanted to get out among people again.

Jaeger had walked for some time, paying little attention to where he was going. His thoughts were all focused on the young man, Connor Coffey, who had been hired to not really burglarize Jaeger's apartment. Why would anyone want to do that? Jaeger could think of only one answer, the one Coffey himself had given him—that the unknown employer wanted Jaeger shaken up. The next question was simple. Who had anything to gain by Jaeger's confusion? The answer did not come so easily. The only one Jaeger could find after some thought was silly. At the moment, only the Aensalords were the subject of his investigations. And a phony burglary just didn't seem to be the Aensalords' most likely response.

The big man stepped up his pace; he passed through a narrow passageway between buildings and emerged into the Marktplatz. Here it was like being in the eye of a storm: a huge, dark, open place, hauntingly quiet while light and life swirled not so very far away. The light and life never seemed to spill over into this center. During the day, the Marktplatz was one of the vital sectors of the city, crowded and abuzz with produce wagons, vegetable stalls, painted umbrellas, merchants, other people. At night, though, it sometimes seemed to Jaeger as though a glass wall had been silently lowered between the big, darkened square and the surrounding community. His footsteps echoed hollowly through the wet night. Dominating the square to his right was the Frauenkirche, the Church of Our Lady, a black Gothic mass looming and glinting in the occasional moonlight like a grim guardian ghost. In the upper left-hand corner of the square the gleaming finger of the Schöner Brunnen, the Beautiful Fountain, stabbed the sky to many times the height of a man; the inscrutable, cryptic faces of kings and knights and gnomes engraved on the ancient fountain stared introspectively out into the hostile, foreign blackness of the modern world.

A gust of wind swirled dead leaves across the pavement like abandoned dreams. They made a rustling noise on the wet stones that sounded to Jaeger like the dry rattle of a dying man. Suddenly cold, he turned up his collar and walked a bit faster through the night.

The Junkyard in Nürnberg, officially known as Grossvaters, was housed in an ancient World War II bomb shelter. If one walked east at night near the Imperial Castle of Nürnberg, above the Marktplatz, one could easily pass the entrance to the Junkyard and never know it was there; the club, though nominally open to the public, usually served only a hard-core cadre of regular customers who attended with almost neurotic loyalty. If one knew of the club's existence, one turned left into a shadowed side-street, pushed open a rusty gate across the entrance to a small concrete blockhouse, and descended a broad, crumbling flight of stairs that slanted steeply down. A warm patch of light spilled through an open door at the bottom of the steps. Below was a narrow winding tunnel, carved from naked rock, that disappeared around a tight curve; from somewhere ahead came the faint sound of voices and the deep vibration of loud music. On the left wall of the tunnel at about eye-level, a crude sign and arrow had been sketched over the rough gray rock in white paint: *Grossvaters noch 10m.*

It was still early, by the clocks of the Junkyard's patrons, a new psychedelic band was playing live, and the club was filled almost to capacity. Karl Jaeger dutifully paid the four-mark admission fee and squeezed through the narrow stone tunnel that connected the club's two main rooms. Here, buried under the earth in an old bomb shelter now filled wall-to-wall with people, the music was not merely heard, it was felt in the bones and in the nerve endings of the skin: a solid thing that filled the brain and almost became an unnoticeable part of the background after a while. Soon, one often found oneself breathing in time to the rhythm, in an unconscious sympathy or an equally involuntary surrender. When the music finally stopped, as it did at infrequent intervals, the silence was much more startling and upsetting.

Jaeger skirted the postage-stamp dais where the musicians performed, squeezed to the back of the long, narrow room, by some miracle found a vacant seat, and settled himself with an air of permanent occupation. The pains in his body had faded; his energetic walking had worked the knots loose from his strong frame. His head had ceased to throb, and there was only a dull ache now where that ridiculous young hoodlum had hit him. There came, at long intervals, memories of evil fangs that glowed in the dark—after all, that adventure had ended less than a full day before—but the Junkyard, Grossvaters to the municipal inspectors and the tourists, was Jaeger's favorite unwinding spot in Nürnberg.

One of the musicians on the dais finished a long, somewhat

pyrotechnic solo improv, and the crowd applauded appreciatively. Tonight seemed to be a study in classic forms. The group was made up of two electric guitars, an electric bass, a drummer, and a male vocalist. The group had no name, of course; but their influences seemed obvious to Jaeger: the immortal Rolling Stones, naturally, and, more interestingly, the more obscure but oddly satisfying psychedelic group, the Kinks. It had been over a century since those two psychedelic groups charted out new areas in music, but their music wouldn't die. It was revived, according to the whims of those who made popular taste, at fairly regular intervals.

The band on the dais began a long, slow song, which Jaeger recognized as "Dark Star," an ancient hit by a group known as the Grateful Dead. Jaeger had never heard the Grateful Dead's version, of course, and neither had the band. Jaeger hoped that the original had a little more spontaneity than the current version. The bass player was wearing what looked like a smile button from the early 1970s; if it were authentic, it would be worth several hundred dollars. It was probably fake, a cheap copy of the details of a hundred years ago.

He sipped beer and drank in the snug but wild atmosphere of the place. Overhead, empty egg cartons had been nailed to the ceiling to absorb sound; five small hanging lanterns splashed discrete pools of pastel light over the intently silent psychedelic enthusiasts. The same spotlights beamed the same bloodless light whether the music of the decade happened to be psychedelic, or fifties harmony, or Big Band. Some things about Grossvaters never changed.

He finished his beer and ordered another. The band finished playing "Dark Star," waited for the lusty applause to die, and then launched into a screaming instrumental number that Jaeger couldn't identify. He would have guessed that it was something of middle-period Who. He listened appreciatively for a while, gently tapping his beer bottle against the table in time to the music; when the song was over, he drained the beer in one smooth swallow, rose to his feet, and made his way through the close-packed crowd.

As the lead guitar began the opening phrase of the Beatles'

classic "Taxman," Jaeger entered the lavatory and closed the door behind him. The room was a stark cubicle about eight feet wide, dimly lighted. Jaeger attended to the necessary, grinning meanwhile at the chalk-scrawled obscenities in five languages that adorned the walls, mingled with such obscure graffiti as "Viva Cosmopolities," "Bird Lives," and "Flick Lives." Jaeger went to the sink basin to wash his hands.

Outside, the voices of the band members chanted in unison. The amplified music was almost loud enough to cover up the sound of the double click—the lavatory door opening and then closing. Jaeger lifted his eyes to the mirror above the sink; behind him, a familiar face smiled at him. It was Connor Coffey, the young man who had so incompetently bungled the mock burglary at Jaeger's apartment. Jaeger opened his mouth to voice his surprise at the coincidence of their meeting again; before he could say anything, Coffey pulled a familiar-looking gun from the pocket of his brown imitation-leather jacket. Jaeger stared, his mouth still open. Coffey took deliberate aim at the back of Jaeger's head.

"You ought to consider that pistol a present from me," said Jaeger.

"At this range," said Coffey, grinning, "all that will be left of you is a thin red slop in the cracks of the mirror."

"You hear a lot about the younger generation not having proper respect," said Jaeger. "And to think, I've always defended you kids, too."

"Not that I love you less," said Coffey. "It's just that I love me more."

"A hundred dollars? You're going to do this for a hundred dollars? I'm humiliated."

"Naw," said Coffey, "this is another deal altogether. It came in a completely different envelope. Just about a half hour ago. Five hundred dollars, plus one hundred for expenses."

"Oh," said Jaeger. "That makes me feel better." His motion was instinctive and instantaneous; his arms and legs moved violently as he threw himself down and away from the sink. Jaeger's body hit Coffey across the gunman's thighs. Startled, Coffey fired: the mirror dissolved in a shower of glass fragments, but the spitting pop of the gun was drowned by the banshee wail of the psychedelic band.

Jaeger got one leg underneath himself and pushed up, ramming his massive shoulder beneath the gunman's breastbone; Jaeger slammed the youth hard against the wall. They wrestled there frantically together, tied in a scrambling knot; for an instant, Jaeger found himself looking down the terrible polished barrels of the gun. Then his strong fingers locked around the wrist of the attacker's gun hand. Jaeger took two quick steps forward, wrenching and dragging Coffey along bodily, and slammed the youth's hand violently against the hard porcelain of the sink basin. There was a sharp yelp of pain and the gun went clattering away.

Coffey brought his knee up viciously into the small of Jaeger's back. As the big man grunted and involuntarily loosed his grip, Coffey tore free and made a dive for the gun. Jaeger tripped him, picked him up heavily by the loose material of the jacket, and smashed Coffey's head against the wall with enough force to stun. Snarling, Coffey tried to ram his knee into Jaeger's crotch, but Jaeger sidestepped and caught the youth right on the point of his chin with a hard uppercut. Coffey collapsed against the sink basin. Jaeger panted for a second, aware of the insane shrieking of the band in the other room and of the impossible tempo of his heart.

Leaning against the sink, Coffey produced a small knife. Jaeger recognized the bright orange of the parachute troops of the Anglo-European League's armed forces. Coffey pressed a button on the knife's side, and the short blade sprang open. It was not long, not like a stiletto, but it was long enough to open a fatal wound. And Jaeger was willing to bet that it was sharp enough. Light gleamed from the knife blade. Jaeger feinted a barehanded attack and leaped. The psychedelic band's drummer began a loud, flashy solo. Jaeger's full weight came down across Coffey's chest, dumping the youth to the floor beneath him. Jaeger's knee ground the knife hand against the floor; suddenly, the knife was gone.

Coffey began to realize that his chances of success were gone, and that his chances of escape were likewise running out. He grew desperate. He butted his head hard into the pit of Jaeger's stomach. Jaeger hissed in pain and hammered his two clenched fists solidly against the potential murderer's head. Coffey fell against the lavatory door; the flimsy handle gave under his weight and he rolled out into the corridor. The sound of the wood splintering was hidden by the high keening of the lead guitar.

Jaeger leaned against the doorframe, breathing in harsh gasps. He had to go after Coffey, if he could ever get his breath back. This had been the first genuine fist-fight he'd had since a few memorable drunken brawls during his old University days; he was out of practice. Damn it, Coffey was starting to stir among the slivers and shards of wood in the hallway. Slowly, the guitars reached their climax and then abruptly there was silence.

Coffey, who had been lying crumpled on the floor of the corridor, shook off his daze and climbed shakily to his feet, just as the crowd in the adjoining room began applauding enthusiastically for the band. The entire battle had gone unnoticed.

Jaeger made a weary lunge for him, but Coffey twisted away and rushed into the main room; without his gun or switchblade he had no interest in tangling with his burly opponent. With Jaeger limping in pursuit, the gunman elbowed, shoved, and kicked his way through the crowd around the dais. A girl with horn-rimmed glasses gave a slight scream when she was knocked roughly aside; a huge University student bellowed in gutteral German as a hard elbow slammed his ribs. Coffey leaped for the corridor leading to the exit, careened into a middle-aged man carrying a glass of beer, and was gone; one or two shouted insults followed him out. Muttering darkly, the crowd reformed, blocking Jaeger's path.

The big man prepared to cleave his own way through the mob, then shook his head in disgust and forgot about it. There was no sense in chasing Coffey; he would be up the stairs and vanished into the maze of dark side streets by now. Besides, the way things seemed to be going, Coffey would show up again. Sooner or later.

Later that night, Karl Jaeger, slightly drunk and nervous enough to be sick, stood in the doorway of the apartment building and ran his finger along the list of residents. It had been a long time since he had been able to work up the courage to try this again; the scars on his soul from the last time were still not fully healed. His finger ghosted along the name list, then stopped, and a familiar sweet tension knotted his stomach. There—Fräulein Nati Fernfelder, and an apartment call number. He hesitated for a moment, his quickened breath steaming in the cool, damp air. He tried to gather his nerve, succeeded, and with a shrug punched the apartment call number on the house phone installed in the doorway.

There was a pause, then a loud metallic click, and the wall speaker began to buzz softly as it was activated. "Yes?" said a familiar voice, soft, sleepy, and feminine. Despite the tinny electronic distortion, it was a voice Jaeger knew, and it stirred him more than he had anticipated. "Karl? You look awful. Go away."

He tried to say something, found he couldn't, wet his lips and managed to say, "Nati." His voice croaked like a thirsty frog.

"Yes?" The girl's voice was less sleepy now, more alert. She sounded annoyed; she was watching him on her little tv scanner, and she had already remarked that he looked beaten. Why would she be annoyed? Hadn't they shared—"Karl, what do you want?"

"You, Nati. I still love you."

There was a sharp, startling sound of indrawn breath, and then with a click the speaker went dead.

Jaeger punched the call number again. No response. Swearing angrily, he leaned on the call button, broadcasting a steady attention signal to the apartment above. After a minute or two of this, the speaker clicked on again.

"I have nothing to say to you, Karl." Her voice was tense, but rigidly under control.

"Well, I have. I want you to drop the princess act. God damn it, do you think you can turn me on and off like a machine? Do you think I can just switch myself off and suddenly stop caring, just because you think you may have lost interest? What kind of an adolescent game is that?"

"I'm sorry, Karl. I don't love you. I'm sorry, but that's

just the way it is." Was there a hollow note in her voice, or was he only deluding himself again? Jaeger wanted to be able to see her face to face, to judge whether she meant the things she was saying.

"Nati, it's cold. Let me come up. I have to talk to you."

"Please go away. We've got nothing to talk about anymore." Her voice was becoming ragged now, but whether from anger or some other emotion it was impossible to say. "We tried it, and it just didn't work. It's over."

"Damn it, it isn't!"

"Damn it, it is!" Her voice was harsh. "Listen, I don't belong to you anymore. I used to, but I don't now. Understand? I don't belong to anybody but me. Listen to me, damn it! Something killed what we had, and it's gone. It never worked between us and it never could. It never will."

"No!"

"Yes!" She didn't speak for several seconds; when she did her voice was tautly controlled again, with only a hint of quiver. "It's over. Over and done with, always. Ashes to ashes, dust to dust, Karl. World without end. How final do you need it to sound? The answer will always be the same, do you hear? I don't want you, and I've never needed you."

"You can't say that."

"Karl, listen to me. I'm going to go back to bed now. If you ring the buzzer again, Anthony will get very jealous and very angry. Do you understand? Is that simple enough for you? God damn it, Karl, get the hell out of my life!"

Jaeger stood with his forehead leaning against the rough painted bricks of the wall. His breath swirled around him like a pearly shroud, and he was very, very cold. He massaged the bridge of his nose wearily with the thumb and forefinger of one hand. "Nati," he said slowly, "two nights in a row I was almost killed. But I'm not afraid of that. I just feel empty." There was only silence. Jaeger guessed that she had gone back to Anythony, whoever that was. In an even lower voice he said, "I need you, Nati."

There was a long silence as Jaeger stood against the wall, thinking, more alone than he had ever been before, in the heart of one of the oldest cities in the world. He stared out of the glass doors of the apartment building; nothing moved, nothing looked the least bit alive. Jaeger shoved his hands into his pockets and started for the door. When Nati spoke, it was like the rasp of an alarm buzzer cutting into a dream. Jaeger had time to weigh each word as it was spoken, and they were like seven icy nails driven into his coffin.

"I don't need you, Karl," she said. "Get out."

Sitting before a teletype terminal linked to the large civic computer center, Herr Gert Stahl was wrapped completely in concentration. The problem was difficult, and he was grateful. It had taxed his ingenuity and skill for five days, and he had never enjoyed any task more. He thought carefully, considering what had gone before, what errors he had made at just this stage of the problem in previous attempts at solving it. Finally his plump fingers reached out and touched the teletype's keyboard. He entered his solution: the computer considered the data for a brief moment, then replied. The computer, through the teletype terminal, said, "Knight to King's Bishop Six. Forced Mate in seven moves." Stahl sighed; he cleared the problem and ordered the computer to return the chess board to its original position. He would try again in a few minutes. It was satisfying to work late at night with his home terminal. Now, though, he got up and left his living room and walked quickly to the small laboratory that he had installed in his extra bedroom.

A large plastic bubble was set in a glowing red ring; inside the bubble, a viscous solution was churning. Stahl noted the temperature, looked at his notebook, and smiled. His small, muddy brown eyes darted from the contents of the bubble to his cramped handwriting on the page in front of him. Things were going along well. The boiling material, when cooled, would be the metallic coating of a new model blindcoat, one that might well be an acceptable compromise between the old type and the infeasible model Herr Jaeger desired. According to Herr Stahl's predictions, the new blindcoat would effectively block light visible to all earthly mammals, and a large range beyond.

Stahl permitted himself another brief smile. Herr Jaeger

would be very happy. Stahl turned and put the blindcoat out of his mind. He hurried back to the terminal and began working on the chess problem again.

Corcail Sendijen had another brush with death as soon as he slipped into the huge, malodorous common room where the black gang slept.

He had waited in hiding for D'jebistred the overseer to make the last of his twice-nightly rounds. D'jebistred departed at last, hissing and growling to himself as he shuffled ponderously along, continually turning his armored head from side to side, tasting the foul air with his flickering pink tongue. The far door closed behind him. Corcail Sendijen had not been missed. Perhaps a little too confident, perhaps a little too preoccupied with the sights and sounds of that night's foray, Corcail Sendijen immediately scurried out into the common room.

Almost at once, something hit him a sledgehammer blow.

The world exploded with pain. Dazed and confused and blind with agony, Corcail Sendijen felt something slimy and enormously heavy land on his back, bearing him down to the floor, crushing him under its bulk.

Blindly, Corcail Sendijen pulled himself into a ball and rolled, lashing out desperately with tentacles and fighting claws, trying to squirm out from under. He landed a solid hit on something with one of his main locomotor legs, and the weight and pressure eased. He rolled away and drew himself up to face his attacker.

In a second, as his breathing eased and his vision cleared, he perceived what he had done. In rushing forward into the sleeping chamber, he had inadvertently blundered right through the psychic space of a Tugore in ovulation. The Tugore, the only one in the black gang and one of the most physically formidable of them all, was in female-stage this cycle; she was in ovulation and, naturally enough, in heat. There was no male-stage of her race within 20,000 light-years of Earth, but that made no difference to her hormonal and metabolic clock. So she had smeared herself enticingly with saliva from head to toe, renewed every hour, and spun an invisible circle of inviolable psychic space around her.

Within it she would sit sleeplessly watching for three days, killing anything—except a male-stage Tugore—that came inside the circle. Even D'jebistred and the Aensalords would leave her strictly alone. She was only four feet tall, but she was more than twice as broad and heavy as the giant Malmo had been.

She was still angry. She hunkered forward, ponderously shifting herself on her enormous toad-like legs until she reached the edge of her psychic space, and then she reached for Corcail Sendijen with four tree-thick arms. He could hear her chewing-plates grinding together, and from her belly issued a noise like rock crushing rock. He did not move.

Just as her hands were about to seize him, Corcail Sendijen stretched out one of his tentacles and touched the Tugore, alongside her anterior eye. Instantly, her tiny mind lit up in his, as visible as a specimen on an illuminated microscope slide.

Her mind was like a still-black pool with a rod of red-hot iron rising out of it, boiling away the water, raising a cloud of angry steam. Corcail Sendijen gathered all the skill of a trained Adept, and then thought *peace* at her, sending the telepathic message deep into her dim and almost defenseless mind. At the same instant he hit her on a somatic level, working directly on her motor nerves and involuntary systems, pinching shut certain glands, stimulating others, slowing down her breathing and the beating of her hearts, interfering with the firing of the synapses that were sending rage/hate messages from her forebrain to her body-coordinating hindbrain. *Peace,* he projected at her. *Quiet, rest, be still.*

Her hands did not close on him. The red-hot iron rod slowly withdrew beneath the surface of the water, disappeared. The surface of the pool once again became black and stagnent and rippleless, as the Tugore sank back into the patient, mindless, waiting daze of rut.

Corcail Sendijen maintained his controlling touch, thinking how fortunate he had been to catch her before her anger became ungovernable. She probably could have torn him apart quite easily and gone on to kill many others before her beserk rage faded. Even the Aensalords might have had trouble stopping her. She was a match for any ten of the Aensa, even with their deadly pistols, and a fight between her and the Aensahounds would be something to see.

His eyes narrowed. All at once he knew how he could use Malmo's death against the Aensalords; the idea that had eluded him earlier had returned to his mind fully hatched.

Still maintaining contact with the Tugore's mind, he built her a vivid image of Malmo's death: the Aensalord firing, Malmo toppling, his shattered body twitching on the stone floor. As feedback, he received an echo of fear and unease—the scene was disquieting to the Tugore. Carefully, with photographic realism, he played the scene for her again, only this time replacing Malmo with an image of the Tugore herself, so that as the scene played out it was she herself whom the Aensalords shot, herself who fell, herself who bled and died. At once there was a massive upwelling of alarm, as the Tugore made the—for her—enormous conceptual quantum jump from the general to the specific: If Aensalords had arbitrarily murdered one member of the black gang, they might also kill *her.*

Rage began to build hotly within the Tugore again, and as it did, at exactly the right moment, Corcail Sendijen burned an inflexible command deeply into her blood and bone: *When you hear my voice, you will obey it. When you hear me call for hate, you will hate the Aensa, you will kill the Aensa, you will hate and you will kill all the Aensa, because they will otherwise kill you. When you hear my voice say to kill you will obey me, and you will kill the Aensa.*

Corcail Sendijen planted this construct deep in the Tugore's unconscious mind, reinforced it, primed it. Then he drained away her residual rage and sent her back into sleepy dormancy.

Swiftly, he moved to the next fitfully-sleeping member of the black gang, touched him to establish dominance, and started the whole process again.

By the time he had repeated it with everyone in the black gang, it was almost morning. Corcail Sendijen was exhausted, but for the first time in months he was also filled with a certain sense of satisfaction and concrete accomplishment—he had sowed a tiny ticking seed of discord, he had created a weapon for himself when he had had no weapon.

All at once, he stopped feeling quite so guilty because of his inability to save Malmo.

Corcail Sendijen settled down to wait for D'jebistred the overseer to come and wake the black gang from their fetid and uneasy dreams.

Chapter Four

When Karl Jaeger awoke, he wished that he hadn't. At first, the feeling was abstract, unfocused. It wasn't that he ached or that he dreaded tending to some unpleasant duty; it was just that he knew for certain that opening his eyes would prove to be a painful business. He was right. For a few seconds he did not move, letting his body suffer in the agony of the hangover sickness it so richly deserved. Bright morning light cut through the narrow gaps between the bedroom windows' curtains; the light stabbed into Jaeger's eyes and increased the tempo of the pounding behind his forehead. He sat up slowly. He felt terrible all over; he began a catalogue of his pains: the back of his head, which still throbbed where Connor Coffey had sapped him, the counterpoint of headache that was pure hangover, the sharp jabs of his neck, back, and leg muscles, still rebelling from their misuse during the race against the Aensa. There was more, but Jaeger had other things to think about.

Beside him, still asleep between the sheets, was a girl named Aldonna. She was the girl with the horn-rimmed glasses in the Junkyard from the night before. Jaeger had returned to the club in a vicious mood, an attitude that had intrigued Aldonna enough to persuade her to spend the night with him. He had learned nothing more about her beyond her name and the fact that she was a student. He did not even know where she pursued her studies. He did not care. He didn't think she knew even his name. Her glasses were on the night table next to the bed, on top of her plastic dentures, which she had wrapped in a tissue for the night. Her hair fell in dull swatches across her face. She breathed through her mouth, loudly, as she slept. She smelled faintly of a very cheap, very sweet perfume. Jaeger assumed that they had made love, although he could not remember the actual bout. He was grateful for that.

He got out of bed quietly. He did not want to disturb Aldonna, whoever she was. He was very sure that she would have wanted it that way. He winced as he walked slowly across the bedroom to the dresser; he looked at the clock there, saw that it was already almost ten-thirty, and scooped up his clothes from the floor. They were stained and foul-smelling. He dropped them again and went into the bathroom. He took a shower, brushed his teeth, shaved, and combed his blond hair. He didn't like the way his face looked in the mirror. It looked too old, too bruised, too lumpy in the wrong places. He had to look at it, though, at least while he shaved. He contemplated growing a beard.

When he finished cleaning himself up, he came back into the bedroom and dressed in clean clothing. Aldonna had not awakened. Jaeger took out his wallet; he couldn't remember if Aldonna had told him where she was from or how long she would be staying in Nürnberg. He passed over the small denominations of local money; he took out a ten-eurodollar bill and folded it, then slipped it under the wrapped package of her cavity-proof dentures. Moving her teeth made him feel a little strange. He hoped that she would not be insulted when she found the money. He knew that there was little chance of that.

No one at JAEGER, INC. would be the least bit curious about why he was coming in so late. His adventures of the night before last would be reason enough. And the ridiculous theatrics of Connor Coffey would give them all things to ponder. Grimacing, he slipped his own gun into the pocket of his jacket for the first time in a long while, checked to be sure that he had his keys, and left the apartment as quietly as he could.

As he pulled the door shut, he heard a sound like a distant cat spitting. Then there was a tocking sound at the end of the hallway opposite the first noise. A faint smell of burnt leaves came to Jaeger's nostrils. It was Connor Coffey again, with his amateur marksmanship. The sound of Coffey's feet hurrying down the service stairway made Jaeger release his grip on his own pistol, which he hadn't even drawn from the jacket pocket. Jaeger thought for a moment of running after the youth, then decided against it. Still, he knew that sooner or later Coffey was going to have to be stopped. Before he did something right.

Jaeger spent a quarter of a minute staring at the door to his apartment, getting his respiration rate down. "The hell with it," he said to himself. He took out his keys and opened the door again. He went back into his apartment, made himself a weak drink, and went across the living room to the Dark Lightning. He sat in the padded vinyl chair, tilted it back comfortably, and swallowed a gulp of his liquor. Then he shrugged, put the drink down on a small round table, and clicked Dark Lightning on. He was asleep almost instantly. There was only an instant of dim grayness, and then the therapeutic dream began.

Jaeger was dressed in a long silk robe of a rich red color, decorated with stylized flowers done in gold and silver thread. He was reclining on a canopied litter, which was borne by four huge servants. They were making their way along what seemed to be a quiet rural road, rutted and dusty. On one side was a blunt granite cliff jutting up over their heads; on the other were fields of grain colored the same as the dry road. Jaeger grew weary of watching the scenery pass by in its slow, unchanging way. He let his head drop back to a small pile of soft pillows. He dozed in the warm air.

Some time later he was wakened by the apologetic voice of Kanoyu, his chief counselor. "Forgive me, Radiance," said Kanoyu in his habitual obsequious whisper. "I believe we have come upon something that might provide some entertainment."

"Here?" asked Jaeger skeptically. "Where are we, anyway?"

"We are yet some twenty-five miles from Edo," said Kanoyu. "And we have overtaken an elderly sage who identifies himself as Shuin."

"Shuin? That same self-professed wise man that gave the

barons so much trouble a few years ago? I thought he was dead."

"That is he," said Kanoyu. "And he is evidently not dead."

"I would like to speak with him," said Jaeger, yawning. "The gods only know why."

"I will bring him right away," said Kanoyu with a quick bow. Jaeger waved the man away irritably and sank down again on the pillows. He listened to the murmur of voices some yards away. In a few minutes Kanoyu returned. "This is he," said the counselor.

Jaeger propped himself up on one elbow and stared at the old man whom Kanoyu presented. The sage looked like a sage: ancient, harmless-looking, tough, bent by age and hardship, with a calm expression and piercing eyes. Jaeger was not impressed. As Emperor, he had seen many such wise men. "Are you then Shuin?" he asked.

"Yes, my Emperor"' said the old man.

"And I assume you have achieved your own spiritual enlightenment."

The old man said nothing. Jaeger chewed his upper lip. "Is becoming enlightened a difficult task?"

"One cannot say," said Shuin, shrugging. "For some it is no more difficult than spilling out the stale water of a vase of flowers. Others pursue the goal for a lifetime and die as they began. Enlightenment strikes one like lightning. It illuminates one's entire mind, but it is unpredictable."

"This is not entertaining, Kanoyu," said Jaeger in a harsh voice. The counselor paled.

"So far from Edo, one must expect less sophistication," said Kanoyu.

"How then did you find your own lightning bolt?" asked Jaeger.

"I had studied at a temple near my village," said Shuin. "I was tutored by the master Ryoki for nearly ten years. He asked me questions daily, of a complex and seemingly nonsensical nature. I would try to give him the answer I thought he expected. I always gave him complex, nonsensical, incorrect answers. There were no answers to the questions he asked. This was something I did not learn until later, however. Whenever I answered him, he would stare at me for several seconds, his face showing no emotion. Then he would slap me very hard across the face. This happened every morning for ten years. One day he asked me the question for that morning, and while I silently framed my reply, he slapped me before I said a word. The instant he hit me, my mind seemed to open like parting clouds after a dark storm. That is the way with enlightenment."

"You are a long-winded wise man," said Jaeger. "That is in itself an entertaining novelty. Not very entertaining, though, and already somewhat wearisome. How, then, might I become enlightened? I don't have ten years to invest in the process."

Shuin smiled faintly. "The Emperor is already enlightened," he said.

Jaeger looked at Kanoyu, who avoided the glance. "I will state categorically, and with some disappointment, that I, the Emperor, am not enlightened."

"I must contradict you, Your Radiance. The Emperor is already enlightened."

Jaeger yawned again. "You are calling me a liar, in effect. Kanoyu, has it ever been your experience that someone has called the Emperor a liar, either behind my back or, incredibly, to my face?"

"No, Radiance," said Kanoyu, his voice hoarse and shaky.

"You must take this sage away," said Jaeger. "Do something with him."

"He will be beheaded, Your Radiance," said Kanoyu fearfully. Jaeger did not reply. He took out a silver knife with a carved ivory and jade handle and began to trim his fingernails. A few minutes later he heard the chocking sound of an ax severing the gray head of Shuin the sage. Jaeger stared silently at the fingernail he was cutting. Shuin's life and the fingernail. All nothing, all a happy nothing. With a sudden, ecstatic flash of insight, Jaeger the Emperor was enlightened.

He woke up. It had been a dream enlightenment, one he had experienced many times through Dark Lightning.

Already the insight was fading. The intense, final emotions blew away like powdery snow on the wind. Jaeger stood up, stretched, and grabbed the glass he had set on the table. He swallowed the rest of the drink in one long gulp. When he turned to make another, the girl, Aldonna, was standing behind the padded chair. "Good morning," he said. He saw that she had put her teeth in but had neglected to get dressed.

"I thought you might want me before you left," she said. "I want you."

"That's very nice," said Jaeger. "I have to leave, though. I left you cab fare by the bed. Do you want a drink?"

"No, thanks. I found the money. Thank you." She came around by Dark Lightning. "We used to have a Kurasu. My family did, a few years ago. But my father traded it in on a Peugeot. Can I use it?"

"Sure," said Jaeger in dull voice. He was wondering why Dark Lightning had programmed that particular vision. Did it understand his subconscious worries, about the Aensa problem, about the curious trouble with Connor Coffey and his invisible employers? Was it saying that the answer to everything was in plain sight, as simple as cutting an overlong fingernail, that all Jaeger needed was a proper kick in the pants and the world's dilemmas would solve themselves? He hated to believe that, for that was an easy way to be lulled into a confident inactivity, when what he needed was plain strenuous work, both mental and physical. He would have to think about Dark Lightning.

Jaeger found himself humming the same Scott Joplin rag that had run through his mind during his escape from the Aensa. "The Maple Leaf Rag," one of his favorites. The song reminded him of Nati, of what she had said to him the night before. He shrugged, trying to erase that memory. When he turned to Aldonna again, she was standing up from Dark Lightning.

"How was it?" he asked.

"Strange," she said. "One I've had before. I was hanging from a vine, over a gorge. On the top of the cliff was a gigantic tiger, so I couldn't climb up. On the ground below me was another one, so I couldn't climb down. Above my head there were two mice, one black, one white, and they were gnawing through my vine. Right in front of me, growing out of a little bulge in the cliff, was a wild strawberry plant. I picked a strawberry and ate it. The only thing I could think of was how wonderful that strawberry tasted. Then I woke up."

"Easy enough," said Jaeger. He had had that same vision, too. Dark Lightning was saying to concentrate on the here and now, to take happiness and pleasure wherever one found them, and to ignore the tigers that waited. They would be there forever, and they were patient. There was such a short time in which to pick the strawberries in life. If Jaeger had believed in such things, he would have interpreted the one tiger as the threat of the Aensa, which even someone like Aldonna must feel in some way. The other tiger would be whatever troubles occupied her subconscious mind. Jaeger smiled bitterly when he realized that he was just the strawberry in her dream, just a casual, already spent pleasure. It was a role he was getting tired of playing.

"I kind of understand it," said Aldonna. "I don't know what I'm supposed to do about it, though." She went into the bedroom and dressed quickly.

"Go back to the Junkyard tonight," said Jaeger.

"Will you be there again?"

Jaeger sighed. "That isn't important at all," he said. "Ready?" She nodded, and together they left the apartment. They rode down in the elevator but parted at the street level. Jaeger walked a couple of blocks, hailed a taxi, and rode to his office.

Marga Geier, Hans Wiessmann, and Gert Stahl were sitting around the reception desk, playing three-handed bridge. They all looked up, startled, when Jaeger came through the outer door. "Good morning," he said. He took off his jacket and threw it onto one of the couches.

"Good morning, Karl," said Weissmann, with a concerned look on his face. Marga Geier stood up from her chair and walked toward Jaeger. Herr Stahl studied his cards.

"What time is that appointment with the IC attachés?" asked Jaeger.

"Three-thirty, Karl," said Marga Geier. "Hans told me what happened. What are you going to do?"

"I think I'm going to sit down to a quiet game of bridge," said Jaeger. "Anyway, Hans doesn't know the details. What did he tell you?"

The girl looked embarrassed. "Nothing, really. That you were on some kind of a mission in the Aensa territory. That you managed to escape. I could see that you were in bad shape, Karl. I worried all last night."

"So did I," said Jaeger.

"How are you feeling today, Karl?" asked Weissmann.

"Better," said Jaeger. "Just a little terrible, that's all." Jaeger picked up the coat from the couch and walked toward the inner door. He stopped there and turned to Herr Stahl. "Shuffle them up, will you? I need some kind of fun where I can be fairly confident I won't end up dead." Weissmann pushed the button on the reception desk. Jaeger opened the inner door, went through, and held it open until Weissmann joined him. Together they walked down the narrow corridor to Jaeger's office.

"Somebody's been trying to cancel me, Hans," said Jaeger. He opened the door to his office. While he flicked on the lights and settled himself at his desk, he filled Weissmann in on the events of the last two days.

"Why, Karl?" asked Weissmann, sitting in the client's chair beside the desk. "Why would anyone want to kill you?"

Jaeger shook his head and walked to his chair. "I don't know, Hans, I can't figure it out. You'll have to get me the Central Data file on this kid Coffey, but I'm willing to bet there won't be anything there. He's worse than an amateur. He claims that he's been hired by somebody; whoever that somebody is, they want their agent to have a clean record. I don't know why. I would have gone with experience."

Hans Weissmann wrung his hands together. He stood and began pacing back and forth distractedly. If he'd had more hair, he might have run his fingers through it. "It's outrageous. Absurd. This is like something out of an old American movie. People don't get attacked in respectable nightclubs.

People don't get shot at in their own apartment buildings. Such things don't happen, nicht wahr?"

"Nevertheless," said Jaeger wearily, "it happened."

"But why?" Weissmann spread his hands wide. "There is no motive. You say that the man didn't ask you to surrender your money. He said that he's working for someone he doesn't even know. He has nothing against you personally?"

"Right."

"No," said Weissmann, with an air of finality, "that doesn't make sense."

"I know."

Weissmann reached the limit of his understanding and began to run his fingers through his nonexistent hair. "Karl, have there been any, ah, indiscretions on your part lately? With another man's wife or lover, perhaps? Something that might somehow become public knowledge and inspire the man to an, ah, crime of passion?"

"Why don't you go back out and help Stalh shuffle those cards?"

"Well, then, do you know of anyone who bears enough hatred toward you to actually attempt murder? Perhaps someone who might hold a grudge from a previous assignment?"

"As far as I know, most of the people who would have real reason to hate me are still in work camps, to which they were legally sentenced. And nobody's going to shoot me over a little scandal or two." Jaeger lifted his feet from the desk, swung them around to the floor. "Hans, did you refund my fee to Herr Schiller yesterday, as I instructed?"

"Jawohl, I mailed it out to him before four o'clock."

"That's the only possibility that I can see, but it's still pretty far-fetched. A big man like Schiller wouldn't behave like that. It occurred to me that maybe he thought I was trying to cheat him out of his money, and so decided to have me gunned down over a few hundred eurodollars." Jaeger grimaced sourly. "No, that doesn't make the least bit of sense, does it? But I guess I do owe him a report today."

Jaeger stared at his desk silently for some time. Weissmann ceased his pacing and took his seat again. Jaeger studied a typed report on his blotter; it was the lab report on his blood sample, which Herr Stahl had prepared the day before. "Interesting," said Jaeger to himself. "Interesting but meaningless, I suppose." The paper showed that Jaeger's suspicions had been correct: the intense panic he had experienced in the Aensa territory had been artificially induced. It had not been characteristic of Jaeger to flee in such blind terror; he did not mind running when he had to, that was a valuable technique he had come to rely on more than once. But he had always kept his thoughts sorted during the process. The substance that Stahl had found in Jaeger's blood was a fairly common drug, used by the military and others to create a sense of almost unbearable fear and helplessness in persons who had resisted all other methods of interrogation. In mild doses it was very effective. In large doses, it turned the victim into a mindless, screaming animal, an effect that was irreversible. The chemical was apparently absorbed through the skin in Jaeger's case; he had received a very minimal dose, much less than the standard. Jaeger whistled to himself, feeling sympathy for the unfortunates who had it even worse than he had.

"A pretty good defense," said Weissmann. "It would confuse any trespasser enough to make him easy to catch. Except you, of course."

Jaeger looked over the page at his friend. His eyes seemed focused on some scene far from the quiet office. He said nothing.

"There has to be a drug to counteract the effect," said Weissmann. "I've already taken the liberty of asking Herr Stahl to acquire some."

"Why, Hans?" asked Jaeger, frowning. "Are you planning on sneaking over the line yourself some night?"

Weissmann flushed but did not answer. The two men stood up and left the office. They went back out to the reception room, took seats, and played bridge until lunchtime. Stahl and Weissmann were winning by a large margin over Jaeger and Geier. Jaeger just couldn't seem to concentrate on the game.

Herr Maximilian Schiller lived in a secluded country house halfway to Ansbach. Jaeger had to pay triple fare to get a taxi to take him that far, and a substantial bonus to get it to wait—already his interview with Schiller was going badly, he thought with foreboding; he could pad his expense account to cover it, of course, but that was only stealing out of his right pocket with his left hand. Grimacing, he got out of the cab. The sunlight was warm and dusty, and the wind through the fir trees made a lonely, desolate sound.

"A great place for a murder," Jaeger said aloud. Then he smiled.

The Schiller mansion had been built in one of those comparatively unpopulated and underdeveloped regions that often remain oddly inviolate even when they are within easy range of the biggest and most expansive of cities. It was surrounded by miles of verdant farming country and dusty sleeping villages, gently rolling hills and fir forests. Except for the occasional intrusive automobile or passing stratojet, it might have been a baronial stronghold straight out of the sixteenth century. Its appearance was deceptive, Jaeger knew. The half-timbered facade was authentic, the wood and stone having been taken from a thousand-year-old house in Nürnberg, but underneath the ancient shell the core of the building was made of carbon steel and reinforced fiberbond. According to a report in one of the sensation-hungry local newsfiches, the house was strong enough to withstand anything short of a tactical nuclear bomb. Jaeger wondered what grim black iron was hidden behind Schiller's respectable business front, as here armor hid beneath old soft wood.

It went without saying that no one amassed Schiller's kind of money by entirely legal means. The question was: How far beyond the routine deceit and dishonesty tacitly approved of by a status-hungry society had Schiller gone?

No one came to answer Jaeger's doorbell ringing. Instead, the door slid open by itself, revealing a small antechamber and an iron inner door. Jaeger looked over this setup warily, then shrugged and stepped inside. The outer door slammed shut and locked itself with an ominous click, leaving Jaeger in musty darkness. There was the faintest of humming noises, on the very edge of hearing, and an almost subliminal prickling of the skin. Jaeger sensed that he was being thoroughly examined by dozens of sophisticated security devices, and was glad that he'd finally decided to leave his gun behind at the office when he came out here. Schiller seemed to be such a complete paranoid, there was no telling what would have happened if he'd been armed.

After a moment, the inner door swung open. Beyond was a long well-lit corridor ending in another massive door. Jaeger's ears registered a pressure change as he stepped inside the corridor—Schiller must keep the house pressurized, probably as a defense against germs. Or airborne poisons.

So far, Jaeger had not seen a single human being. He wondered if there were any servants, or if the whole house was run by robot machinery. It was spooky to think of Schiller sitting alone in the center of this vast empty house day after day, running his huge publishing business by holophone, pulling the strings that controlled his financial empire, tended only by silent mechanical ghosts.

The door at the end of the corridor led to a spherical library/study, brilliantly lit and entirely carpeted in shaggy red plush all the way around the inner curve of the sphere, overhead, underfoot, everywhere. From the doorway, it was like peeking into a hollowed-out tennis ball and discovering that a big black beetle has crawled inside it to live. A beetle who could afford the most sumptuous of furnishings, a library of rare books and manuscripts, and had perhaps a million-dollars' worth of fine paintings on his walls.

"Come in, Herr Jaeger," Schiller said.

Jaeger walked gingerly down the curve of the wall toward Schiller's enormous teak desk, which was located in the exact center of the spherical room. The two men rose, half-bowed to each other, shook hands formally, and then Schiller nodded Jaeger to the room's only other chair. They sat down.

"Schnapps?" Schiller asked, pouring himself a drink from a bottle that magically appeared on his desk.

"No, thank you."

"Ah," Schiller said thoughtfully, as though Jaeger had just said something very wise. He was not what Jaeger had expected. He was a big, robust man in his middle fifties with a lumpy face, a bulbous nose, and an almost-bald head. He looked like a dock worker, or a truck driver, or—Jaeger taking in the fact that the maroon turtleneck sweater he wore, while still only a turtleneck sweater, was made of the finest and most expensive of materials—more accurately, a retired major-general about to diligently engage in the hour of jogging prescribed by his doctor. He seemed not at all impatient to get down to business, as if he was perfectly willing to spend the afternoon drinking schnapps and chatting about the weather. The very rich were never in a hurry, Jaeger thought. They had all the time in the world.

"You may perhaps have received the return of my retainer?" Jaeger asked.

Schiller dismissed this with a probably unconscious flick of his little finger: It was literally of no importance.

"I have decided that I am unable to complete my assignment," Jaeger continued, "but I feel that you deserve a full report why."

"Ah," Schiller said.

Jaeger delivered his report as succinctly as possible, trying hard to avoid the sing-song professorial monotone he almost instinctively slipped into at such times—occasionally, Jaeger had to fight hard against a hated tendency toward humorless pendantry that was particularly German, and probably the residue of his academic years at the University. He told Schiller everything, leaving out only the odd events that had taken place after his return to Nürnberg. Schiller listened impassively to Jaeger's tale of fangs in the night and relentless pursuing horror. His eyes flickered constantly around the room, peering into every shadow, but this did not seem to be an effect produced by Jaeger's eerie report; his eyes had roved and probed thus before Jaeger had even opened his mouth to speak. Perhaps they always did. He even stared with deep suspicion into his glass from time to time, as if he feared that someone might have dropped a pill in his schnapps.

When Jaeger had finished, Schiller put his glass carefully down on the gleaming surface of his desk—the glass disappeared—and shook his head in dissapproval. "I must say, I am not pleased, Herr Jaeger."

"Ah," Jaeger said cynically.

"I had hoped for better from you." He made the flicking gesture with his little finger again, dismissing Jaeger and his generation and all the degenerate world. "But I should have known better. You are not tough enough, Herr Jaeger. None of you are tough enough anymore, you are all effete and soft—not like we were. Not like I was, in the old days. We kicked life in the teeth, and it was life that gave way, not us. We were tough."

"I don't need to be tough," Jaeger said. "I'm efficient."

"Pfui. Who cares for that? I had been told that you were tough."

"Don't give me that," Jaeger said testily. "The tough detective mystique—that's image, it's good for business. People expect it. Don't try to tell me you were taken in by the image; you're too smart for that. You didn't hire me because I'm tough, and you goddamn well know it. You hired me because I get the job done."

"You didn't get it done this time."

"No, but that's because, in my opinion, the job is impossible. I said I was efficient—I didn't say I was God. At least I got back alive. Which is more than most men could've done."

"The other two didn't," Schiller said, "so perhaps there is something to that."

Jaeger stared at him. "You son of a bitch," he said softly, after a long pause. "You knew all along how deadly dangerous this assignment was, and you let me go toddling off without even telling me."

"If I had told you, you might not have gone. Besides, if you were enough of a man, you'd be able to handle yourself against anything."

"I ought to tear your head off," Jaeger said thickly. "I'm enough of a man to handle that."

"You're not supposed to be tough, remember?"

"For you, I'll make an exception. You son-of-a-bitch."

"You know," Schiller said, in an interested, affable tone, "when you get rich, you soon find that there are many things from which your wealth will shield you. People calling you hard names, for instance, to your face. I'm not used to that anymore."

"Get used to it again, quick. I'm not half finished yet."

"Jaeger," Schiller said with sudden intensity, leaning

forward in his seat. His restless gaze locked on Jaeger. "Will you go back there? For triple the fee?"

"No."

"You're a coward."

"Yes, certainly. Of course."

"Ah, Jaeger," Schiller said sadly. "You're not *tough* enough, Jaeger. I should've sent someone with guts."

"The situation didn't call for guts, old man. It called for brains and a lot of luck, and the fact that I happened to have both was the only reason I got back alive. What do you expect your brave hero to do, punch the Dktar in the snout?"

"I don't know, Jaeger," Schiller said, "but let me tell you one thing. If I was twenty, or even ten years younger, I would have made it. *I* would have made it." Schiller's voice had become earnest, and he leaned still further out over his desk, almost beseachingly. Jaeger sensed that, for the first time, Schiller had stopped playing games and was speaking his heart. "Don't ask me how, but I would have gotten the job done, some way, any way. I did many harder and more dangerous jobs when I was young. Because I will not accept failure. I never have and never will, d'you hear?" Schiller's lumpy face was flushed and sweating. Jaeger could imagine him looking just so as he jogged, worked out in expensive gyms and saunas, practiced karate with programmed robot assailants, and did all the other things a somewhat hysterically desperate rich man does when he is fighting a losing battle against the inevitable disintegration of his youth. More than ever he reminded Jaeger of the kind of retired general you see on stereop shows—he had a stereop general's eyes, unblinking agate-hard eyes that were beginning to cloud and dim, so that the hawk-like intensity of his gaze now seemed suspiciously like the weak-eyed squint of someone straining to see.

"You attack and attack in this world," Schiller whispered, "and you don't stop until you've won. Because you are a man."

There was a moment of silence.

"You know," Jaeger said conversationally, "one other thing wealth can do for you is enable you to sit around in great comfort when you're old and pretend that you're still tough. Or maybe that you ever were."

Schiller froze into ice.

Jaeger continued pleasantly: "And most people will sit by and let you play *machismo* games with them because you're rich. Even if you've swallowed your own crappy fantasy game like a wormy apple, and are obviously mad as a hatter, people will let you act out your fantasies on them. Because they know you've got a lot of money. That must be nice! Eh?"

Schiller sat frozen for a million years of ice, and then, in a flat, deadly voice, said: "I don't suppose, Herr Jaeger, that you've considered the fact that there are other things that rich people may often get away with? Especially in their own house? In their own soundproofed house in the country?"

"You're too smart for that, too," Jaeger said.

Schiller thought about it for a minute, and then said, "Yes, I am, aren't I?" He relaxed and sat back in his chair, seemingly dismissing the whole matter from his mind. When he spoke again, his voice was almost affable. "I think that terminates both our conversation and our association, then. Correct?"

Jaeger stood up. "Quite correct."

"Good day, then," Schiller said. A snack of cheese and pickles on toast had appeared on his desk out of nowhere, as well as a steaming mug of hot chocolate. He didn't look at Jaeger again.

Outside in the dusty sunlight, Jaeger reflected that his confrontation with Schiller had gone as badly as he had expected. Doubtless it would also be terrible for business, once Schiller got through bad-mouthing him near and far. He had not even bothered to accuse Schiller of hiring Coffey—what good would it have done?—so the trip had been wasted as far as that was concerned as well.

As he neared the taxi, he choked off an exclamation of dismay and started walking faster.

The meter was still running.

At three-thirty, Jaeger was sitting at his desk again, calm

again, pretending that he had quite a lot of work to do. Weissmann had produced a fiche on Connor Coffey. Jaeger had guessed right; the young man had nothing on his record more serious than a couple of minor traffic violations. Jaeger snorted in disgust and tossed the datafiche into the wastebasket.

A buzzer sounded on Jaeger's desk. He picked up his telephone, and Marga Geier's voice said, "Three gentlemen to see you, Herr Jaeger. The gentlemen from the International Congress. They have appointments."

"Thank you, Marga. Send them in."

Weissmann arrived, politely herding the three men like an anxious shepherd with an unpredictable flock. Jaeger rose, was introduced, and everyone shook hands all around. Herr Stahl entered briefly with another report, and he too was introduced. Everyone shook hands all around again.

Jaeger cleared his throat softly. "How may I be of assistance, gentlemen?" He sized up his visitors with an experienced eye. The one from the Northeastern Monocity, a Mr. Huston, was tall and grizzled, with a hawklike face and a dangerous air. The other NAUL representative, Mr. Healey, was short, rotund, and officious. Teresky, the attaché from the Slavic Confederacy, was gray, slender but strong-looking, with a bitter face. He sat noticeably apart from the other two men.

Healey coughed and tapped his fat fingertips together. "We, representing the Security Bureau of the IC, in addition to our various homelands in this affair, of course, would like to engage your, ah, services for an indefinite period, Herr Jaeger. We realize that your regular fee—"

"One moment, please." Jaeger's eyes weighed Healey briefly, then discarded him from the conversation. Healey was a pompous bureaucratic ass, of a type that Jaeger immediately recognized and just as quickly hated. Healey had sounded vaguely like someone pricing women in a brothel. "Engage your, ah, services" indeed! Jaeger decided to ignore him. He looked at the other two men. "I find this all rather hard to believe, gentlemen," he said. He leaned forward slightly. "The IC Security Bureau has a large network of its own agents, all the trained men it could possibly use. Why could you possibly need me?"

Healey coughed and started to reply, but Huston cut him off smoothly; the fat man glared. "Special tasks require special talents, Herr Jaeger," said Huston. A smile crinkled his hawk face without lighting his eyes. "It is possible that you possess the necessary special talents for this particular task. In the past, you have demonstrated a knack for doing the improbable. We hope that it will prove so again, this time."

Jaeger studied him for a second, wondering what the man would think if he could speak with Herr Schiller for a few minutes. The cold eyes of the IC attaché were serious and unflinching. "What's your problem, gentlemen?" asked Jaeger. He hated the tiredness of the phrase, even as he spoke it.

Huston glanced quickly at Hans Weissmann. Jaeger caught the hint. "Hans," he said, "would you be good enough to make us some coffee, please? I know that I'll be needing some in a little while, at any rate, and I expect that these gentlemen might like some as well." Jaeger nodded toward the door. "I'll buzz you when we're ready." Weissmann smiled, nodded good-naturedly, and left.

Huston tugged on his chin, glanced up sharply as the door clicked shut. "Herr Jaeger, I don't have to remind you that everything we will say in this room is covered by the Official Secrets Act as provided for by the World Charter."

Jaeger raised an eyebrow slightly. The big guns were being brought up. "I'll keep silent, gentlemen. You don't have to worry about that. I'm not an Eastern spy, either."

A brief, rather grim smile creased Huston's face. "We know. Your security clearance has been checked extensively. And you do have a record of confidential government work. I'll proceed on the assumption that you're in the clear."

"Thank you." Jaeger's smile was hard and equally grim. "What do you want me to do? Or rather, who do you want me to kill?"

Teresky stirred in his chair for the first time. His melancholy eyes flickered over Jaeger. "Who do we want you to kill? Perhaps the Aensamaster, perhaps someone else. Perhaps no one. It depends."

"On what?"

"On the circumstances; on what you find out. On how well you do your job. On whether you can remain alive long enough to worry about it."

"What do you want me to do?" asked Jaeger. His face had clouded at the mention of the Aensamaster; it would take a while to uncloud. "How do the Aensalords figure into it?"

"Basically," said Huston, "we want you to move stealthily into the Aensalords' territory and do a little reconnaissance job for us. We want to learn a few basic facts."

Jaeger made a small grimace, unnoticed by the other men. He wondered which insane god had taken charge of his life. Not again! "Why me?" he asked. "Why not send one of your own men? You must have men who would make better commandos than me."

Huston snorted, Healey fidgeted nervously, and Teresky gave a rumbling laugh. "Ah, but we have," said the Slav. "We've sent seven of our best men into Aensa territory to spy in the past month. Not one of them has been seen again. They vanished without a trace."

Huston shook his head. "Well, parts of the last two men were found near Schwäbisch Gmünd. That was established conclusively by the laboratory tests."

Teresky nodded. "Yes, thank you. I had forgotten. However, the men were hardly in any condition to report. Or to do anything, for that matter. So our knowledge in this vital area remains next to nothing, and we have lost seven good men."

Jaeger chewed his lip thoughtfully. "And you're in some kind of hurry to make it eight. Why? What do you want to know about the Aensalords?"

Healey interrupted. He looked nervous. "Huston," he said, "I still think you should reconsider. We know little of this man, and a matter of this magnitude—" Huston shriveled Healey with a murderous scowl. Muttering, Healey sank back into his chair.

Jaeger smiled slightly; his picture of the trio was beginning to firm up. The Northeastern Monocity and the Southern

Megalopolis had long been major political rivals within the body of NAUL. There was a definite hostility between Huston and Healey that Jaeger might have dismissed as a product of his imagination, had he not known the names of their home cities. The two men were traditional enemies; old ethnic patterns did indeed make stubborn ghosts!

As for Teresky, although he was aloof enough in the political manner of the Slavic Confederacy, Jaeger could sense a certain sympathy toward Huston and himself that was difficult to explain—until one realized that Teresky came from Warsaw, and not someplace like Moscow that had more reason to bear a lingering grudge against Western Europe.

Huston crossed his legs impatiently. "You are familiar with the basic facts concerning the first landings of the Aensalords?"

"Yes."

Huston smiled. "Good. Now forget all that and let me tell you what really happened." He arose from his chair and began to pace; Huston's pacing was more relaxed and self-assured than Hans Wiessmann's frantic marching. Huston's voice was even as he wandered about Jaeger's office. Jaeger supposed that Huston was actually trying to get a better evaluation of the investigator by looking at the contents of the room. Jaeger wondered if Huston would have the nerve to open one of the empty file cabinets.

"A few weeks before the first official contact with the Aensalords outside our planet's atmosphere, somewhere around Mars, I think," said Huston, "reports of UFO sightings began to trickle into IC Headquarters from all over the world." He paused. "Now this was nothing new, of course; there have been periodic flying saucer scares for centuries, none of them ever amounting to anything. But these reports were made mainly by our own spy network, one of the finest in the world. Our satellites track anything moving over the surface of the world, whether it seems to be flying in a ballistic pattern or not. So if our spy network reported that it had seen UFOs, then it had seen UFOs, and we couldn't afford to laugh it off as just another silly-season scare. It had us worried."

Huston grimaced as an unpleasant memory flickered

through his mind. "Then one of our IC warships vanished without a trace during a routine patrol beyond the moon. Impossible. Any kind of an accident would have left some trace for us to pick up, particularly that close to home. It had to be outside interference." A muscle twitched in his cheek. "Well, we came pretty damn close to the Big War then, I can tell you. The only thing that prevented it was that we didn't have any idea who to aim at. It's a miracle some bureaucratic fool somewhere didn't lose his head and hit the panic button. For about two weeks before first contact, diplomatic relations were strained to the limit. The Slavic Confederacy naturally assumed that we were up to some kind of mischief and—"

"And the NAUL naturally assumed that the Slavic Confederacy was up to some kind of mischief," Teresky said dryly.

"Precisely," said Huston. "Neither government figured that a third party might be responsible. At that time, there weren't any likely third parties. A provincial attitude, I guess. It was a bad shock for both of our nations when the Aensalords appeared. For decades we had been taught that trouble could only come from the East—" a quick glance at Teresky "—or the West, as the case may be."

"Thank you." Teresky's cool eyes were ironic.

Huston smiled briefly. "Yes. Well, at any rate, the turmoil caused by all this was mostly isolated in the highest diplomatic circles. As is usually the case, the man on the street never got the word."

Jaeger nodded. "This is the first time I ever heard anything about it."

"It should be. Uttermost top secret. Drop Dead Before Reading, and all that." Huston tugged at his chin. "Did you see the telecasts of the first conference with the Aensalords? Yes? Then you know that the Aensalords insisted that they had just happened upon us in the course of a long trading voyage, that they had no previous knowledge that our system contained an inhabited planet, that the contact near Mars was the first time they had ever entered our solar system from deep space. Well, they lied! They did an extensive reconnaissance job on us for two months before letting themselves be seen at Mars. They sniffed out every aspect of our planet, right down to capturing and interrogating humans—the poor devils from the IC ship. They knew well enough what they were getting into."

Jaeger rubbed his forefinger against his nose thoughtfully. "Why? What are they after?"

Huston grunted. "Remember that conference at the NAUL capital in Denver, then the one in Moscow, in London, and all the others? Well, they were just window dressing. The real business was settled during a meeting between the Aensalords and the IC Security Bureau a week earlier. It wasn't a conference, really; it was a vehicle for the delivering of an ultimatum."

"I imagine the Aensa would be very good at the ultimatum routine."

Huston nodded. "With their superior firepower and equipment, the Aensalords could destroy our entire civilization, or at least cripple it beyond recovery. But we had ships and relatively crude atomics, too, and the victory would likely be a costly one for the Aensa. In addition, it would ruin the commercial value of Earth for hundreds of years. That didn't fit in with their scheme." He shrugged. "It was a standoff. So the Aensalords demanded that we pay, ah, what was your word?" Huston looked at Teresky.

"Danegeld," said the Slav. "What the tenth century British paid in tribute to the Norse raiders."

"Yes," said Huston, sitting in his chair again. "Thank you. If we could meet the Aensalords' price, then they would refrain from attacking us, and everyone would be happy. If not—R.I.P. the entire world."

Jaeger's jaw muscles tightened. "Bribery. Appeasement. Protection money. The same old thing over and over again; it never ends." He sighed. "What was their price?"

"A damn odd one," said Huston. "They demanded ten square miles of land meeting detailed climatic and geographical specifications, total immunity from outside interference, and complete privacy. There were also some concessions made in precious metals and fissionable material, but the land was the major term in the agreement."

Jaeger arched an eyebrow. "Why?"

"Damn it, we don't know!" said Healey, loosening the

unskillfully tied knot of his necktie. "Nobody knows."

Jaeger shook his head, grimly thoughtful. "Minos of Crete demanded his maidens, the Danes wanted gold, Hitler took the Sudetenland. And now the Aensa have their ten square miles of land. Why? They could have just as easily have raped the Earth."

Huston nodded. "We've tried to figure it out for years. If you have any better luck than IC Intelligence, let us know. We evacuated the population of the area that most precisely met their specifications and let them settle in. Their warships, three damn big monsters, went into parking orbit around Earth to make sure that we kept our end of the bargain, and that was that. Naturally, we clamped down hard on publicity. The first contact near Mars had triggered the Thirty-Day Riots; there was no telling what would have happened if the public had found out that death would be hanging constantly above their heads, from that moment on. The Aensalords cooperated; they didn't want any internal troubles bothering their precious solitude."

Healey coughed softly. "For the last time, I must make an official protest at this flagrant breach of security."

"For the last time, shut up," said Huston, growling. Healey flustered briefly, then subsided as Teresky turned a dangerous glare on him from the opposite ideological camp.

There was a short-lived silence. At last Jaeger said, "And just where in all of this do you think that I figure, gentlemen?"

Teresky flipped open a briefcase, fished around inside it, and came up with a tiny glass vial. In the vial gleamed a few drops of bright blue liquid. "This is where you figure into it, Herr Jaeger," said Teresky.

"What is that?"

"That," Huston said, nodding toward the vial, "is probably one of the most dangerous substances on Earth. It is the kind of thing the military has been dreaming about for centuries. It is the kind of thing that paranoid citizens have believed in, but even their most nightmarish visions could never come up with something like this. It took the Aensa to do that. Let me explain. Five years ago, unconfirmed reports of the effects of a powerful new drug began to circulate through unofficial channels. Within a year, reports of its use had tripled. We could no longer ignore the rumors, although the drug itself had neither been isolated nor even identified. The estimated use of the stuff has been rising at a fantastic rate ever since."

"And—" said Jaeger.

"—that's it," said Teresky. "Yes. Looks harmless, doesn't it? Have you ever seen the effect of cobra venom or curare on the human body? Yes? Well, the effects of this chemical are incalculably worse. The drug goes beyond addiction. Once it is introduced into an organism's system, death is inevitable unless additional doses of the drug are taken at regular intervals."

"So then—"

"Clever, isn't it?" Huston smiled coldly. "Just the kind of treachery you might expect from the Aensa. Just the kind of insane scheme that used to make horror thrillers for children's entertainment." His face suddenly became a brittle mask, taut and incredibly weary. "It forges an unbreakable bond between its victim and whoever supplies the drug. The stuff is immediately habit-forming, yes, but the motivations for obtaining more are stronger than mere withdrawal pain. If the continuing doses are not administered on time, about every eighteen hours, death follows quickly. There is no known substitute or cure. Moreover, unlike many conventional drugs, it can be given involuntarily. It's easily soluble, and it's tasteless."

Teresky spoke up. "The drug is a priceless political weapon. It's so easy to dissolve in the food or drink of some key man and then—suddenly—he is your creature, and no one is the wiser. Or, if you'd rather play at assassination, simply give it to your victim, make sure that he can't get more, and then watch him die inch by inch before the eyes of the world. I'm told that in diluted doses it also makes an effective truth serum, although the subject isn't likely to be worth very much afterward; the brain tissues tend to break down. Tactically speaking, that little vial is worth a small, well-trained army."

Jaeger's eyes glinted. "The cup of hemlock is mightier than the sword?"

Teresky smiled without mirth. "Exactly. Look at Renaissance Italy, where it was raised to a fine art, along with everything else. But this blue poison is worse than anything they knew about. I doubt if Socrates would have approved; it's a hemlock that kills the soul before the body."

Jaeger nibbled a thumb. "You said this was a political weapon. How effective?"

"Supremely effective," said Huston. "Too effective. Too damn effective, in fact." Healey coughed in his irritating way, started to say something, glanced at Huston's face and thought better of it, turned the sound into a choke. Huston continued softly. "In the last five years, a determined and efficient attempt has been made to undermine the world's body politic by use of this drug." His voice grew cold and flat and final. "And it's succeeding."

"We have no way of determining, of course, just exactly who is under the influence of the drug," said Teresky, "but there are ways of guessing that an increasing number of high officials are. For example, every month more and more pressure is put on the IC Security Bureau to leave the Aensalords alone. We're not going to be able to ignore it much longer without going into open rebellion against our own diplomats. And the death rate among the higher officials has risen drastically. From the drug, we believe."

"That's a state secret, by the bye," said Huston. "All this stuff is. Maybe you'd better start carrying a cyanide capsule in a hollow tooth or something."

"Or something," Jaeger agreed. He rubbed a thumbnail along his jawline; things were beginning to fall into place. "Then you have definitely traced the origin of this stuff—"

"—to the Aensalords," said Huston. "Yes. Definitely. Our biochemists say that it couldn't possibly have originated from any earthly substance. The protein complexes are wrong or something. I don't know, I'm not a scientist. But take our word for it: That stuff is coming from the Aensa territory."

"How's it getting out?"

"A human pipeline, same as with more conventional

narcotics. Hand to hand to hand. It's damn near impossible to trace back from the middle; you have to start from one end or the other. This time we managed to do part of the job, though." Huston gave a short, bitter laugh. "It took a third of our entire staff two years. We couldn't trace the pipeline to its end, unfortunately, or we'd have the men who are aiding the Aensa and trying to overthrow the International Congress; but we did manage to trace the pipeline back to its beginnings. It comes from the Aensa base, all right; the pipeline from there is continent-wide and directed by a clever man with an airtight, respectable front. A man named Schiller, the publisher from Munich."

None of Jaeger's surprise reached his face. Schiller! "What do you intend to do?" he asked calmly.

"Nothing. We've been watching him for some time. We know that he hired you, but we can't understand why. We could easily close down his part of the pipeline, but that wouldn't do any good; the Aensa could easily build up another one. Besides, it would alert the big boys, and Schiller would be hard to grab outright, without evidence. No, we've got to destroy either end of the pipeline; eliminate all the users, or eliminate the source. That's where you come in."

"I was afraid of that," said Jaeger. "What do you want me to do."

Teresky's voice was unusually sympathetic when he spoke. "We have a much more difficult task for you than Schiller did."

Huston looked grim and sad. "We want you to go back into the Aensa territory, discover the source of the drug, and destroy it if possible. If you agree, it's more than likely that you're signing your death warrant." His voice was calm, but with a hint of nervous strain held under iron control. "But then, you won't be the first, and you won't be the last, if you fail. This is our last chance; we're mounting an all-out offensive against both ends of the pipeline, attacking with everybody and everything we have, in every possible way. You're the first wave, and the last chance for stealth and subtlety. If you fail, too, then we try an armed peace patrol next, and then wipe the place out with a low-yield atomic as a last resort."

Jaeger raised an eyebrow. "And what about the three Aensa warships in parking orbit above Earth? Do you suppose they'll watch passively?"

Teresky leaned forward; there was a desperate urgency in his voice. "Herr Jaeger, a government is like a man in many respects, and our government is dying. A dying man will do many things, some completely irrational, when he knows that he has lost. A dying man will do anything to hold on to life. Our government is dying and it is desperate. It can feel control slipping away through its drug-numbed fingers, and at the final showdown it will risk the retaliation of the Aensa ships rather than relinquish that control." He paused, wearing the haunted, haggard look of a man caught in the middle. "A fleet of our best warships is waiting behind the moon now, although the Aensa are probably aware of it. If the word is given and the atomic device dropped on the Aensalords' base, our fleet will close with the Aensa ships and attempt to destroy them before they can retaliate. With the sophistication of Aensa ships and armament, it'll be like a pack of wild dogs against three tigers; just barely possible but not very likely. If our fleet wins, fine. If not—" he shrugged, made a sweeping gesture "—Bang."

Huston fidgeted. "Right or wrong, that's what *will* happen, unless—" He winced. "Do you accept the assignment, Herr Jaeger? However slight it might be, you're one of the few hopes we have left." His hands clenched where they rested on the arms of his chair, his knuckles turning white with strain.

Jaeger stared at his desk for a long while, until he could look up without showing the fear that had grown in his eyes. He pressed a button on his intercom and spoke to Marga Geier. "Miss Geier," he said, "would you prepare a standard contract, the short form, usual fee, usual waivers, please? Thank you." He shut off the intercom and looked at his visitors with a frown. "Yes," he said slowly, wearily pressing a thumb and forefinger against the bridge of his nose, "damn fool that I am."

Jaeger smiled. "Now that everything's settled, gentlemen—" a glance at Healey "—I could use a drink. How about that coffee? Laced with whiskey, if you'd like."

Huston grinned. "How about some whiskey laced with coffee?"

"To hell with the coffee," Teresky said.

Corcail Sendijen wrapped his tentacles around the pull-bar and heaved. The huge ore wagon trembled and swayed. He opened his big fighting claws and grasped the pull-bar with them. He shoved again. Beside him, a miserable, motley assortment of creatures—winged, scaled, armored, protoplasmic, hairy, furry, smooth-skinned, with everything from talons to hooves, from eight eyes to none, from tentacles to fingers to pseudopods—also struggled with the task. There was a warning hoot; the attention of the black gang turned to D'jebistred, the overseer. The captive crew caught his stream of thought speech: "—faster—quick—quick—now—faster—" The team pulled harder. Slowly the ore wagon began to move.

Corcail Sendijen was wheel man today; this meant that he had the responsibility of guiding the wagon by using his body weight to balance the careening car. It also meant that he would be killed, crushed like a bug between the side of the wagon and the walls, if his calculations weren't correct. If you wanted to keep a low-grade labor slave alive, or at least in reasonably good working condition, this was not the kind of job you assigned to him. But, naturally, the Aensalords didn't really attach much importance to that. They had plenty of slaves, from many different worlds. Nevertheless, Corcail Sendijen planned to stay alive, if for no other reason than to frustrate the whim that had caused D'jebistred to pick him out of the roster for wheel man.

The ore wagon moved ponderously down the tunnel on its double rails, slowly but relentlessly gathering momentum. The team was running now as they pushed; soon the wagon would be up to speed, and the team would release it to coast the rest of the way—with only Corcail Sendijen left aboard, riding the narrow footplate and keeping the wagon on its rails by skillfully shifting his position. With only two wheels, the wagon could easily tip forward or backward; at high speeds, that kind of sudden accident would be quickly but messily fatal.

Ayai! The wagon gave a sudden forward lurch; they had released it. Corcail Sendijen was on his own. The first curve. Shift the weight to the right, cautiously, cautiously, a little more. Ah! Not too much or the wagon will overbalance. Easy, now. The wind of his passage whipped at Corcail Sendijen, seeking to tear him from his precarious perch. A touch of the brake. Yes. Just enough to keep the wagon at speed but not out of control. Tricky business. Damn, another curve—

Corcail Sendijen leaned carefully to his left. The wagon took the curve, shuddered, but stayed on the rails. Here was the worst place ahead, the spot where the tunnel narrowed. Corcail Sendijen's eyes shrank to hard golden slits. This was where the wheel man of a few days before—a winged creature with a crimson beak and emerald eyes—had failed; the wall had scraped him off as he hurtled by and he had died almost instantly. The trick was to remain rock-steady on this stretch. Rock-steady.

Committing himself to his gods, Corcail Sendijen tightened his hold on the pull-bar with all his tentacles. He tried to pretend that he was a rock; he succeeded only in intensifying the slight queasiness in his gut. The narrowed tunnel walls were flowing by like black syrup. Slowly he applied the brake, a simple affair using the friction of a metal brake shoe pressed against the metal wheel rims. The landscape began to resolve itself again. With a final shower of sparks from the brakes, the wagon bumped to a stop against the railhead.

As Corcail Sendijen leaped down from the wagon, a giant metal hose, made flexible by dozens of hinge-like joints along its length, extended from the ceiling of the tunnel, plunged into the tons of quarried matter carried in the wagon, and sucked it all up neatly and efficiently. From there, the load of rock and earth would be transported down to the main generator buried somewhere below, where a processing plant would transform the material into a form that could be converted directly into the energy to operate the Aensalords' power-hungry mechanical devices.

Breathing deeply, Corcail Sendijen waited for the rest of the black gang to arrive, so that they could drag the ore wagon back to the other end of the tunnel again; it was a blessing that they only had to make this run once a day. As he waited, Corcail Sendijen tapped a tentacle sharply against one of his fighting claws (the Eighteenth Gesture of the Rites: utter contempt with insulting sexual overtones) and stared up at the massive ore wagon. This entire set-up was completely absurd. Any other race of intelligent creatures he'd ever seen would have automated the whole system, but not the Aensalords. Automated, this system would run hundreds of times more productively, and would relieve an unnecessary drain on valuable slaves and man-hours besides. And yet the Aensalords refused to automate. Why? Well, there was the natural perversity of the Aensalords, for one thing. They desired to do everything the most difficult, most unpleasant way possible. And they seemed to glory in the extravagant wasting of lives not their own. Then, too, if his suspicions were correct, Corcail Sendijen believed that there might be another very good reason . . .

Impatiently, Corcail Sendijen began pacing about the now-steady wagon. He inspected it closely. Those wheel rims were just about worn out from the friction of the brake shoes; it was time to have them replaced—Corcail Sendijen's eyes grew narrow and he leaned forward sharply. A tentacle flicked up and played about the ruts left by wear on the wheel-rims. Those ruts had been deep last night when the black gang had quit work, yes, but not that deep. And it was impossible for that much to have been worn away during the single run made today. But then how had the ruts been deepened? The ore wagon wasn't used at any other time. Or was it?

Before he could pursue this interesting train of thought, the black gang arrived from the other end of the tunnel. Making his equivalent of a shrug, Corcail Sendijen turned to receive his orders in thought speech from that prince among fellows, D'jebistred the overseer.

Chapter Five

His mind churning patiently like an idling engine, Karl Jaeger sat in the back of the taxi as it drove him back through the city toward his apartment. He thought about what the IC men had told him; how quickly his orderly world had been turned over! And now an awful lot of responsibility had been shucked onto his shoulders. An awful lot. In fact, Jaeger realized for the tenth time, it just might be that the sorry lot of humanity rested with him alone. That was a thought that Jaeger found impossible to accept emotionally.

The Marktplatz had been nearly deserted when Jaeger left his office. There was only a low-slung silver-gray sports car, its motor turning over with a tiny hollow tinging sound. When Jaeger entered the cab, the sports car turned on its headlamps. The strange car, whether by accident or design, pulled out from the curb as the taxi started across the square. Jaeger watched the sports car with professional curiosity. He had been followed before. His suspicions were put to rest when the car turned away at right angles to Jaeger's route home. He snorted in disgust; if he were going to be any help to all of mankind, he was going to have to get his thoughts together.

The taxi turned up the hill toward Die Burg, the Imperial Castle of Nürnberg, a grim, gray mass that gleamed nakedly in the glow of spotlights from the roofs of houses in the street below. A narrow, winding way led up to the forecourt of the castle; here the taxi turned right.

Jaeger paid the driver in silence when they reached his apartment. Accompanied only by the whispering rain, he stalked across the small court to his apartment building and clattered up the narrow stairs to the top floor. He thought the stairs would be quicker than the leisurely elevator; besides, he had to get into better shape. He laughed aloud at this thought: Sure, a couple of quick trips up and down the staircase, and he'd be ready to fight off the entire race of Aensa.

He let himself into his apartment, hit the light switch without looking, and closed the door. A dim, soft light radiated from the ceiling. The apartment was small, but cozy; a tastefully furnished living room was important to him when he came home from the JAEGER, INC. office depressed by an assignment. Now, more than ever, he needed a comfortable place to hide and think. He was a little disappointed. He had half expected to find Aldonna waiting for him.

One wall was covered with bookshelves and oil paintings—his own, mostly landscapes and a few miniature character portraits, including a remarkable likeness of Nati. The right wall was dominated by wide, shuttered windows. Jaeger looked wistfully at Dark Lightning, then decided that he couldn't allow himself any such pleasures. He went to the window and opened the shutters. For long minutes he stared out at the fog-distorted shapes of buildings, watched the flickering lights and listened to the impersonal pat of the rain. He put Debussy's "Prelude to the Afternoon of a Faun" on the omni system, and settled back into a comfortably overstuffed chair.

As the first lonely notes of the French horns echoed and hung in the air, a plastic patch in the wall by Jaeger's elbow glowed red. There was a low warning buzz. Jaeger cursed, snapped on the small stereop screen, and then flicked a special black switch set next to the regular control knobs. The picture came on darkly, then quickly lightened and focused; it was a view of the last landing of the stairwell, just before Jaeger's floor. Jaeger had little patience with the gadgets used in popular dramas and the stereop shows, most of them being either ridiculous or highly impractical, but this little trick—a miniaturized television camera concealed invisibly in the stairwell wall, and its mate by the elevator, with a telemetering system to avoid a clumsy wiring system—had been so easy and cheap to install that he hadn't been able to resist. It also came in handy on occasion. Jaeger moved in circles where it was often vital to see one's visitors first; he made a point of glancing at everyone who triggered his inexpensive electric alarm. He was alone on the top floor, except for the old woman across the hall; anyone who set off the alarm would most likely be coming to see Jaeger. Most of the time, there wasn't any cause for excitement.

This time it wasn't a false alarm.

Jaeger caught a glimpse of two men running silently up the stairs, saw light glint from the polished barrel of a machine pistol, saw the squat shape of a hand gun. He was up and moving. He leaped for a wall closet; he had only seconds, perhaps too few, to act. Fighting anxiety that would make his movements clumsy, Jaeger searched in the closet and came up with something that looked vaguely like an overcoat made of a thin, shiny material like mylar. Footsteps sounded at the top of the stairwell. Grimacing, Jaeger swung the blindcoat up and let it settle around his shoulders, like Siegfried donning his cloud-cloak; to the human eye he was now a six-foot fun-house mirror, throwing back distorted images of the apartment walls around him. Jaeger pressed a plastic switch that Herr Stahl had fastened in the cuff of one sleeve. To the human eye, he was suddenly nothing at all.

Jaeger pulled the blindcoat closer around him, and then reached into his pocket for his own gun. To his intense dismay, he could not find it. He patted dumbly at the empty pocket for a heartbeat, then cursed bitterly. He quite simply had forgotten it. It had been so long since he'd worn a gun with any kind of regularity, so long since he'd had any need for one, that he'd simply put it down and forgotten to pick it back up again. It was resting right now in a drawer of his desk at his office, where he had put it before going out to visit Schiller. Only a mile away. It might just as well have been ten thousand miles.

This made the situation much more serious. Now the only weapon he had was the blindcoat and the invisibility it conferred. In dealing at very close quarters with men armed with automatic weapons, that might not be enough. From the invisible sniper he had hoped to be, he had instead become invisible prey.

Nervously, Jaeger glanced at the door. Better get out of the line of fire. He edged noiselessly to his right. The "Afternoon of a Faun" played unnoticed in the background. More footsteps thudded in the corridor outside. As an afterthought, Jaeger took a heavy, silver-headed walking-stick from a stand and slipped it beneath the blindcoat; the walking-stick disappeared also.

A hush, lasting all of a few seconds, settled over the room; the two men had reached his door. Jaeger felt the skin tighten over his skull. Tiny ant feet pattered up and down his back.

There was a muffled cough, the door shuddered violently, and then the lock tumbled onto the carpet with a soft clunk, smoking. Two sharp spitting sounds and the magnelocks twisted uselessly. The door swung open. A gun barrel poked its way into the room, followed by a man. The man was a blunt-headed blond giant with cloudy blue eyes and splotchy skin. The gun was a machine pistol with a silencer. Both man and pistol were ugly and dangerous-looking; Jaeger had never seen the man before, and he had no desire to become better acquainted with the gun.

The blond raked the room with his eyes, then stalked toward the bedroom door, passing Jaeger, who had stopped breathing and was standing very, very still. The other man appeared in the doorway; he had tucked his gun away, and Jaeger saw that he was carrying a bulky hand grenade, wired as a crude time-bomb; in his other hand, the man held a long hypodermic needle—half full of a shimmering, bright blue liquid.

This man was evidently the brains of the operation. Jaeger studied him carefully. He was a chunky dark-haired man in a sweatshirt and vest, with a touch of the Balkans in the eyes and hook nose. He looked to Jaeger like a Turk. Jaeger had never met this man, either, a fact for which he was duly grateful; he and the blond looked very unpleasant indeed.

The blond paused by the omni system, glanced down, and then twisted the volume knob all the way up; Debussy filled the room. To drown the noise of their work? The blond flung open the bedroom door and went in fast and low. In a moment he came out of the room, shook his head in puzzlement, then gazed narrowly at the far wall as if looking for secret passageways or other escape hatches.

Jaeger paid little attention to the blond; it was the Turk that captured his fancy. Actually, not the Turk, but rather what the dark man was carrying. Jaeger frowned. He studied the hypodermic for a moment, then glanced at the grenade and grinned savagely. The blue drug made an extremely effective truth serum in diluted doses. The IC attachés had told him that. What a sweetly diabolical scheme these two intruders had dreamed up for him.

The blond was suspiciously tapping walls; the Turk had planted himself firmly in the doorway and didn't show any signs of changing position. The "Afternoon of a Faun" squawked and died in the middle of a proud horn call as the blond absently killed the omni set. The sudden silence was shattering. Was it possible to edge through the doorway without alerting the Turk? No, not nearly enough room. Damn, he had to breathe in a short while, and it was sure to be heard, the way Jaeger's luck had been running.

Seeing that his prey wasn't immediately forthcoming, the Turk relaxed a bit, and the syringe and the bomb dipped slightly toward the floor. Jaeger shrugged resignedly, stepped up next to the Turk, measured him briefly, and then brought his walking-stick down on the man's head. The walking-stick crunched solidly against bone. The Turk staggered dazedly across the room. He fell and lay sprawled on his back, staring blankly at the ceiling, dribbling blood from his forehead; the bomb rolled across the carpet and bumped up against a table leg near the shuttered window.

As soon as the Turk moved away, Jaeger leaped for the door. Bullets tore a geyser of wood from the door frame, and then Jaeger was through and running. The blond chased grimly after him. Jaeger ran past the entrance to the stairwell; the blond, thinking that Jaeger had gone that way, started down the steps. Several seconds later the Turk appeared, staggering but determined. He carried his gun in a rather limp grasp, walked to the elevator, and disappeared into the waiting car. Jaeger sighed; he waited a few moments, then went back to his apartment. The door stood as the blond man had left it, its locks forever useless. Jaeger switched off the blindcoat and took it off. He stood silently, staring thoughtfully into his living room. Behind him, a door opened. Jaeger spun, raising the walking-stick. It was only his elderly neighbor. "Herr Jaeger," said the old woman with a scandalized frown, "I don't know whether to call the landlord or the police. I've never heard such noise. You should be ashamed, waking up an old woman in the middle of her nap. If you insist on making such a racket, I'll have you thrown out of here."

"Fine," said Jaeger. "I don't like the kind of people I've been meeting in this neighborhood." The old woman's eyes opened wide, she started to say something, then slammed her door. Jaeger shook his head and stepped into the living room, shutting his own door behind him. His telephone was ringing.

He crossed the room and answered it. The face of Connor Coffey filled the screen. "Hi," said Jaeger, "you're late. Your friends already left."

"What?" said Coffey. He looked worried.

"Let it go," said Jaeger tiredly. "It would take too long to explain it to you. Anyway, how do you think you're going to kill me over the telephone? Are you planning to hypnotize me into jumping from my window?"

"What?" said Coffey. "I don't want to kill you anymore."

"That's a relief," said Jaeger scornfully.

"No, really. I called you up because I want to hire you."

Jaeger snorted. "I have an office. I have a telephone there, which I answer during office hours. I'll talk to you tomorrow, after I break a chair over your head."

Coffey looked worried. "No, listen," he said quickly. "I can't wait until tomorrow. I have to talk to you now. I was hoping you wouldn't hold it against me for trying to snuff you. I was only doing a job. You're the only one I can turn to."

Jaeger stared in disbelief. "I don't hold it against you, Coffey," he said. "I figure you're the product of a broken home or something. It don't bother me that you almost killed me too many times. I have a lot of love for humanity."

"Go to hell," said Coffey. "Will you listen or not?"

"What is it?"

"Look," said the youth. He held up a sheet of paper to the phone. Jaeger could read it easily. It said, *Your services are no longer required,* typed neatly in one line. Below that, in a scrawled handwriting, were the words, *Believe it. You're dead, you idiot.*

"Your employers have the right idea," said Jaeger.

"Go to hell," said Coffey. "I need help, and I need it fast. You want to help me?"

"You want to pay me?"

"Sure," said Coffey. "I don't have much, though."

Jaeger smiled. "You got five hundred to kill me."

"I only have two hundred left," said Coffey.

"Two hundred it is."

"I don't want to argue. Just get over here fast." Jaeger nodded, took Coffey's address, and clicked off the phone. Coffey lived in the old part of the city, near Nati's apartment. Jaeger shrugged again, folded the blindcoat over his arm, and called a taxi. In a few minutes, he was on his way. When the cab driver let him out, while Jaeger was getting his change from the fare, he noticed that the same silver gray sports car was parked across the street from Coffey's apartment. Jaeger knew who would be sitting in that car, where they had come from, and why they were there. He went up the short walk to Coffey's building.

Connor Coffey lived several blocks to the west of Nati Fernfelder's apartment building, in a half-timbered building hard against the side of the main castle keep, opening on the enclosed fore-court. This had once been a warden's hut, originally built around A.D. 1200, to house a medieval bondsman; now, on the top floor, it housed Connor Coffey. Jaeger wondered what significance that had, as far as what the human race had done with its last thousand years; he spat on the ground in front of him, forced himself to look away from Nati's building, then went in, identified himself to the cautious youth upstairs, and began climbing the dim flights to Coffey's apartment. He knocked on the door. "Jaeger?" came the nervous voice from the other side of the door.

"Look," said Jaeger, "even if I wasn't, I could say that I

was, I might be somebody here to kill you. What are you going to do now?"

Coffey opened the door a crack, peeked out, then swung it open all the way. "If you were here to kill me, you wouldn't have said that."

"I don't know," said Jaeger, walking past Coffey into a musty, dark, unpleasant room. "I've done it before."

"Sit down," said Coffey. "I don't think we have too much time."

Jaeger thought about the silver sports car but said nothing.

"Here's the note," said Coffey, handing Jaeger the last letter from his unknown employer.

"Is it like the others?" asked Jaeger.

"Exactly," said the bearded young man. "Except that the others never had the handwritten message. They must be pretty confident, to do that. I saved the envelope. I thought you might want it for fingerprints or something."

"Sure," said Jaeger. "After the post office clerk smothered it, and all the post office employees who routed it, and after the man who delivered it pawed it all over, and after you got your own prints on top of all theirs, and especially since whoever sent it probably knew enough not to leave any in the first place. Did you get any money with this?"

Coffey looked at Jaeger in surprise. "How did you know? Yeah, they sent me another five hundred, in eurodollars. Can you trace it?"

"Let me see the bill." Coffey brought the pale blue note out of his pocket. Jaeger took it, folded it, and put it away in his own trousers.

"Hey!" said Coffey. "I thought you only wanted two hundred."

"I thought you only had two hundred."

"Well, two hundred and that fiver."

Jaeger shrugged. "Expenses," he said.

"Well," said Coffey, "what are you going to do?"

"I'm going to wait here a few minutes until your friends arrive, and then together we're going to beat their brains in, find out who they work for, and put you in the clear."

"How do you know—" Coffey's question was interrupted by the buzzing of his doorbell. Jaeger smiled. "Give me your gun," he said. Coffey got up anxiously and answered it.

"Let them up," said Jaeger. "They know I'm here, anyway. I owe them something on my own."

A short time later, Coffey answered the door and let in the two men, the blond giant and the shifty-eyed Turk. Jaeger held Coffey's gun toward them and nodded. "Take a seat, gentlemen," he said. "I want to talk to you about paying for my door." The two men sat together on a torn couch. Jaeger watched them carefully. He spoke over his shoulder to Coffey. "Do you know these guys?" he asked.

"Never saw them before," said Coffey.

Jaeger turned back to the two hoods. "Before we get on with the important business," he said, and then was interrupted by a heavy blow that glanced off the back of his skull. Coffey had barely missed again. Jaeger jumped up, turned to freeze Coffey in the act of raising a heavy bookend, turned again to freeze the two men, who were reaching for their own weapons, and then ran for the door. "God damn that kid," thought Jaeger, as he threw himself flat on the dull wood floor beyond Coffey's apartment. Bullets whipped over Jaeger's head, tore into the top landing of the stairwell. Jaeger rolled over the topmost step and clattered recklessly down the stairwell. He heard shouts and cursing from Coffey's apartment.

Somehow, Jaeger reached the bottom of the stairs without breaking his neck. He paused only to swing the blindcoat over his shoulders and activate it. Thank God he had had the foresight to bring it with him; it was probably his only chance. As he ran from the building, a loud pock from the Turk's gun shivered the pavement near Jaeger's heel. Rapid footsteps echoed in the stairwell behind him. Jaeger dashed into the forecourt, stopped, and looked around him quickly. Which way to go? Straight ahead was the long winding path to the street below; he would be without cover all the way down, an invitation to the kind of lucky shot he had no wish to court. Behind was an ancient tunnel leading to the dry moat on the other side of the Imperial Castle. To the right, the cobblestoned path slanted up to the Sinwellturm, the round tower keep that overlooked the city; that was much too far away to risk. To the left was a path that led to the castle gardens; that ended in a cul-de-sac. That was no good, either.

Where to go? Quick, decide! Jaeger chewed his lip, trying to remain calm. It would have to be the tunnel.

Jaeger whirled, and ran noiselessly for the mouth of the tunnel. The blond emerged from the apartment building, hesitated, then fired aimlessly across the forecourt in the direction of the Sinwellturm. Good, thought Jaeger, the gunman couldn't hit what he couldn't see; maybe Jaeger had a chance of getting out of this, after all. That was when the blond turned, fired again, and put a bullet through the fine mesh circuitry of the blindcoat. Jaeger was flickering in and out of visibility like a dying firefly. The blond shouted; Jaeger ducked into the tunnel mouth. A bullet screamed off stone behind him. The blindcoat was dead; Jaeger was completely visible now. He wriggled out of the thing as he ran and dropped it; his chances of survival dropped with it, almost to zero. Jaeger lowered his head and ran like hell.

The blond reached the tunnel mouth and peered into it, pistol at the ready. He waited a moment for the Turk to join him. While he waited, he slipped a fresh clip of ammunition into the magazine of his machine pistol. The fog had finally swirled over Die Burg; thick tendrils of fog were pushing their way up the tunnel from the lower elevation of the dry moat on the other side. The blond cursed. "Hey, Limal!" he called to his comrade, "How the hell are we supposed to hit anything in this stuff?"

The Turk said nothing in reply. The blond man sighed and pointed his pistol in front of him; the Turk grasped his gun. Together they trotted cautiously into the tunnel.

The fog bank had swept over Jaeger a few moments before, giving him the first, lonely glimmer of hope. His pursuers wouldn't be able to pick him off with long-distance shots, at any rate; they would have to come close. An ambush was the thing. But where? Jaeger clattered out onto the wooden bridge that spanned the dry moat. Not here. The bridge was too narrow for a fight, particularly outnumbered two to one; Jaeger would never get across to the other side before the blond and the Turk charged out of the tunnel behind him. Jaeger looked over the railing and down. Through the fog, he could just make out the bottom of the dry moat, about forty feet below. He shrugged. There were thick wooden crossbeams all the way down to provide handholds.

Jaeger slipped awkwardly over the wooden railing and began to climb down; a short time later his feet touched ground and he slid into the darker shadow of a crossbeam. The blond and the Turk appeared on schedule, studied the situation carefully, and then came to the correct conclusion. The Turk waited on the bridge, watching carefully, as the blond tucked his pistol away in his trousers, hauled himself over the railing, and began to climb down.

The blond jumped from the lowest crossbeam, landed crouched in the grass of the dry moat bottom, and signaled up to his partner. He took the pistol from the waistband of his trousers, waited poised for a moment, then slowly stood up. He took a cautious step forward, then another, edging around the crossbeam. Jaeger smiled a grim smile. The blond moved around the crossbeam and began to turn. Jaeger's hand slashed down, outlined in the murky light of a fog-shrouded spotlight. The edge of his hand swung in a clean arc and smashed sharply down on the blond's gun hand, just behind thc thumb; a bone in the man's wrist broke with a snap and the pistol cartwheeled away into the night.

"Hey," shouted the Turk, "got him?" There was no reply except the pained grunting of the blond man.

The blond lunged at Jaeger. Jaeger turned slightly and rammed his elbow up into the blond's chest, just below the sternum. Whimpering, the blond giant staggered backward; Jaeger's eyes glinted. He raised his hand and cracked the blond solidly across the face with an open palm.

There was a muffled explosion; the Turk was firing, caring not whether he hit Jaeger or his own blond companion. Jaeger threw himself to the side, wrenching his ankle, raised the hand that still held Coffey's gun, and fired twice. The first shot splintered the edge of the wooden rail. The second shot flattened the Turk's head, from the nose up. The Turk, now as dead as the glory of the city around him, tottered mindlessly and slumped over the railing. Slowly the corpse shifted, then slipped over the railing and fell with a ugly clump beside Jaeger.

Jaeger grunted with satisfaction as he turned back to the

blond giant; the danger was over, and he was now in control of the situation. He realized what a novel circumstance that was, particularly in the last few days. He wanted to talk to the blond, but that opponent had had more than enough. Whining deep in the back of his throat, he broke and ran. Jaeger cursed and tired to run after him, but his sore ankle forced him to a painful limp after a short distance. Swearing, Jaeger hobbled along the moat bottom, trying to keep the blond in sight.

After a while, the blond man came to a flight of stone steps and climbed back up to the castle; Jaeger followed, cautiously and slowly, circling wide around the Sinwellturm and the tower of the Tiefe Brunnen instead of going back through the tunnel. When he reached the forecourt, the blond gunman had already staggered down from Die Burg to the street and was crawling into the low-slung sports car. The car sputtered, then roared away and was gone.

Jaeger shook his head. The entire episode since his rather ungainly exit from Connor Coffey's apartment had lasted no more than five minutes. It certainly had not caused a large amount of excitement in the neighborhood. Jaeger thought for a moment of returning to Coffey's building, but he figured that the young man would surely not have remained in the vicinity. But then, Jaeger thought, with Coffey one couldn't be too sure. Jaeger pulled his light jacket closer around him as the wind blew cold. He began walking home. After a while he stopped a taxi and rode the rest of the way.

The taxi was already pulling away from the curb, and Jaeger was fishing in his pocket for his keys, when a tongue of flame lanced from the side of his apartment building, turning the night red; the roar of the explosion echoed hollowly off into the distance among the roofs of Nürnberg. It wasn't a huge explosion; the force of it didn't knock Jaeger over. It shook him enough, though. A plume of black smoke streamed from the top floor of the building and twisted lazily into the sky. Lights began to come on in the neighboring houses, one after another. Jaeger gaped upward angrily. The Turk's bomb. Damn! He hadn't had time to think about it. He had quickly assumed that the two intruders had gathered their playthings together when they left. Jaeger's jaw muscles tightened. He thought of the Turk, lying on the damp ground of the moat bottom, the top of his head missing and his bones broken. He sighed and watched the smoke pouring from the hole in the wall where his apartment had once been. The insurance company wasn't going to like this . . .

Footsteps on the cobblestones. Jaeger made a wry face. He was very tired. He considered letting whoever it was take a quick shot at him. It was probably Connor Coffey.

It was Nati, her eyes wide and frightened, biting into white knuckles as she stared up at the jagged rent in the wall. She flashed wild eyes at him, seeming to see him for the first time, and then something changed in her eyes and she sobbed, and then she was in his arms, and he crushed the long warmth of her to him and their lips touched.

He held her like that for a moment, ignoring all the shouting of the people around him. There were sirens coming closer, but Jaeger had played out his part in that drama. He closed his eyes and worked at holding Nati.

Something in a pocket in her windbreaker jabbed at his ribs. He laughed softly and removed it. It was a piece of paper wrapped around a small, empty plastic vial, empty except at the very bottom, where there gleamed a tiny drop of liquid, a drop of the deepest blue. The paper had words that said simply, *Your services are no longer required.* Nati sobbed against his chest. Jaeger felt the warm tears soaking his shirt. He closed his eyes and listened to the sirens.

Karl Jaeger emerged from the underworld at five a.m. When the police and the fire department had let him go, he had gone straight into the home grounds of the muck and dregs of human society, searching for answers. His search had started in the cheap, brightly lit bars and drugstores of Nürnberg's Strip, then continued through the smothering slums of the city, and ended in the narrow ring of shabby shops and factories that circled the city; the unsavory shadow-world that inevitably grows up like a diseased tumor on the decent creations of men.

The shadow-world was Hell, but Hell was inhabited. People lived there, too many people, squeezed together like dead fish in a great, smelly container. Some of Hell's citizens were big, stoic, hard-faced men in oil-spattered coveralls, who worked the night shifts in the various factories. They were the lucky ones. Less fortunate men and women—the poor, the insane, the addicted—made up the majority of the shadow-world's population. They, and those who preyed on them, and the ones who preyed in turn on the lesser predators of the awful jungle. One of these scavengers would have the answers to Jaeger's questions.

At five a.m. on a cold autumn morning, Jaeger emerged from the shadow-world, with the lines in his face etched a little deeper, a little less money in his wallet, and the knowledge that having answers sometimes doesn't get you any farther than you were before.

It was Schiller who had tried to have him killed, all right; the blond man had been identified for a price as one of Schiller's "work crew." The Turk was well-known in the shadow-world as one who would do anything for anybody, for a proper consideration. A free-lancer who would rent his talents no more.

Why? It didn't make any sense, even yet. Why would Schiller hire a man to spy on the Aensalords' castle, when Schiller was on the inside already and knew what was going on? And once having hired such a spy, why try to have him killed as soon as he returned from his mission, without even giving him a chance to report? There was no logical pattern to it at all; somehow, a piece of the puzzle was still being withheld.

Jaeger shook his head and limped through the night. To hell with it. The air held the biting chill of approaching winter, a grim promise that there was worse yet to come. Car headlights beamed through the persistent fog; a fine mist left tiny drops of moisture on Jaeger's forehead and dampened his bushy eyebrows. The big man shuddered slightly and quickened his pace.

He entered the old, walled part of the city, walked past his darkened office, and continued up Koenigstrasse. Schiller! What to do about Schiller. Jaeger swore softly to himself. If his mission had been to trace the pipeline to its end, then his course of action would have been clear. He would have tackled Schiller somehow and tried to work his way back through the chain of command. But that was not his mission; his job was to find and destroy the source of the alien drug—and to do it before a panicky world government tried to intervene and caused a nuclear Ragnarok. Time was running out; with every tick of the clock the government grew more desperate and less cautious, and fingers would be tightening on the trigger. Jaeger realized again that it might all depend on him. Everything. He was one of the few things left between the blissfully ignorant human race and the three black monsters that circled Earth in an endless killer's stalk high above.

And there was Nati. Would the IC give him some of the blue poison? If not, Nati was dead. That's all.

That's all.

He shuddered again, a bit more violently, and his shoulders hunched slightly. It was a lonely thing, this business of saving the world. Jaeger decided that on the whole, he didn't really like it very much, after all.

Very far from Jaeger, in a giant warship hidden behind the moon, Colonel John Robert Devaney watched a telemetered picture of the three Aensa ships. The stereop screen in his operations room was large, bright, and a restful green; it cast odd shadows in the room, and it turned Col. Devaney's face into a grotesque mask. It would have been impossible to tell from looking at his expression what his thoughts were.

On the stereop screen the Aensa ships fell through space. They looked small and harmless; Devaney felt like he could just reach out and crush them. That was the illusion of the holog process. In reality, the Aensa ships were each over twice as huge as his own ship. The Aensa cruisers were long, slender, and black, much like their masters. And, Devaney knew, they were every bit as deadly.

Devaney stared at the stereop screen, but his thoughts traveled much farther. They traveled in space, back to Earth, back to what had once been the state of Maine, what was now part of the Northeastern Monocity of NAUL. His thoughts traveled in time to the years of his childhood on the beaches and rocky shorelines of his youth. He waited for the order to attack. He pushed a control button and the picture on the screen changed; he pushed the button again. He searched the black sky around him for his lucky star, the middle star of Orion's belt; it was hidden by the gray-brown bulk of the moon. Luck was eliminated from the equation that now ruled his life and the lives of everyone else; reason had been eliminated some time before. All that remained was hope. That, and duty.

Devaney returned the picture of the Aensa ships. Then, for the first time in twenty-five years, he muttered a prayer.

Corcail Sendijen opened his eyes and carefully sniffed the air. Nothing. Near him, the other members of the black gang twitched, moaned, or rippled in their sleep, according to their natures. The air was filled with low noises—snores, hisses, wheezes, bubbling sounds, rasping snarls—and the stink of many alien bodies in an enclosed place was almost overpowering. But nothing moved through the dim shadows. At least, nothing moved; that was something to be thankful for. Corcail Sendijen could tell that all the pitiable creatures around him were deep asleep, lost in their strange dreams; now was the time to act.

Slowly, Corcail Sendijen stood. Softly now. Listen for a flicker of awareness in the low-grade minds of the black gang. Nothing? Then move! A tentacle swung to the right and probed cautiously, found an empty square of pavement; Corcail Sendijen shifted his weight in that direction and whipped his sensitive upper tentacles around the surrounding area. He balanced easily on his locomotor legs, searching among the huddled, ragged forms of his teammates, swaying slightly as he picked out other squares of empty pavement among the sea of bodies.

Corcail Sendijen smelled and heard movement; he was aware of an approaching consciousness. Instantly, he crouched, coiling his longer tentacles beneath him. The familiar form of D'jebistred the overseer appeared on the steel catwalk that ran around the edge of the sleeping chamber. The overseer made a slow circuit of the catwalk, his ponderous unshod feet rasping unpleasantly on the metal plating. Corcail Sendijen hugged the floor and followed D'jebistred with fiercely slitted eyes; his fighting claws twitched.

D'jebistred paused, grasped the railing with his stubby, eight-fingered hands, and leaned out. His faintly luminous eyes searched over the sleeping creatures. Corcail Sendijen closed his eyes, relaxed, and waited for the overseer's gaze to pass over him. The chamber was too dim to make out more than shapes and shadows, and D'jebistred was too stupid to be able to sense consciousness in any of the forms below. Corcail Sendijen glared up when the eyes had passed and the overseer had turned away; he thought a message of death and murder-lust at D'jebistred, but the overseer was too insensitive to pick up the thought directly. Some of the raw emotion must have managed to trickle through into the overseer's subconscious; D'jebistred fidgeted, looked around uneasily, and then shuffled out, hissing softly to himself.

Corcail Sendijen counted slowly to a thousand, then stopped; that should have given D'jebistred enough time to get well clear. He uncoiled his tentacles, rose up on his locomotor legs again, and began to pick his way toward the far wall like some great spider. In a moment, he had scrambled up the catwalk and away.

Usually, when Corcail Sendijen went exploring, he made his way up the ventilator shaft to the surface; but tonight he wanted to prowl the lower levels. The worn wheels of the ore wagon had made him suspicious. Corcail Sendijen postioned himself in a concealed vantage point near the ore wagon's rails and waited. Soon the air was filled with a low humming, and the rails began to vibrate slightly. So, the ore wagon was used at night after all! But why? And by whom?

The ore wagon appeared at the far end of the tunnel, rambling slowly forward. Corcail Sendijen backed away and flattened himself close to the floor in a patch of shadow. The ore wagon crawled opposite his position and inched by. Corcail Sendijen's golden eyes narrowed and he snarled softly. So! The ore wagon was being pushed by Aensamen—members of the Aensa race, but of the lowest social order—while a proud Aensalord stalked along the tracks to supervise. The Aensamen weren't compelled to risk their lives on the ore wagon, in the way that members of the black gang were during the day; these were Aensa, after all, and they pushed the wagon along at a cautious, safe speed.

Corcail Sendijen lifted his head slowly and carefully; he had to see what was inside the ore wagon. His fighting claws stiffened and his eyes shrank in unmixed hatred.

The ore wagon was brimful of a luminous bright blue liquid.

Corcail Sendijen watched the wagon creak by, then gathered his legs under him and scurried silently after. He had to find out where the wagon was taking the drug. This could be the opportunity he'd waited for all these weary months.

The ore wagon continued slowly on through the tunnel to the railhead and then stopped. Corcail Sendijen watched intently from a distance as the metal hose dropped from the ceiling and pumped up all the precious blue liquid. He had thought that the metal pipeline only led to the converter of the main generator, but evidently it also had a branch line to some great storage tank buried beneath the castle. Clever. If that was quite the correct word to use about the Aensalords.

Corcail Sendijen slipped back into the darker shadows. The Aensa were tricky fiends, one had to grant them that. But Corcail Sendijen's patient weeks of observation had finally paid off. Half of his job was done; now all that he had to do was find the source . . .

There was a noise behind him. Corcail Sendijen whirled, throwing up his fighting claws.

The scaly bulk of D'jebistred the overseer loomed menacingly in the tunnel like an iron statue. Next to D'jebistred stood a slender, bright-eyed Aensalord. The gun in the Aensalord's hand was of a type Corcail Sendijen had seen before. It was also pointed directly at Corcail Sendijen's chest.

D'jebistred smiled.

Chapter Six

"To hell with the whole thing!"

Karl Jaeger smacked the silver head of his walking-stick angrily into his palms, then tapped it against the edge of his desk. "This damn business has finally upset me. I'm annoyed. I am very annoyed."

Hans Weissmann fidgeted, looked concerned. "Was the damage to your apartment very great?"

"No." Jaeger made an impatient gesture. He had related to his friend most of the details of the events that had occurred the evening before. He had left out all mention of Nati, however, especially the disturbing fact of her forced employment by Schiller. Along with the entire Aensa situation and the problem of his own survival, Jaeger was faced with finding Nati a source of the blue drug. At the moment, all these things added together to make a circumstance too overwhelming for Jaeger to confront alone. But he had to work alone; he knew it and, with supreme reluctance, he accepted it. Still, he didn't have to like it.

"Well," said Weissmann, "for the record, and for the insurance claim, and for tax purposes, if you made an evaluation—"

Jaeger cut him off with a quick swipe of one hand. He could hardly believe that such things could be going on in the same world with the difficulties he was facing. "One wall and the windows blown out," he said. "Smoke damage to the furniture. My paintings and the books weren't badly damaged. The Dark Lightning was unhurt. It was really nothing. I spent the rest of the night with, ah, with a friend. But—"

Weissmann smiled patiently at his friend's tirade. "What did the SEPG have to say last night?"

"Wasn't much they could say. I told them it was a malfunctioning solar accumulator that exploded; I can't get the SEPG involved in this business." He laughed in rather nasty delight. "They didn't think much of my story, but there wasn't much they could do about it; my name carries at least that much weight, these days. Besides, they couldn't really figure it out otherwise. That's all right with me." Jaeger smiled ruefully. "That's one of the reasons for my foul mood this morning. I hate to admit that this whole deal doesn't make sense yet. By now, I ought to be getting a clearer picture. But something or somebody is doing a very good job at holding me up. I keep hitting roadblocks, no matter which route I try." He rubbed a finger along his nose and frowned. Why would Schiller first try to have him killed, and then try to have him interrogated? It ought to have been the other way around. No, it wasn't his imagination, thought Jaeger. There still wasn't any logic in it.

Herr Stahl entered, stood stoop-shouldered at the edge of the desk, and blinked. He looked down uninterestedly at Jaeger. The big man smiled back encouragingly and waited for Stahl to respond. Stahl said nothing. Jaeger shrugged his shoulders and handed Herr Stahl a folded piece of paper. Herr Stahl lazily unfolded the paper, glanced at it. Jaeger drummed his fingers and let the proper tone of authority enter his voice. "Herr Stahl," he said, "I would like these materials prepared by noon, if possible. Is that satisfactory?" Stahl grunted, glanced at the paper again, nodded slowly, and walked out of the room. Jaeger sighed.

Weissmann chewed his lip. "What are you going to do, Karl?"

Jaeger smiled tightly. "I figure it's time that I stopped letting everyone beat on me. I'm going to force everybody's hand, all at once." He riffled through a file and handed Weissmann an index card. "Hans, will you ask Marga to please contact Mr. Huston of the IC at this number? I must speak to him as soon as possible. Within the hour would be best.'' Weissmann took the card and left, looking worried.

Jaeger fingered the silver head of the walking-stick and gazed out across the bustle of Koenigstrasse. He was tired of being a target. By God, it was his turn to hit. One thing for certain, he couldn't hang around Nürnberg for very much longer. If he stayed here, they would get him sooner or later—poison in his food or in the air of his apartment, a sniper on the street, a fast car driven to kill, another bomb in his office. It was only a matter of time. No, the thing to do was move, to strike fast and unexpectedly, gain the offensive and then keep on attacking until the opposition crumpled away or you were dead. But what could he do? The opposition was so much bigger than he, the cards were stacked so heavily against him. How could he make a dent in that iron front? Jaeger smiled. His only hope was in brazenness and unorthodox strategy. He would have to do the unexpected, and attack from an entirely new direction.

Jaeger thought, and his expression turned somber, his eyebrows merging into a bushy line over the bridge of his nose. He had tried to infiltrate unnoticed into the Aensalords' keep; he had failed miserably and survived, for which he was grateful but still astonished. Other trained men had tried to infiltrate the keep as well; they had failed and died. Face it, it couldn't be done. Jaeger's fingers tightened about the head of the walking-stick. Well, then, he thought, if you couldn't sneak in through the back window, walk around and kick on the front door. Sometimes the most open approach is the best. All right, then: barge in through the front door and to hell with it! He would have to bluff; bull his way through and depend on his luck and his wits to keep the enemy off-balance. If it worked, he'd have a fighting chance. If it didn't—well, big as he was, he'd provide a fine supper for the carrion-eaters near Schwäbisch Gmünd. He'd never have to worry about the bombs from the Aensa in the sky.

Jaeger's brow creased. If he made it, what then? How to find the source? It had to be skillfully hidden, or it would have been spotted by the IC recon planes before this. He rubbed his finger along his nose. He would find it. In every mystery there is an invisible factor: some obvious thing that is the key to the whole enigma, but which often goes unnoticed because the minds of ordinary men function in well-worn grooves. Ordinary men can't peer over the edges of those grooves to grasp the significance of anything beyond.

Jaeger had no such mental blinders; his mind was open, and it functioned as much as possible on a basis of pure logic. When he was on a job, he tried to empty his mind of preconceived notions; he tried to do his thinking with his brain rather than with his habits. Using Occam's Razor and the theory that nothing, however unlikely, was completely impossible, he often succeeded simply because of his ability to see the forest in spite of the trees. If someone told Jaeger that the sun wouldn't rise in the east the next day, he would have considered it highly improbable, but still not impossible. Given the proper equipment, it might be possible to stop Earth's rotation and start it again in the other direction. More than just rather unlikely, certainly; but not impossible. Yes, Jaeger would find the Aensa's invisible factor—if he lived long enough.

The big man thrust the problem from his mind. Time enough to worry about that later. Right now he had other things to consider. Jaeger glanced at the phone on his desk; his fingers played idly with the bottons. The smooth texture of the plastic reminded him of the velvet fineness of Nati's skin. Nati! Damn it, there was the main problem. He had to find some way of convincing Huston that Nati took precedence over saving the rest of the world. It would be a difficult argument.

They had rested in each other's arms that morning, side by side in the pink light of dawn. She had explained how Schiller's men had attacked her in her own apartment, the morning after Jaeger's escape from the Aensa territory. From her description, Jaeger recognized both the Turk and the blond giant. The last trace of sorrow over the Turk's death disappeared; Jaeger swore a silent oath to hunt down the blond man, when he had the chance. They had injected Nati with the blue drug and left her. A letter came later that day, informing her of what she had to do in order to earn a daily dose; what she had to do was upset Jaeger. She had done that job well: There had been no Anthony. The craving for the blue narcotic overpowered her feelings toward Jaeger. Then, when the Turk and the blond had failed where Connor Coffey had also failed, Schiller had discarded Nati. Simply. Without the least twinge of conscience. It occurred to Jaeger that Schiller himself was likely an addicted tool of the Aensa; still, that didn't lessen Jaeger's hatred of the man.

Jaeger listened to Nati's story, and his fear grew. They lay in the cool morning breeze that streamed through the high open window. Still, Jaeger felt the perspiration running down his face. It had been an odd night, a strange awakening, with fearful love mixed with the unspoken knowledge of what waited for Nati unless Jaeger—what? Unless he did what? He didn't know; he only thought that if he had cracked the assignment earlier, Nati wouldn't be facing a certain death within eighteen hours.

The telephone buzzed, interrupting Jaeger's memories. He clicked on the intercom, and Marga Geier's voice informed him that Huston was on the line. Jaeger told her to put the call through, and a few seconds later Huston's tired face filled the screen of the phone. "Hello, Huston," said Jaeger.

"How are you, Jaeger?" said the NAUL representative.

"Listen. One simple thing. I need some of that blue Aensa drug. Schiller was trying to get to me through my girl friend. They shot her full of the stuff, and now they've cut her off. I need some by about four or five this evening."

Huston's expression looked even more weary, more sorrowful. "I'm sorry, Karl," he said. "There isn't any. I can't get any. You could have it if we had some."

Jaeger felt a chill in his guts. "What about the vial you showed me? That would hold her another day."

"It's gone to the labs. All the stuff that's around is going to the people who use it. No one is going to let you or me have their ration."

Jaeger was growing angry. He felt futile, impotent. "Look, Huston," he shouted. "I'm not asking for a ton of the stuff. I just want—"

Huston interrupted him by raising a hand. "Cool down, Jaeger. I'm not going to discuss this any more, not over the telephone like this. I'll meet you at your office about two o'clock. I'll see what I can do." Jaeger said nothing; he clicked off the telephone with a furious gesture. Huston wasn't his only hope, but the IC attaché was the best hope.

Jaeger hurried from his office. It was already quarter past twelve. He stopped just long enough to tell Marga Geier that he was going out for a couple of hours, and that she could expect Huston at two o'clock. Then Jaeger ran out.

He repeated his late-night journey through the shadow-world of Nürnberg; he saw the same streets, the same filthy buildings and shabby people. But he didn't have the same luck. No one had answers for him this time. No one had a drop of the blue drug. One tough young hoodlum said that he knew of the stuff but had no idea where Jaeger could get some. Like Huston said, it was doled out by Schiller's operation in carefully controlled lots, just enough for those the Aensa wished to keep alive. And Jaeger could get a single dose from every poor addict that he could kill; if he could identify those people, of course, and if they hadn't already taken the drug themselves. Jaeger felt sicker as the afternoon went on. He could only see Nati's haggard, trusting face when he looked at the derelicts he questioned. He could only feel that he was responsible for the torture that she was probably already beginning to feel. And if he couldn't find her dose.

Jaeger panicked then; his mind was overwhelmed by a wave of unbearable fear and impotent panic rage that carried everything before it, swept it away, both professional training and common sense. He would not have panicked in that way for himself, however great his fear; his self-discipline was too strong. But Nati was alone and in pain, and he could do nothing but swat uselessly at shadows, wrestle futilely with smoke.

What happened next was never entirely clear in Jaeger's memory, but somehow he must have gotten back to his office; the next thing he knew, he was talking to Schiller on the holophone and, amazingly enough, trying to talk Schiller into giving him some of the Aensa drug for Nati. Jaeger could never afterward remember exactly how he had broached this indelicate proposition to Schiller, but Schiller's immediate reaction was unequivocal enough and entirely fitting with his character, and one Jaeger would have foreseen if he had been in his right mind.

Schiller's face closed up like a bank vault. "You're trying to entrap me!" Schiller whispered, in horror.

"No!" Jaeger bellowed. "God damn it, no, listen to me! I don't care about your damn drug traffic, you understand that? I don't care! Run it forever, poison the world, I don't care, I just want—"

"Oh, you're clever," Schiller was whispering, unheeding, "but I'm cleverer still." He began to shout in a loud, stilted voice, pronouncing each word distinctly, like a stupid tourist trying to communicate with a native who doesn't speak his language: "I know nothing about any drug traffic! You hear that, Jaeger? I'm recording this conversation, and my lawyers are now monitoring this line. I KNOW NOTHING ABOUT ANY DRUG TRAFFIC! I don't have the slightest idea what you're talking about! I don't know what kind of entrapment scheme you've masterminded, but it won't work; a man in my position takes precautions against these kind of smears. I DON'T KNOW WHAT YOU'RE TALKING ABOUT!"

"Schiller, listen," Jaeger tried, "I'll take the pictures for you—" But it was too late for that.

"I told you it wouldn't work, Jaeger!"

"You won't give me any!" Jaeger raged, almost incoherent with fury. "I'll come out there and take it from you, you son of a bitch! I'll kill you, I'll break you in half if you try to stop me!"

"This conversation is being recorded, as I mentioned," Schiller said, suddenly calm and smooth as silk. "You have just made a death-threat against me, a serious one, on the record—that gives me excellent probable cause grounds to have you shot if you even look like you are about to make anything that even looks like it might be a physical attack on me. Furthermore, if you try to break into my house—and that can be construed as merely setting foot on my property once you have been expressly forbidden to, as you have now officially been, I can shoot you for that, too. So come on out here, Jaeger! We'll be waiting for you."

Schiller smiled and broke the circuit.

Jaeger reached for a desk drawer, opened it, and took out his gun. He felt numb and dead and very grim. He weighed the gun in his hand, checked to make sure it was fully charged, and slipped it into his pocket. He stood up, and only then did he become aware that Huston had been standing in the doorway, watching him.

"Jesus Christ!" Huston said. "I don't believe you did that."

Jaeger started to brush by the IC man, but stopped as an idea hit him. He reached out and grabbed Huston by the lapels and jerked him half off his feet; Jaeger's face was wild and flushed and frightening. "Huston!" Jaeger shouted. "Listen, you've got to stage a raid on Schiller's place immediately, right now. He'll only be expecting me, not an attack in force. If we can crack his place fast enough, we can salvage a great deal of the drug."

"No," Huston said firmly, not even trying to free himself from Jaeger's grasp. "I'm sorry, Jaeger, but absolutely not. You've probably already let Schiller know that we're onto him with that berserk phone call. I won't tip our hand any more than that. The time's not right."

Jaeger released him. "Then I'll go alone," he said suddenly.

"I won't let you do that either. If necessary I'll call out the IC cops to stop you. Jaeger!" Huston grabbed Jaeger's wrist to halt him.

Jaeger swung around, looking as if he was going to hit Huston. The two men pitted leverage against leverage for a second. "I don't want to have to fight you, too," Jaeger rasped. "But I will. I don't have time to fool around with anyone. I've only got a few hours left to save Nati."

"You don't have any time left, Jaeger!" Huston cried. "More than likely, it's probably already too late. Listen to me!"

Jaeger stopped struggling.

"That eighteen-hour limit," Huston said, "that's just an approximation, an average. It varies a lot from individual to individual. For some it's sixteen, fifteen, even twelve. It depends on individual metabolic rates, among other things. For a small, slender woman, the safe limit would be a lot less than eighteen hours. You've got to face the fact that she's probably already dead, and that there was nothing you could have done about it anyway. Jaeger—"

But Jaeger had started off again, towing Huston behind him like a toy boat. "Jaeger," Huston panted, "listen to me. This girl is important to you. I can understand that. But think of the rest of the problem. Think of the rest of the world, of the life we can all look forward to under the domination of the Aensa. Or, if not that, then—"

"I don't want to hear about it. I don't want the lecture about duty. I had that in college. I had it in the SEPG. I've had it, period." He looked around the small waiting room, his eyes wild. He focused on nothing. Suddenly, Jaeger grabbed the IC man's arm and began pulling him toward the door. "Come on," he said. "There has to be something we can do."

"Nothing," said Huston. "It's better if you realize that. You're going to have to face it."

"It's not far. We'll call a doctor. Maybe if she's sedated enough, she'll pass through the crisis."

"Nothing, Jaeger," said Huston. Jaeger would not be denied. Down on Koenigstrasse, he hailed a taxi. Jaeger and Huston rode to Nati's apartment building; Jaeger flung a large bill at the driver, and did not wait to hear the man's startled thanks. He dragged Huston to the glass doors, forced them open, and hurried to Nati's apartment. He called her name; there was no answer. Weeping, and not knowing that he wept, Jaeger kicked in her door. He ran into the room, and Huston followed. It was empty. Jaeger looked into the bathroom, and then in the bedroom. He stifled a sob as he found her. She lay on her bed. Her eyes were rolled up, and her expression was one of such inhuman suffering that Jaeger had to turn away. The wall just above her head was stained with a large red patch, where she had beat her head in the extremity of her pain. Her fingers were like stiff claws, twisted on the ends of her outstretched arms. Her once-lovely hair was fouled with her clotting blood. Jaeger walked over and touched her. He would never know a winter night that would be as cold as her skin.

"Let's go," said Huston.

Jaeger cried. He stared at the other man. He tried to speak, but he couldn't find any words.

"Sure," said Huston, "I'm sorry. We have to go. The IC will take care of her. You don't want the SEPG to find her. Come on, man. Let's go back to your office. We'll call that doctor, for you."

"Let me go," Jaeger said in a voice like old wood. "Leave me alone, can't you? There's got to be something I—"

"Jaeger," Huston said, very firmly, "she's dead."

"No," Jaeger said, pulling away.

Huston wouldn't let him go. "Jaeger, *she's dead.*"

Jaeger's shoulders slumped, all at once, and his eyes glazed.

Numbly, he let Huston lead him from the bloody room.

"Are the IC cops done in there yet?" asked a workman in gray overalls.

A uniformed guard yawned. He had two more hours before his shift ended. He wondered if he could stay awake that long. He stared at the short man and nodded. "Sure," he said in a bored voice. "They finished about half an hour ago. I heard them mumbling to themselves. They didn't learn nothing. I'll tell you, it's scary how often they don't learn nothing."

"Sure, yourself," said the short workman, turning to his companion. "It don't surprise me at all."

The other workman smiled. "They were IC cops. Those guys are paid not to make trouble. They wouldn't find a potato in an Irish stew."

"Let's get to work," said the short man. The guard nodded to the two men and let them into the apartment. The short workman pulled out a yellow slip from a pocket. "Here," he said to the guard, "you'll have to sign it and put down the time we went in and the time we finish." The guard said nothing, but did as the man said.

The two workmen went into the apartment; they ignored the quiet elegance of the furnishings, the incongruous paper sheets the IC Security Bureau had left on the carpet, and the nauseating smell of death, with which they worked every day. They went into the bedroom and stopped for a moment. They looked at the still, stiff, cold corpse of Nati Fernfelder.

"Nothing to it," said the taller workman.

"I thought this was a special job," said the small man.

"Me too."

"Well, we won't have to do anything but carry her out. I remember this one guy, oh, maybe two weeks ago, just like this on his bed. He had one hand wrapped around the metal post of his headboard. By the time I got to him, his fingers were so stiff, I had to saw them open. And his legs were spread out too wide to carry through the door; me and this other guy had to spend half the day shoving the guy's body around before we could even wrap him up and cart him away."

"This one won't be no problem."

"Naw, no problem. I wonder why she did it."

"I don't," said the tall man. "They're all crazy."

"Grab her feet together," said the small man. "Dump her on the floor."

There was no answering voice; Karl Jaeger was alone. The ghost had disappeared.

Jaeger woke up. He was sitting in his Dark Lightning. The dream faded, and he stretched a little. He stared through the hot darkness of his apartment. He sat in the padded chair of Dark Lightning for many minutes. Then he stood, went to his bar, filled a glass with ice cubes, changed his mind and threw them into the sink, put the glass down, and went back to Dark Lightning. He sat down again. He clicked the machine on again. He was asleep again instantly.

It was the same dream. Jaeger was sitting on the floor of his small hut, dressed in simple, poor clothing. Next to him lay his beautiful, young wife. She was very ill, and Jaeger did not have the money to buy her medicine. He loved her more than he had ever loved anything in his life. He had sold all of his possessions to buy her things to ease her pain. He had stolen money. He had robbed strangers passing by on the highway. The medicine had not stopped the young woman's illness, though it had eased the discomfort a little. Now, after many months, there was no more money, and there was no more hope. Jaeger's wife was only minutes away from their final parting. He watched her through tear-filled eyes.

The woman looked up at him. Her face was full of love, even though her pain had drawn deep furrows in her once-youthful skin. Her forehead was hot when Jaeger touched it. Her lips were cracked and dry. Still, she tried to smile. "I love you so much," she said, and her voice was like the faint rustle of insect wings in the autumn night.

"I love you, Keishi," said Jaeger.

"I love you so much. Please, don't make me leave you. I couldn't bear it if you drove me from your heart, just as this fever is driving me from your side."

Jaeger shook his head. "Don't think such things," he said, weeping. "How can you say that I would ever forget you?"

Keishi smiled again, more weakly than before. "I know the ways of men," she said softly. "And I know your ways, Karl. Do not go to another woman after I am gone. I could not bear it, my love. I would come back to you, as a ghost, and I would bring you bad fortune."

"You are ill, my wife," said Jaeger. "Rest now."

Before the hour had ended, Keishi had breathed her last, letting the air out in a peaceful sigh. Jaeger collapsed from grief and from his nervous reaction. He awoke many hours later, summoned the village's priest, and arranged for a proper funeral. He placed himself as an indentured servant to pay for the funeral, and he worked for a year and a half to remove that debt. In all that time he respected his wife's final wish. But near the end of his servitude, he met another woman and fell deeply and sincerely in love with her. After another year and a half, when Jaeger had recovered his fortune enough to offer the young woman security, they became engaged to be married. This was three years following the death of Keishi.

Immediately after the engagement, the ghost of Jaeger's dead wife began to visit him, tormenting him for not keeping his promise. Jaeger tried to reason with the ghost, saying that it was wrong for him to shut himself away from love for the remainder of his stay on earth. The ghost would not be persuaded. Jaeger's torture proceeded.

The ghost was amazingly knowledgeable about Jaeger's affairs, with the young woman and in his business dealings. The ghost of Keishi would repeat entire conversations, word for word, and would give details about not only what Jaeger had done, but also what he had thought. Jaeger pleaded with Keishi's ghost to leave him in peace; the ghost would not listen. Jaeger was prevented from sleeping. He was prevented from taking his meals in quiet contemplation. The ghost appeared at odd intervals throughout the day, so that Jaeger was reduced to constant fear and dread.

At last, seeing Jaeger's condition but not understanding the cause of it, a friend counseled Jaeger to see a wise old man who lived in the next village. The sage's name was Shuin, and he had a reputation for being able to solve even the most intricate of dilemmas. Finally, in total despair, Jaeger agreed to journey to the neighboring town and consult Shuin the sage.

"So," said Shuin, after they had met, "your first wife died and became a ghost, as she threatened. Now it seems that she knows your every action and word and reproaches you for what the ghost claims is your faithlessness. Everything you say or do, whatever gift you give your new love, the ghost knows. She must be a very wise ghost. I think that one should be proud to know such a clever ghost. The next time that she appears, try to strike a bargain with her, for there is no fooling such an intelligent spirit. You must admit to your wife's ghost that you cannot hide anything from her, in word or deed. Then say that if she will answer a single question correctly, you will swear to break off your new engagement and remain unmarried for the rest of your life."

Jaeger hesitated. "What is the question that you think I should ask?" he said.

"Take a large handful of soy beans," said Shuin. "Ask her how many beans you hold in your hand. If she is unable to tell you, it will prove that she is a product of your guilt, a figment of your imagination. She will trouble you no longer."

The next night, Jaeger waited impatiently for the appearance of Keishi's ghost. When finally she arrived, Jaeger did just as the wise man suggested. He flattered the ghost and told her that she knew everything he did and said.

"Certainly," said the ghost. "And that includes the visit you had with Shuin, the wise man. You cannot fool me, just as he said."

"Yes," said Jaeger nervously, "and as that is probably true, tell me how many beans I hold in my hand!"

There was no answering voice; Karl Jaeger was alone. The ghost had disappeared.

Corcail Sendijen crouched low and made a snarling sound. He faced the Aensalord and D'jebistred the overseer. What a hell of a thing to happen! Could he possibly take both of them? A sudden leap, perhaps? But the weapon in the Aensalord's hand was held by a nerveless being; the weapon's muzzle stared unswervingly at him like a sinister black eye.

D'jebistred the overseer took a shuffling step forward, his pale eyes shining; a fat tongue licked out from between ivory fangs and played over his cracked gray lips. He glared at Corcail Sendijen with evil hunger, his studdy hands clenching greedily. D'jebistred turned and fired a burst of thought speech at the Aensalord. "— kill—him/it—now— me—yes?—" His bloodlust hung tangibly in the air.

The Aensalord looked at D'jebistred with distaste; he raised his slender hand reluctantly—the Aensalords hated to use the crude mixture of telepathic speech and sign language that was the basic tongue of the lower-grade creatures. The Aensalord stared and flashed a staccato burst of thought speech that was much crisper than D'jebistred's slurred efforts. "— not—yet—later— question—now—what—he/it—doing— here—spying?—why?— know— you?—"

D'jebistred looked away with poorly concealed displeasure, shrugging impatiently, and glared at the floor with a surly expression. The Aensalord turned thoughtful eyes, deep pupil-less orbs that glowed fitfully golden, on Corcail Sendijen.

Corcail Sendijen returned the stare levelly, his eyes crackling golden slits. His only chance was to play dumb.

The Aensalord probed with his mind at Corcail Sendijen. Corcail Sendijen left a few confused thoughts typical of a low-grade mentality on the surface of his mind for the Aensalord to riffle through; he withdrew the rest of his consciousness behind an impenetrable mental shield. Corcail Sendijen was trained as an Adept, several degrees higher than the being who faced him, as a matter of fact. The Aensalord would learn nothing telepathically.

Shaking his head in puzzlement, the Aensalord switched to a vocal tongue and thundered in standard Galactic: "Who are you? Death comes swiftly—" Corcail Sendijen stared at him blankly; the Aensalord mustn't suspect that he was anything other than a common laborer. The Aensalord switched to modern Language, the accepted universal tongue among the interstellar races. Still Corcail Sendijen didn't respond. Frowning, the Aensalord spoke in his own tongue of bell-chimes and rasping buzzes, then shifted into flowing, sibilant Slanchi, another widespread trading language; neither of these attempts had any effect. The Aensalord tried a few words of Terran, the artificial language devised a few years back after the first contact with Earth, as a last resort. Thought speech crackled again from the Aensalord. "—what—are—you—doing—here? — answer— true— swift—"

Corcail Sendijen's eyes narrowed. This was going to be tricky. He couldn't pretend that he didn't know thought speech; D'jebistred knew better. But at the same time he mustn't give himself away. He could feel the weight of D'jebistred's smoldering eyes.

Corcail Sendijen raised a supple tentacle and sent a slow stream of thought speech at the Aensalord, remembering to slur his syntax and make his delivery as crude and halting as possible. "—lost—hungry—(untranslatable)—season—need—mate—must—find—you—have?—where / when—(untranslatable) —season—eggs—need—mate—where / when—lost—"

The Aensalord glared suspiciously; Corcail Sendijen could almost hear the whir of his busy mind. It was possible that this was Corcail Sendijen's mating season (as a matter of fact, it wasn't; Corcail Sendijen's people, like humans, had no specific mating period) and that he had been driven out into the corridors by brute instinct, in a futile search for a mate. But it was also very possible that he was a liar. Indecision flickered in the Aensalord's mind, but did not show in his terrible, cold eyes. He raised the muzzle of the weapon slightly.

Corcail Sendijen felt blood rush to the small chitin horn that protruded from his forehead, an involuntary preparation for a last-ditch attack. His fighting-claws ached with tension. The slimy Aensa creature was going to shoot; any god, shrivel him! What a time to be killed; his goal had been almost within his grasp—

The Aensalord made up his mind, and his finger loosened slightly on the trigger of his weapon; thought speech rattled toward D'jebistred. "— take—him/it—to—interrogation—room—lower—level—question—later—keep—him / it—immobilized—but—unharmed—" D'jebistred absorbed the message, grunted sourly, and turned away, disappointment evident in his thoughts.

Corcail Sendijen gave his equivalent of a sigh of relief. At least the moment of truth had been postponed for a while. He waved a tentacle in the Sixteenth Gesture of the Rites (Obscene) at the Aensalord. The Aensalord looked startled, then flashed "— what—he/it— doing?—" to the overseer. D'jebistred shrugged. The Aensalord grunted suspicously, then pointed imperatively back down the tunnel; D'jebistred shuffled cautiously forward, keeping a wary eye on Corcail Sendijen.

Corcail Sendijen felt better; he had won a small victory. He again made the Sixteenth Gesture of the Rites, and then happily followed D'jebistred the overseer down the tunnel, the Aensalord's weapon at his back.

Chapter Seven

The ground slipped slowly along below. Karl Jaeger squinted his eyes against the glare of the sunlight on the plastic windshield; the roar of the helijet's vanes was a constant coughing chatter in his ears. It was a small, two-man IC helijet, and the tanned IC pilot beside Jaeger was competent, taciturn, and completely uninterested. He had his orders, and he didn't really care to know anything else about the mission. This suited Jaeger, who was in an introspective mood and had troubles of his own to think about.

The urban center of Schwäbisch Hall appeared below, the last large signpost of civilization, human civilization, before the edge of Chaos. It looked lonely and futile and pitiably brave, like a painted balloon. Within minutes, the countryside had swallowed it up; the last traces of concrete and glass disappeared behind, and all was the melancholy autumn green-brown of withering grass and dying leaves, everything sleeping before the first angry leap of winter. Somewhere above this loneliness rode three black ships, waiting, but Jaeger didn't want to think about that quite yet.

Beneath the helijet, the land itself began to run in folds and ridges, the first warning that the ground would soon hurl itself up toward the sky in the jagged, tortured mountains of the south; a network of rivers and streams gleamed below like silver ribbons. The humped looming peaks of the Swabian Jura stretched across the horizon ahead, purple with distance. Jaeger leaned forward, his brows drawn together. The silent earth spun below, empty.

This was a haunted land, filled with ghosts, and with the

ghosts of ghosts. For many centuries this land had seen nothing but war; not a generation had passed here without the violent deaths of many men. It hung in the air: the memory of war and its slumbering possibility. The rocks had been scratched and shattered by hooves and caissons and tanks alike. The wooded glades had rung with shots, the clash of cold steel, and the almost continuous screams of human agony. The trees and the grass had been nourished with human blood, the soil had been soaked in it, until the land and the people had formed a curious amalgam and kinship. It was a closed environment in which the sum of the parts was much less than the whole, and the bond of those parts was shared blood. It was a relationship between the mother earth and her children that had been forced into so tightly drawn a knot, so disfigured by the weight of ages, that the land *was* the people, and the people *were* the land. Forged into an eternal circle of love and hate, the land and the people drifted unchanged down through the years, timeless and impenetrable to outsiders. Here memory was more than a thing of the mind, it was a dimension as real as length, breadth, width, and duration. The land itself brooded; the people were nourished from birth on the fruit of the soil, and when they died, their bodies were returned to the soil. It was a closed cycle, gaining nothing, losing nothing, somehow managing to exist in the past, present, and future simultaneously. The land below was a ravaged battlefield, occasionally cloaked in living green, waiting with complacent knowledge for the devastations to come.

Schwäbisch Gmünd was also impressive in a negative sort of way, like a chambered nautilus that has withdrawn into its inner shell and left its outer portions empty and lifeless. Once it had been a much larger town, but the threat of the Aensalords had drained the community of energy and inflicted it with a wasting illness. Rows of buildings stood deserted and desolate; only an inner nucleus was still alive, the fitful glow of a dozen lighted buildings in the darkened, empty town marking the last stand of a hard-faced group of men and women determined to remain in their ancestral home.

The emptiness of the town began to seep into Jaeger's

mind, thick and foul as noxious fumes. Grimacing, Jaeger walked into the main room of the gasthaus and ordered supper from an elderly frau who wore an old-fashioned apron. She dragged slowly away into the kitchen; a moment after she opened the kitchen door, cooking smells flowed into the room. Then the door closed with a heavy thunk. Jaeger frowned sadly. There was no vitality to these people; the mere struggle to survive here in the face of the grisly menace to the south had drained them of all excess life. Five large wooden tables filled the main room of the gasthaus, but there were no customers except Jaeger, and no sign that there ever were any save a half-empty coffee cup on one of the tables near the kitchen. Jaeger moved in his chair, and the sudden creak of wood echoed horribly from the bare walls of the room.

An hour later, Jaeger strode through the moonlit streets of Schwäbisch Gmünd, toward the edge of town. The streets around him were deserted; nothing stirred, and the innumerable dark corners attracted no young lovers nor staggering drinkers, as they might have in a normal town. Jaeger's imagination peopled the hushed blackness with creatures from the area's own mythology: gnarled, hunched trolls, demons, pixies, and elves. His feet made a startling click-clack through the night.

Jaeger reached the edge of the village and looked out, a chill prickling at the back of his neck; the ravaged land rolled black and lonely into desolation, the dead vegetation lit coldly by a waning moon. Somewhere out there the Aensalords were waiting, going about their incomprehensible tasks, thinking incomprehensible thoughts. It was unsettling to consider that inhuman eyes were gazing from the depths of the forest at the same moon and stars that he was seeing now; the primitive vestige in Jaeger howled in fear. He smiled when he felt the instinctive reaction, the bristling of the short hair on the back of his neck, but it was a tight smile, devoid of pleasure. Out there was something beyond his power. Perhaps the primitive nature in Jaeger was right in wanting to flee, and it was Jaeger the civilized man who was insane for going on. The black land lay before him, ignoring him, neither luring him nor forbidding him. Three black ships sailed serenely overhead, and in Jaeger's imagination they glared contemptuously down upon a frozen, helpless Earth.

Stiffly, Jaeger turned and limped back to his room, to sleep and dream of fangs and golden eyes that glowed in the dark.

The red-tiled roofs of Schwäbisch Gmünd fell swiftly away below. The pilot punched a control button; the helijet swooped sharply to the right and chattered through the damp mists of early morning in the mountains. Schwäbisch Gmünd dwindled slowly behind and disappeared as the helijet dodged around the shoulder of a mountain. Below, an abandoned road appeared. A tiny village went by, deserted, choked with black, dead vegetation. They were now in Aensa territory.

A chill shivered along Jaeger's spine. Days ago he had followed this same route on foot, and he knew what it was like down there: an empty, unnaturally silent land, like a forgotten stage set, filled with nothing. Jaeger's knuckles were white as they gripped the edge of his seat; he noticed it, smiled sourly, and loosened his deathgrip. Jaeger glanced at his companion. The pilot's face was pale, and he was unconsciously moistening dry lips with his tongue. Several hours of argument between the IC and the Aensa liaison had won Jaeger grudging permission to enter the Aensa land. But who could guarantee that the unfathomable Aensalords wouldn't change their minds and decide to have the helijet shot down . . .

A whoosh and a black flash, and suddenly there was a long metallic object hanging in mid-air alongside the helijet, keeping pace with it easily. The pilot gasped and took a long, shuddering breath. Jaeger shrugged resignedly; the Aensa ship was probably armed, and could certainly fly rings around the helijet. There was nothing they could do but wait. Would the Aensalords fire? It didn't seem likely. The Aensa craft maintained a steady course alongside and made no other move to interfere. Jaeger nodded to himself. They had been given an escort to make certain they got into no mischief on their way. Diplomatic courtesy? Like hell. A watchdog by any other name would still smell.

A mountain grew steadily over the horizon's edge, and the helijet headed for it. Memory clicked and a name appeared in Jaeger's mind. This was Hohenstaufen; near its foot was a deserted town; on its flank was the Aensalord's central keep. Jaeger had not made it this far on his solitary foray.

The Aensa craft accelerated, swept twice around the helijet in contemptuously tight circles, evidently only to demonstrate that the Aensa could do it, then waggled slightly and moved down and to the right. The meaning was unmistakable. The pilot wiped nervous sweat from his brow, muttered something under his breath, and followed the Aensa craft in. The mountainside leaped toward Jaeger, jigged and tilted crazily, and then slid smoothly away as the helijet made a slow traverse across its face. The Aensa craft led them around the shoulder of the mountain, occasionally leaping back to scream dizzily about them if they strayed even slightly from their course, avoiding collision by only a hair's breadth. The pilot was cursing steadily in a low tone now, and his face was white. Jaeger clenched his teeth and remained silent.

The ground climbed closer, opened up into a large plateau terraced into the mountainside. At the far end of the plateau stood the Aensa keep, the ruins of an ancient Bavarian castle which the Aensalords had renovated and redesigned to suit their own mysterious purposes. It was an ugly, monolithic sprawl of pale stone; the square, ramparted bulk of the keep itself was surrounded by a thick wall, the wide inner courtyard appeared empty. A broad lake, diked at the edge of the plateau, lapped against the outer wall on three sides; the fourth side was nestled snugly against the sheer side of the cliff.

Jaeger frowned at the dark waters that rippled peacefully beneath the helijet; the lake neatly cut off a ground attack from this direction. How did the Aensahounds get out of their keep for their nightly hunts? Unless they swam the lake or knew a secret way up the cliff, the Aensalords must airlift them out. Jaeger tried to imagine what the scene inside an

Aensa ship would be like, filled with black Aensalords and the howling monster Dktar. He shuddered and stared instead at the flashing scene before him.

The Aensa craft made for the ramparts of the central keep, buzzed about like a hunting wasp, and then touched down. The helijet settled in toward the ramparts, hovered, swayed as its vanes slashed the air, and then gently made contact. The helijet's landing struts bumped slightly as they touched stone; then the pilot cut the power, and the vanes lost momentum slowly with a shrill, dying whine. "God damn," said the pilot fervently, his voice shaky. Jaeger swallowed and unclenched his fists again. His job was just beginning. He climbed out of the helijet.

Something moved in the shadow of an archway leading to the interior of the keep. A tall, slender figure walked slowly toward them, wrapped in a black cloak and hood. The Aensalord paused before Jaeger; a hand went up and reluctantly drew back a black veil. Jaeger was surprised to see that, in the daylight, the thick fur on the Aensalord's arm was of a silver color. He fought down a wave of primeval dread; somewhere inside him, the primitive self was gibbering that this Aensa creature was alien, evil. Two large, pupil-less eyes, glowing golden, smoldered at him from the shadow of the black hood.

Jaeger narrowed his eyes and returned the gaze. The Aensalord's bored implacably into his. Jaeger's eyes were as hard as steel and as cold as a winter sea; his gaze held. After a moment, though, Jaeger discovered that he had to look away. He glanced back at the creature inconspicuously. The Aensalord's features were roughly humanoid, although somewhat distorted and even bestial. Light shone wetly from needle teeth in the half-opened mouth, which Jaeger might even have termed a muzzle. The silver fur of the Aensalord was dappled with black on the face, around the eyes and the throat. A flickering golden aura shimmered around the Aensalord, faint in the sunlight; it would be much brighter in the dark, as Jaeger well knew.

The Aensalord winced and darted a brief, angry glance at the sun as it came out from behind a cloud. The Aensalords were creatures of the dark; they didn't like the sun. This particular Aensalord seemed almost in pain; undoubtedly his eyes were too sensitive to stand the glare of a bright autumn day for long. Jaeger chewed his lip. These creatures were apparently evolved from carnivorous ancestors, instead of omnivores, as mankind's forebears had been. The hunting instinct was still strong in the Aensa—that was evident in every supple movement of the tense, nimble body, every sharp glance from the constantly roving, wary hunter's eyes. Such beings could not honestly be called evil; certainly by their own standards they weren't, but those standards were so permeated with a natural cruelty, with the calculated savagery of a large predator, that the distinction was an extremely fine one, and would make little practical difference to the people of Earth.

"I am Aensamaster here," said the Aensalord in rasping, gutteral Euro. He spoke with a slight lisp and drew out his sibilants much too long. He nodded toward the helijet. "We have granted your urgent demand to confer with us. For your sake, soft one, what you have to say had better be of most extreme interest." He held up a silver-furred hand. "Do not try to explain your business now; you will do so before a Council of Lords tonight." The Aensamaster squinted at the sun uncomfortably and hissed. "This harsh light injures my eyes; I must depart. You will be guided to a room where you will wait for nightfall. You will not leave that room unaccompanied under any circumstances." It was not an order or a threat, but a statement of fact. The Aensalord's expression dismissed Jaeger, and turned toward the helijet pilot. "You, flyer, will go now. Return to Schwäbisch Gmünd"—his tongue rendered the town's name almost unintelligible—"and wait. If this one ever has occasion to leave here again, you will be called." The Aensamaster pointed a long arm toward Jaeger, then swung it back toward the pilot. "Go," he said. "Swiftly." He almost spat the final word. A snarl gathered behind the needle teeth.

The pilot, his face white and strained, punched on the jets and prepared to lift off. He looked toward Jaeger, his expression worried. He hesitated, then shrugged helplessly and reached out toward his control buttons. "Good luck, brother!" shouted the pilot above the whine of the jets; then the helijet shot skyward.

Jaeger felt a rare glow of human warmth, which was quickly smothered by the chill presence of the implacable creature beside him. The streamlined Aensa craft whooshed silently from the ramparts and floated up to escort the helijet out. The Aensa ship made two reckless circles around the helijet and then settled down into an escort position several yards away. Jaeger shook his head. He was amazed that in his situation he could still feel sympathy for anyone else; that pilot was in for a very rough trip back. The Aensamaster glowered at the sun, snarled, and then beckoned impatiently. An Aensaman scurried from the interior and cowered before the Aensamaster, squinting painfully in the sunlight. The Aensamaster spoke in his own language, meanwhile gesturing at Jaeger with a silver hand. He pulled his face veil closed and stalked away into the interior of the keep, moving with the fluid grace of quicksilver.

Jaeger watched him go, then turned his eyes back to the sky. Above, the helijet and its companion were roaring away around the bulk of Hohenstaufen. Slowly the helijet diminished to a toy, then to a moving brilliant speck, and then it was gone.

Once again, Karl Jaeger was alone.

Corcail Sendijen climbed up from a red well of pain and smiled to himself. Across the room, the slender Aensalord switched off the apparatus and turned hesitantly toward what seemed to by a hypno-probe. Corcail Sendijen's golden eyes flickered around the room. He and the Aensalord were alone. This might be the opportunity he'd been waiting for.

Corcail Sendijen twitched his feeding mandibles in his analogue of a savage grin; his mouth parts were taut with anticipation. He'd been waiting patiently in the interrogation room all day, held prisoner by the Aensalords' stasis field. Minutes ago, the Aensalord that had captured him had entered the room and wired Corcail Sendijen to a small machine; the device was designed to stimulate the pain centers of any typical chordate organism. Corcail Sendijen supposed that, with characteristic thoroughness, the Aensa would have a similar apparatus prepared to use upon every type of sentient organism known in the inhabited parts of the galaxy.

The Aensalord had started the preliminary questioning. Corcail Sendijen sat quietly. An Adept such as he was trained in the necessary discipline to resist mere physical pain; that part of the questioning had been simple. Now the Aensalord had decided that it would be necessary to use harsher methods; he would render Corcail Sendijen motionless beneath a hypno-probe and start in on his naked brain.

But before he did that, the Aensalord would have to remove the stasis field.

The Aensalord approached and stretched forth a silver-furred hand. Corcail Sendijen waited. Everything now depended on how convincing an actor he'd been. If the Aensalord still believed that Corcail Sendijen was only a low-grade laborer, then he would probably not bother to take the proper precautions before nullifying the stasis field . . .

The silver hand touched a glowing plate and pushed with two long fingers. Corcail Sendijen felt a needle-sharp tingle as the restraining field died away.

The Aensalord sent a telepathic message on the subconscious level crackling across to his captive, ordering Corcail Sendijen's motor nerves to freeze him into immobility. Preoccupied, the Aensalord turned away to prepare the hypno-probe. If Corcail Sendijen had really been a low-grade laborer, the telepathic freeze order would have been sufficient; but Corcail Sendijen was not a low-grade laborer. Corcail Sendijen was an Adept of one of the higher degrees. He ignored the freeze order, whipped up two of his longer tentacles, wrapped them tightly around the Aensalord's slender neck, and crushed it like an eggshell. The Aensalord gurgled, writhed briefly, and then hung limply in Corcail Sendijen's grasp. Corcail Sendijen grunted in satisfaction, maintained his grip for a moment longer to make certain, and then casually tossed the corpse aside.

Corcail Sendijen stepped forward into the middle of the room and paused, interpreting the signs received by his various senses and by his superior mental faculties. There was a consciousness somewhere nearby, but it didn't seem to be alarmed; evidently no sound of Corcail Sendijen's short-lived struggle with the Aensalord had penetrated past the walls of the interrogation room. Corcail Sendijen hesitated, then rippled his tentacles in a shrug. He would have to take a risk; he couldn't afford to remain in the interrogation room. Someone was certain to check in on the Aensalord who now lay dead. By then, Corcail Sendijen must be far away from that room.

Slowly, Corcail Sendijen moved to the heavily timbered door, wrapped his tentacles around the old-fashioned handle, designed for other limbs than his, and pulled. The door came open a crack, inched a little wider— The rusted hinges gave a terrifying creak. Corcail Sendijen cursed. That decided it! He threw the door wide and jumped out into the middle of the corridor, landing crouched.

D'jebistred the overseer whirled to face him. His eyes took in Corcail Sendijen, widened, and then blazed green with killing fury. Corcail Sendijen's own eyes narrowed; his fighting claws stiffened. D'jebistred gave an inarticulate shout and ran blindly forward, his stubby hands reaching. Corcail Sendijen's locomotor legs straightened, hurling him up from his crouched position in a spring like that of a great jungle cat. The two massive forms, those of D'jebistred the overseer and Corcail Sendijen the putative slave, crashed together in mid-air, then slumped noisily to the ground.

D'jebistred jerked his head back, opened his mouth to reveal four pairs of hunting fangs; he struck, snarling like a wounded tiger, his yellowed-ivory teeth glistening. Corcail Sendijen twisted to the side and wrapped crushing tentacles around the overseer. He squeezed. They thrashed together, straining, rolling back and forth across the corridor like partners in some insane ritual. D'jebistred grunted, turned, got one leg under him, and lashed out with his armored tail. The tail smashed into Corcail Sendijen and tossed him away. Corcail Sendijen rolled, gathered his tentacles to steady himself, rose again on his locomotor legs to his full height; his eyes closed to fierce slits. D'jebistred rushed forward, swinging his clenched hands as a bone-crushing bludgeon.

Corcail Sendijen moved quickly aside with sinuous grace;

D'jebistred's clubbed fists pounded empty air, then chipped plaster from the wall of the corridor behind where Corcail Sendijen's head had been. Corcail Sendijen lashed tentacles around D'jebistred, and lifted the overseer into the air. He threw D'jebistred heavily to the floor, with an impact that raised a thick cloud of ancient dust from the stone floor. D'jebistred crawled slowly to his feet, shaking his armored head, his green eyes blinking fitfully. The overseer leaped to the attack once more. Corcail Sendijen lowered his head and met the overseer's blind charge with the chitin horn that protruded from his forehead; Corcail Sendijen felt the impact shake him to his tentacle tips, as D'jebistred impaled himself.

With a sharp jerk of his head, Corcail Sendijen freed his chitin horn; D'jebistred howled in agony. D'jebistred flailed wildly, his hands hammering futilely around his agile opponent. Corcail Sendijen saw his opportunity; his great fighting claws scythed forward and snapped. D'jebistred screamed and staggered away, dribbling blood. Corcail Sendijen followed after him. D'jebistred, his thick skin now the pale ashen color of death, the same hue of expiration in so many otherwise dissimilar species, stumbled backward until he felt the cold, damp stone of the wall behind his back. Then he struck desperately at his enemy. Corcail Sendijen dipped easily beneath the blow; the big fighting claws slashed again at the overseer, gleaming and terrible in the stark square of light from overhead. D'jebistred grunted; his body jerked violently at the blow. Corcail Sendijen's fighting claws slashed again, and again. D'jebistred gave a last despairing moan, fell forward a step, trying to bring up his hands, then crumpled forward and slid peacefully to the floor; his bright green eyes slowly glazed, and then he was gone.

Corcail Sendijen leaned against the corridor wall, his breath hissing harshly through the throat membrane-flap. The struggle had been too close; he had enjoyed less of an advantage over D'jebistred than he had expected. Corcail Sendijen pushed himself erect, glancing about the corridor. No shouts, no rapid rhythm of running feet; down on the lower levels, such disturbances might easily go unnoticed. Few people would be about on the level now. Later, though, the traffic would begin to pick up; something had to be done with D'jebistred's corpse. Corcail Sendijen considered the matter briefly, then brightened. Of course! He wrapped tentacles around D'jebistred, and dragged the heavy body into the interrogation room. He arranged it next to the body of the Aensalord. Then he backed out, slamming the door of the interrogation room and sliding the locking bar into position with a sharp click.

Rather pleased with his success so far, Corcail Sendijen glanced at the locked door. That ought to buy him some time. To a casual passerby it would look as though the interrogating Aensalord had finished his business and left, locking the door behind him. Of course, when the other Aensalords realized that one of their fellows was missing, the most elementary of searches would soon reveal the truth. But, with luck, the Aensalord would not be missed for hours, and by that time Corcail Sendijen would either have succeeded in his mission or he would be dead.

Golden eyes narrowed, Corcail Sendijen scurried along the corridor and began his search for the source of the bright blue Aensa drug.

Chapter Eight

Karl Jaeger paused on the threshold and glanced warily around the cell. It was utterly bare—bare walls, bare floor, bare ceiling. A featureless room of gray stone. Only the door behind him and a high slit of a window broke the smooth planes of solid rock. Jaeger heard the Aensaman who had escorted him step closer; with a shrug, Jaeger moved forward slowly, squinting.

In the exact center of the room stood the only furnishings, a large table with a solid slab of granite for a top and a crude wooden chair. The fact that there was neither bed nor toilet facilities indicated that the room was only a detention cell, rather than a permanent prison. Jaeger could think of reasons why that might be good, from his point of view. He could think of just as many why that might be ominous. He grinned ruefully; whatever the meaning, they certainly weren't giving him much to work with. His scheme had been hastily devised only to get him into the Aensalord's keep. From here on in he was completely on his own. He would have to play it by ear, without the aid or the official sanction of the International Congress.

The one certain fact was that Jaeger couldn't afford to stick around to meet that Aensa Council of Lords tonight; they would see through his thin cover story in about five minutes. Whatever he decided to do, it would have to be done quickly. The first step, obviously, was to get out of this damn cell. While he looked around the room again, searching for some meager thing to encourage his hopes, the Aensaman slammed the door. The noise had a too-final sound to Jaeger's anxious mind. The Aensalords had other thoughts about his poking into their affairs.

Jaeger moved to the center of the room and placed his silver-headed walking stick carefully on the granite-topped table. He cast a swift glance around the room and swore softly to himself. He would have to assume that the Aensalords had equipped the cell with some manner of surveillance apparatus; it was the natural thing to do. Microphones, closed-circuit stereop, old-fashioned spy holes? There was no way to tell, but a subtle tingling in the back of his neck told him that his subconscious mind didn't like the situation at all. He wasn't surprised; his conscious faculties weren't too excited either. He wondered how long he would have to go up against the Aensa and their strangely superior technology; it seemed to Jaeger that every time he squared off with the aliens, he was armed only with toys and hunches.

To a certain extent, his decisions had been made for him, his course of action determined by the Aensalords' own actions. Jaeger would have to have his special field equipment before he could proceed, and he'd have to assemble it now. There would definitely be no time later. How could he hide his movements from unfriendly eyes? Jaeger's brows drew together. The room had no fixtures for artificial lighting. When night came, it would be as dark as a landlord's memory in the cell, and he could easily—

The big man shook his head sadly. He was still thinking like a human. To defeat an enemy, think like the enemy, only better. Jaeger told himself that he had to remember that if he was to have any chance at all of surviving. Darkness would hardly bother the Aensalords; their night vision was dozens of times better than that of a human. Why, they could actually see better during the night than during—

Jaeger stiffened and rubbed a finger thoughtfully along the bridge of his nose. They could actually see better during the night than during the day. There was the germ of an idea there somewhere. Hold on to it. He smiled slowly. If you want to hide an activity from a human being, do it in the dark. If you want to hide an activity from a nocturnal Aensalord, do it in—

The light. Jaeger walked around the table, thinking. The

harsh light of mid-morning streamed in through the open high window, hitting a spot near the end of the granite-topped table and refracting there dazzlingly in a prismatic spray. The flecks of minerals in the stone gleamed like a galaxy of bright stars. It was undoubtedly the brightest spot in the room, and would only remain that way as long as the sun was near this particular angle. He would have to act now. Very casually, Jaeger retrieved his cane, strolled about the room in an apparent tour of inspection, and then returned to the table. This time he nonchalantly placed the cane in the middle of the bright spot. Jaeger walked around the table again and went to the window; he spent a few moments there standing on tiptoe, gazing out the window as though lost in thought. He drifted back to the table, giving the impression, he hoped, of absent-minded meditation. He moved his fingers along the swirls and patterns in the granite table top with studied boredom, until his hands moved into the bright spot.

Jaeger stared expressionlessly toward the window, his eyes narrowed in a near doze. He wondered whether his unknown observer could be sophisticated enough about human attitudes to appreciate the pantomime. Meanwhile, his fingers flew with frantic haste. He would have to work fiendishly fast, even while he tried to lull his warden into inattention. Everything would have to be done by touch, and none of the anxiety that he felt could be allowed to reach his face. Jaeger seriously doubted that an Aensa observer could see Jaeger's hands, bathed now in the direct, painful glare of the sun; still, the observer could not be permitted to become suspicious. Any trouble at this point would be disastrous. Jaeger believed that the risk was not that great. Nevertheless, he knew that it was his only chance, and he'd have had to take the risk, no matter how unlikely success might have seemed.

Deftly, Jaeger's hands grasped the walking stick and gave the silver head a slight turn; there was a metallic click and a narrow section of the stick flipped open, revealing a small compartment that ran the entire upper half of the stick's length. Inside the walking stick had been packed three items hastily prepared by Herr Stahl. Jaeger's fingers extracted them painfully; he was not able to move more than the tips of the fingers or risk revealing his actions with the excessive motion. He quickly palmed the three things: a tightly rolled piece of fabric that had taken up most of the storage space, a small transparent tube filled with a greenish paste, and an even smaller plastic ball fitted with a needle-spray nozzle. The three objects were quickly hidden away in Jaeger's clothes, as he clicked the cane's invisible door shut with one hand and reached into his trouser pocket with the other. The switch had been made; there were no excited cries in the hallway. He had not been discovered. Jaeger let out his breath and relaxed.

Calmly, Jaeger picked up the walking stick, made another leisurely tour of the room, and then sank down into the wooden chair with a sigh and a great show of resignation. He passed a hand across his forehead, and discovered that it was dripping with sweat. His fingers trembled and ached with nervous tension. Jaeger laughed silently; relax, he told himself, you're supposed to be bored.

He sat in the chair, barely moving. He had little to do until twilight began to darken the cell. He thought; he had no other means of passing the time. His thoughts returned in an involuntary way to Nati. He tried to think of other things, of the implications of his mission to the world at large, of his responsibility to his planet and his race. But then he would see Nati's twisted body hanging in the air before him, and he would remember the sickness he had felt when he had first rushed through the bedroom door in her apartment. He remembered what Huston, the IC representative who had accompanied him, had said, about Nati being only one more victim of the Aensalords' hateful plan, about the thousands of other human beings who were only hours or days away from the same fate, of the billions of other human beings who could expect the same or worse soon enough. Huston's rallying speech had not affected Jaeger at all. Huston was right enough, in his way, in the way of the crusading politician. But Huston had not been able to touch Jaeger's feelings at all; after seeing Nati's grotesque corpse, Jaeger doubted whether anything would ever touch him that way again. He had agreed to this mission, and now it was the memory of Nati that kept him going. He was on a personal errand of revenge, and, while he knew that such a motivation might make him less rational than he would be under ideal circumstances, he knew by the same token he would be much harder to stop.

Jaeger was going to make it very difficult indeed for the Aensalords to stop him. With the contents of his walking stick safely transferred, he began to feel more confident.

The day lingered endlessly, the seconds passing in a seemingly infinite procession. Time seemed to slow down, lurch into low gear, then stop entirely. For hours Jaeger pretended to doze, all the time wishing that he could. His eyes were closed, but his brain churned like an overheated engine. An Aensaman brought him food and drink in the late afternoon; Jaeger touched nothing—they would have to be a little more clever if they wanted to snare him.

The sun crawled down below the horizon at last. Jaeger sat in inky darkness and waited, snoring peacefully for the benefit of his hidden audience. About half an hour after sunset, Jaeger seemed to sense that the Aensa spy had gone away. It was only another hunch, but it was the best thing that Jaeger could come up with in the situation. Besides, he told himself half-heartedly, he had three things going for him. First, his instincts usually proved to be trustworthy, based on experience (he did not consider consciously that his experience had been chiefly among members of his own race, and that experience might have little value when applied to the Aensa). Second, his placid behavior might well have satisfied the Aensalords (he did not need to think that he might have done exactly the opposite, that the Aensalords expected to see a little more spirit in someone they knew to be an enemy agent). Third, with the coming of nightfall, the Aensalords' own element, they might have become overconfident (and it was pointless to remark that such a confidence could likely be completely realistic). No matter; Jaeger summed things up according to the arithmetic of his mood, and decided that the Aensa sentry had given up his vigil.

Jaeger stood up from his chair, stretched catlike in a vain attempt to relieve his cramped muscles. There was a dry tension in his throat that refused to go away. Now! Silently, the big man took the tightly rolled piece of fabric from its hiding place and unfurled it. If there had been enough light to see, the fabric would have shimmered like a coat of mirrors.

Jaeger swung the new model blindcoat over his shoulders, He attached wire leads on the coat to a tiny power pack on his belt, then pressed the activating switch in the sleeve. A very nervous invisible man walked to the window, grasped the rough stone of the ledge, and pulled himself up. Jaeger had a moment of panic while he forced his big shoulders through the narrow window, but then he was through and standing on the ramparts of the Aensa keep. It was a starry night, and cold, with a bloody thumbnail of a moon just starting to rise.

The mutter of voices reached him, if one could call them voices. They were a mixture of soft snarling rasps and chiming sounds. Jaeger moved in that direction, catfooted. Two Aensalords lounged idly against the wall several yards beyond Jaeger's cell. Jaeger held his breath. The Aensalords were different creatures during the night—they were totally unlike the Aensamaster Jaeger had met earlier in the day. They were like the Aensa Jaeger had come to fear during his race for life. They were all deadly at night, regal, menacing, incredibly self-assured; their luminous golden eyes gleamed like molten pools. The flickering golden aura that shimmered around them emphasized every supple, taut motion of their carnivore bodies. Somehow the cold starlight glinting from the half-exposed fangs was infinitely more sinister than sunlight had been. During the day the Aensa had been beings not so terribly unlike mankind; alien, but still just another kind of mortal creature. In the night, they were every foul and horrible thing that man has ever conjured for himself from his darker imaginings. They were as lordly and implacable as any Satan or Lucifer; they were the embodiment of pain and fear.

Thinking these thoughts, somewhat paralyzed by the Aensalords' proximity, Jaeger found himself looking straight into the deadly, smoldering holes that were an Aensalord's eyes. Jaeger froze into immobility, more stiffly than before, completely helpless. The Aensalord's eyes slid uninterestedly away from Jaeger and returned to the other Aensa. Jaeger pried his fingernails out of his palms and let out his breath quietly. His data had been correct, or, at least, his suppositions. And Herr Stahl had come through again, in the most important way of their long association. The Aensalords' eyes were fooled by the blindcoat, now that it blocked a greater band of the light spectrum. Jaeger wondered if the Dktar, the Aensahounds, would be similarly deceived. He supposed that he could only learn that the hard way. Ah, well. The blindcoat had already helped to even up the odds, although only by a small amount.

Jaeger stood silently, waiting for a plan to take shape in his mind. For ages men had yearned for some mystic device—a cloud-cloak or a magic ring or something like that—that would give them some special power all their own. Now Jaeger had a kind of mystic device, and he had that power; but if he happened to trip one of the Aensa alarm gimmicks, he was still in big trouble, and neither mystic device nor special power of invisibility would do him much good.

The two Aensalords continued to converse in low tones, one or the other gesturing occasionally toward the window of Jaeger's cell; to Jaeger's mind, it seemed that the Aensalords' attitude was one of amused contempt. One of the Aensalords carried an odd-shaped metal and plastic tube; it looked like the Aensa version of a hypodermic syringe. The tube was filled with a bright blue liquid. Jaeger nodded grimly. Their intentions were fairly obvious. If the drugged food didn't get him, they'd force-feed his addiction with the needle. Once he was tied in bondage to the Aensalords, by means of his need for the drug, then the upcoming discussion, whatever it was, could be settled quickly and efficiently in the Aensa's favor. And there would be no troublesome questions from the ignorant humans.

Either that, Jaeger thought suddenly, or they were suspicious of his cover-story and intended to wring the truth out of him by using the drug as a truth serum, turning a blank face to IC Headquarters when Jaeger never returned from his mission. After all, IC Headquarters wouldn't dare to press the Aensalords too far on such a minor matter. Jaeger had to realize that, officially speaking, he was a minor matter. What was a murdered representative or two between friendly enemies, anyway, particularly when both are sovereign governments?

Jaeger shuddered; he'd realized it before, but now it had been driven home with greater emphasis: he'd better not get caught. Why didn't the Aensalords go back inside and put their simple plan to work? What were they waiting for? He shrugged. True to their nature, they were behaving in a way that Jaeger couldn't possibly understand. Well, let them play; the more time it bought him, the better. Jaeger turned quietly and faded away into the night.

The way down was long and strange. Jaeger padded along back corridors and down winding stairwells, trying to avoid areas that would likely be filled with the Aensa usurpers, trying to make his way safely down to ground level. His path was blocked repeatedly by blind corridors that ended abruptly or looped back in the direction from which they had come, until he began to feel the grim, bloodshot panic of a laboratory animal trapped in a cruel experiment. On the sixth retracing of his steps, Jaeger found a narrow hallway that ran in the direction he wished to go. He threaded his way down, accompanied by musty shadows and vague fears.

Much of the interior of the Aensa keep was too strange to be entirely grasped by a human mind. There were rooms full of colors and other rooms full of slowly moving shadows. There were halls full of disembodied singing, other corridors that screamed and sobbed. Jaeger walked through cold, flickering flames. He passed among musky odors that excited him in a way that made him feel filthy. There were glimmering machines that sat and hummed and chuckled to themselves. There were chambers full of nothing but a brooding, frightening presence, rooms without ceilings or floors, walls covered with tiny, crawling pictures that seemed much too alive, places where the air itself felt wet and sticky and stung like invisible needles.

Some places seemed almost familiar; with an effort, Jaeger could guess at their functions; after all, the original castle had been built centuries before by his own ancestors. There was an immense room that was almost certainly an eating hall. Jaeger peered into the chamber as he passed silently by, masked from observation by his blindcoat. Aensalords lounged on fur-covered daises, picking up their oddly colored foods with their fingers, tearing at it with their fangs.

Some played at a multileveled game where silver triangles and cones shifted position without being touched. But why did that huge sphere of crackling blue fire roll slowly around the outer edge of the table, and what were those crimson firefly nimbuses that swirled in the center, occasionally licking out to touch each diner?

There was a place that could have been a theater, where groups of silent Aensalords watched gravely while a huge, naked warrior twisted and spun in a lethargic dance, moving around a motionless silver-furred Aensa female. Was the female dead? The warrior reached down and picked her up by the arms. The audience made a high wailing sound and hissed its applause. Jaeger did not want to watch the scene any longer; something in the air smelled so strongly that he felt he would suffocate. He walked on, past a place where Aensalords slept curled in velvet-lined wall niches. And there was an area where a circle of Aensalords sat with their heads caged in intricate mazes of plastic and metal, and a gray cable connected each faintly phosphorescent helmet to a slowly pulsating black wall. Jaeger couldn't understand what that was, either, and he realized—with a touch of panic—that he didn't really want to know about any of it.

Brain whirling, Jaeger at last broke free into the open courtyard, through a narrow servants' entrance reserved for the socially inferior Aensamen. He stumbled and half-ran across the courtyard until the castle loomed a bit less menacingly above him. He tired to repress the sickening inner feeling that he'd already failed before he'd even had a chance to begin, defeated by the sheer power and alienness of the Aensa. He'd been a naive child to think that it might be otherwise. Where could he begin his search? He shuddered. Sooner or later, of course, he was going to have to enter the keep building again, and probe its miles of tortuous corridors in more detail. The prospect made Jaeger very uneasy, and he wanted to put it off as long as possible. Explore the more obvious possibilities first; the inner courtyard alone was big enough to hide a thousand secrets. Too damn big! The whole place was too big and too alien. How to find that invisible factor that he was counting on, when he didn't know what he was looking for and probably wouldn't recognize it even he came across it? He didn't even know how the drug was produced; he could have walked unwittingly by the source a dozen times already, for all that he knew.

And even if he did manage to find and destroy the source of the drug, how could he manage to escape from the keep and make his way safely across the frozen miles to Schwäbisch Gmünd? The Aensalords and the Dktar would be on his tail, more determined and more awful than the first time, with a much greater distance to cover. It was impossible. Impossible to carry out his mission; impossible to escape in any event. If he had several nights to spend at the task, then there might be a chance that he could bring it off, but this way . . . He shook himself. More than his life or death was depending on this. Three black ships circled sleeping Earth, pointed like giant cannons, loaded, primed, and deadly. Numbly, Jaeger began to search again.

Minutes later, he found the Dktar pen. It was a discovery he wished he hadn't made. The pen was actually a wall of flashing, snapping blue force that pinned the Aensahounds into a large semicircular enclosure against the side of the outer wall. Set in the wall, surrounded by the sleeping herd of Dktar, were the main castle gates. Jaeger scratched his jaw. There could be no more effective guardians. Anyone who tried a frontal attack, across the lake and through the gates, would be in for an uncomfortable surprise. The Dktar killed what slim chance remained of an overland escape. Somehow, Jaeger would have to steal an Aensa aircraft, when and if the time came. He would have to learn to operate its alien controls. He would have to be mighty lucky—

One of the Aensahounds twitched and stirred slightly in its sleep, a quivering, sickly phosphorescent horror. Its multiple rows of legs rippled gently, as if it were running through its dreams—after prey. The clawed feet left long silver scratches on the stone of the courtyard. Jaeger shuddered and turned away.

He recrossed the courtyard, moving silently toward the keep. He was getting nowhere, and it was getting late. Time, time, time—damn it, he needed time. Soon now they would discover that he had escaped from his cell, and then the pressure would be on. There didn't seem to be anything in the courtyard; he would have to make his way into the main keep building and—

Something moved.

A flicker of motion in the deep shadows. Jaeger stood statue-still, not breathing, sudden perspiration dampening his hair and trickling down his face. His mouth was dry and he felt lightheaded; which did he prefer, a silent, gliding Aensalord, or a howling, ravaging Dktar? A grotesque form separated slowly from the shadows and slithered forward. Jaeger's breath hissed in his throat. God! What a monster! The thing was huge, a few inches taller than Jaeger and much broader. Its body was a nightmarish cross between an octopus and a lobster; thick tentacles swayed like living ropes, and huge pincers were half-concealed beneath a chitinous carapace. Set in a neckless, lumpy head, its eyes were large and golden, and surprisingly intelligent.

The eyes were looking at Jaeger.

He gasped at the realization and took a step backward. His blood roared. The monster could *see* him; his blindcoat was useless. Jaeger fought down gibbering panic; the primitive vestige inside him screamed and threatened to go mad. This was the stuff of insane delusions. How could he fight this tremendous horrible creature? It was all over. Death—

The creature moved forward slowly, feeding-mandibles wiggling around a curved parrot-beak of a mouth. Starlight and moonlight frosted a chitin horn projecting from the thing's forehead. Jaeger raised the walking-stick in a pitiable attempt to defend himself. It was a futile effort, but there was no place to run to. Here it comes, thought Jaeger, becoming strangely calm. Get ready, damn it, just get ready. He stood poised. His blood pounded in his ears.

The creature stopped six feet away, waving its tentacles in a graceful, elaborate pattern. Jaeger glanced at it tensely, his jaw muscles aching with the strain. Why didn't it attack? He became aware that the creature was making a sound, a high screeching noise like a subway train going around a tight curve. What the devil? Was it saying grace before its meal? The creature's soprano wail dropped in pitch, sinking quickly to a gutteral rumbling almost too low for the human ear to detect. The noise alternated up and down the tonal scale, slower each time, as if it were searching for some particular pitch; it reminded Jaeger of someone trying to tune a radio to bring in a faint station that kept fading away. The noise again sank lower in tone; for a moment it seemed that Jaeger could almost understand it, but then it was a subsonic growl. Infinitely slowly, the noise began to rise in pitch again.

"—you understand me?" the creature said. "Can you understand me? Can you understand me? Can—"

Jaeger was stunned. Almost without a conscious decision, he responded. "Yes."

The creature's voice rose no higher in pitch. "You speak Terran?" it said.

Jaeger was still numb with shock. "Yes," he croaked inanely, "I live here."

The creature narrowed its eyes. "Oh, a native you are, yes? I have never seen one before in the fleshes. I Terran tried because you didn't respond to thought speech and didn't look like one of the Aensalords' creatures. The Aensa library here in the keep a complete hypnocourse on Terran has. I thought that it might—" the creature made a washboard rumble which Jaeger could not interpret. It might have been a laugh. It might have been anything. "—sometime be useful. Had on the secret, of course, to take it."

"Of course," Jaeger muttered.

"But contact we have established, yes? That is the thing important." The creature rippled a tentacle. "This is a bit of the luck unexpected." His narrow golden eyes stared at Jaeger shrewdly. "For both of us I think, perhaps, yes and no?"

The first overwhelming, brain-dulling shock was beginning to wear off, but Jaeger still felt rather forlorn and lost. He licked his dry lips. "What—" He coughed apologetically. "Who are you?"

The creature's feeding-mandibles moved in a way that Jaeger found repellent. That must be the creature's equivalent of a smile, Jaeger thought dazedly. At least, he hoped that it was. It could be that the creature was only hungry. It widened its eyes slightly; somehow, incredibly, it made the creature look friendly. "Corcail Sendijen this one is called. What name is yours, please?"

Suddenly the whole thing was too much for Jaeger. Here he was, after tense hours of playing hide-and-seek with an unknown death through the dark, chatting casually with this improbable creature and exchanging polite formalities. Where did the being think they were, standing on the corner of Koenigstrasse during rush hour? Soon now, Corcail Sendijen would invite him out for a drink, and the tentacled beast would bow and present Jaeger with an engraved business card. The sudden release from the night-long tension was worse than the fear had been. Jaeger threw back his head and roared with careless laughter.

"That is not an idea of the best value at this time," said Corcail Sendijen seriously.

After a moment, Jaeger let his laughter die. He eyed Corcail Sendijen ironically. The creature was right, of course. Jaeger struggled to get himself back in control. Corcail Sendijen stared back quizzically; somehow he looked amused, although Jaeger couldn't put his finger on how he differentiated the alien's expressions. "I'm sorry," said Jaeger, "but I couldn't help it. You see, I thought you were going to eat me."

Now, was it Corcail Sendijen's turn to have an ironic gleam in his golden eyes? "Not having a worry," he said. "I never eat anyone without proper provocation."

Jaeger nodded. "In that case, my name is Karl Jaeger." He grinned. "Corcail Sendijen, is it? How do you do. I'm very glad to meet you."

"Customs," said Corcail Sendijen. "Your race burdened is, yes, more than no?" He extended one of his shorter, inner tentacles. Jaeger stared, disbelieving; then he grasped it with a darkly tanned hand.

Solemnly, they shook appendages in the dappled moonlight.

Chapter Nine

Karl Jaeger and Corcail Sendijen continued their discussion in the deep shadows near the inner wall, where they would have been hidden from any Aensa eyes about on the battlements of the keep's main building. For Jaeger, it was one of the most fascinating experiences of his life. For Corcail Sendijen, who had met many alien species on many worlds, the conversation lacked the emotional overtones that it held for the human, but it was interesting in its own right, and desperately urgent. Corcail Sendijen thought that finding a native of the invaded world about in the Aensa keep was the first breakthrough of any significance that had been made in his mission. If he handled this correctly, it meant that he had found an unexpected ally, just when he needed help most critically. The human race was primitive in some ways; even the lowest member of the Aensa's black gang could read thought speech, while it had been obvious that Karl Jaeger was deaf to it. Still, Corcail Sendijen had been impressed by the way Jaeger had faced him and prepared to fight, in spite of the fact that the Terran was obviously inferior to him in physical formidability. The native had courage. Corcail Sendijen was aware of Jaeger's blindcoat only as a slight flickering and blurring of light, but it was obvious to him that the human was wearing some sort of visibility distorting device; the local inhabitants of this world weren't as primitive as their grotesquely shaped bodies would lead one to suspect. But what was the human doing here, alone, in the Aensa fortress, so many miles from the nearest of its countrymen?

They talked as the moon climbed steadily higher across the sky, and slowly the situation became clearer. To Jaeger, it was a glimpse into an unknown world. Corcail Sendijen had been sent by an assembly of civilized races to seek out and destroy the source of a drug traffic that was having much the same effect upon an ancient, but slowly disintegrating, stellar civilization that it was having upon the Terran world government. In the course of his investigations, Corcail Sendijen had learned that recruiting for a "blind cruise" contract—an agreement to do unspecified work for an indefinite period in an unknown place—was going on through the chronically unemployable misfits that gather around any interstellar port of commerce. Posing as a laborer of rudimentary intelligence, Corcail Sendijen had signed up for the blind cruise, and found himself on Earth, an unlisted planet, among a platoon of replacements for the Aensa black gangs.

The black gang had been told nothing except that this was an independently owned outpost operated by an Aensa trading company. The overseers had claimed that Earth had been recently registered with the central galactic authorities. Corcail Sendijen had been fairly certain they were lying; his knowledge of galactic exploration was considerable, and he had never come across a planet matching Terran specifications in the registration files. Now he knew that he was correct. The Aensalords—whether they were acting on their own or were, as he suspected, secretly backed by the Aensa government—had discovered Earth, but had deliberately failed to register or report it, as required by law. Corcail Sendijen wondered if these Aensalords on Earth were, in fact, renegades, or whether the entire Aensa Empire and all its resources could be readied to support the invasion forces. If the latter were the case, and at the moment the truth was not ascertainable, these unfortunate humans were surely in for more trouble than they could cope with. This wasn't anything against the courageous Terrans; few races in the galaxy had been able to stand against the Aensa, once those terrible silver and black lords turned their attention in their direction.

It happened that parts of Earth matched the narrow range of

atmospheric and chemical conditions needed to grow a certain universally outlawed plant. Using Earth as a base, the Aensalords had begun the greatest drug traffic in the history of the galaxy. No wonder the Aensalords had never automated the system of ore wagons; to get the proper equipment to do the job, they would have to admit that they were colonizing a planet, then register Earth, and submit a request for supplies and survey advisers to the central government. They weren't about to do that, thank you! So lack of proper apparatus meant the black gangs and, in the case of the midnight labors, use of the Aensamen themselves. And there was the weakness in the Aensalords' organization.

"What I don't understand," said Jaeger, "is why they're selling the drug to humans, when they have an established market elsewhere. Surely the star-traveling races can offer them more valuable considerations than human individuals can."

Corcail Sendijen rippled a tentacle. "Certainly, but other reasons there are. The Aensalords may a surplus of the drug have. They are doling slowly it out into galactic channels, to avoid the market flooding and the price lowering. As long as rare a thing is, valuable it is, yes? So some of the drug they will have left over to spare without their quotas hurting. Pay them the humans probably will in fissionable material, at least in your upper circles. But the reason most important for supplying humans the drug is that using it they are the Terran government to overthrow, yes and no? From their point of view, good this is. New government of necessity sympathetic toward Aensalords will be, and all meddling with their base will stop. Then the Aensalords about internal troubles won't worry, and making the rest of the galaxy miserable can they concentrate on."

"They're doing a pretty good job here, too. Our government is being torn apart by the strain."

Corcail Sendijen rippled a tentacle sympathetically. "Not having worries. Resilient things governments are. After we the source of the drug destroy, it will back into shape pull itself."

Jaeger smiled bitterly. "Yes, if there is anything left of

it.'' Tensely, he explained the menace of the orbiting Aensa warships.

Corcail Sendijen's voice sounded worried for the first time. ''Bad this is. Of the warships I of course knew, but their significance didn't realize until now. Yes, fits it. The Aensalords capable quite are of sterilizing an entire planet their tracks to cover. Prevented this must be.''

''I'm glad you feel that way,'' said Jaeger.

Corcail Sendijen fell into a thoughtful silence; after a moment he looked up. ''There one way is likely. Other agents signed with me for the blind cruise. I of course not alone would be sent. The Aensa their black gang replacements into two parties split, one group for the low-grade crews aboard the warships to serve and strengthen, and here the larger group was sent. Much maneuvering and risk it took, but to get an agent aboard each of the Aensa ships we succeeded; three of my litter-mates, in fact—brothers, you would call them, or at least that's enough close. As senior, to Earth I came with the other group the major part of the investigation to carry on.''

He snapped a fighting-claw. ''We in this way hoped to be able to trace the Aensa ships for later capture, when they inevitably fled after destroyed their main base here was. But now I think I better ways see. Perhaps we can, ah, wrap this thing whole, as you say, at once up, yes, more than no? Security is much looser on board the ships than here it is. I think that my brothers managed have to retain the tiny radio devices at the start of this mission we were issued; destroy I had to mine on the way here for fear of a search. If I them can contact, to attack get them and the control room of each ship hold—briefly, of course, but long enough for your fleet in to move and the ships to capture, yes—''

Jaeger ignored the pounding of blood in his throat; this was a time for careful thought. ''As I see it,'' he said, ''the thing breaks down into two problems. One, how to find and destroy the source of the drug. Two, how to communicate with the outside for help.''

''No problem is the latter. Here in the castle fine communications equipment the Aensalords of course have. Seen it I have, and understand it well. Once the communications room I capture, no problem it will be to the equipment readjust to broadcast on the secret frequency of my brothers' receivers."

Jaeger frowned. "Do you know the IC frequency?"

"No, but easy enough to find it will be. Monitor any radio frequency on the planet with this equipment I can."

"Then you'd better give them a call, too. I suppose they'll be a little surprised to hear from you. I wish I could be there. Talk to Mr. Huston of the Security Bureau, and coordinate the attack on the Aensa warships. The IC has a peace squad standing by somewhere near the edge of the Aensa territory, too. You'd better have them dispatch that, while they're at it. We might need rescuing. Mention my name and they should cooperate."

Corcail Sendijen's eyes narrowed. "As if you weren't going to be there you talk."

Jaeger smiled. "I'm not. I think that we'd better split our forces. We've little time before the Aensa discover I'm gone and alert the entire fortress, and we can't afford duplication of effort. I don't know how to operate the Aensa communication equipment, but I do have the means to destroy the source—if I can find it."

Corcail Sendijen gestured with a tentacle. "The hard part that will be. Admit that I'm baffled I'll have to. Extracted the drug is, from a lichen, and in plastic containers is grown, so that exposed to the sun it doesn't have to be, but its nourishment artificially infused can be. It could be anywhere hidden. Somewhere in the vicinity raised the lichen must be, and a good deal of ground space must take up, but the courtyard I've searched, the keep buildings all and the lower levels, and yet nothing found. Nothing. As if invisible it was."

Invisible. Invisible. Jaeger had prided himself on his talent for discerning the invisible factor in situations like this; that was his job, his specialty, the only thing that might make him something more than a hindrance for this shrewd creature. His bushy eyebrows merged as he strained to catch an elusive thought. Something was tickling the back of his mind. Something he had seen or heard had touched off a trigger in his subconscious, sent a chain of associations rattling and clinking. He was sure that he had the answer tucked away in his head somewhere; he just didn't realize consciously that he knew he knew. Jaeger pressed a thumb and forefinger against the bridge of his nose and massaged it. Think. What had caused the warning light to flash in the back of his mind? Jaeger blanked his thoughts and tried to let the proper ideas sneak in. Invisible. Takes up a good deal of ground space. Nothing in the courtyard, keep buildings, or lower levels—

Jaeger stiffened. It must be! There wasn't anywhere else. By damn, it had to be. The invisible factor.

Corcail Sendijen stared at him, puzzled by Jaeger's sudden agitation. "What, my friend—"

Jaeger whirled to face him. "I think I know where to find the source. Corcail Sendijen, have you ever played the 'I Spy' game?"

Corcail Sendijen wiggled a tentacle in bewilderment. "I don't think so. I've never of it even heard. What—"

Jaeger smiled tightly. "It's a children's game. One child thinks of some object within plain sight, and then the rest of the children try to guess what it is. It's a process of elimination. One by one the objects in the area are guessed until there's only one thing it could be. Now, the novice at the game will inevitably pick the smallest, most inconspicuous object in sight when his turn comes up to be 'it.' And he inevitably loses; people guess it right away, because it's too obvious a choice. But the expert at the game, the neighborhood champion, the kid who always wins, will pick the largest and most conspicuous thing in sight. Nobody thinks of it; it's too obvious to be obvious. That's a trick of human nature, and apparently nonhuman nature, too."

"But what—"

"The situation's the same here. Although in this case I didn't happen to think of it until you mentioned that the drug was grown in plastic containers and didn't need air or sunlight. What's the one place in this crazy-house that you'd never think of as a hiding place for anything? A place that most people wouldn't even associate with any kind of plant?"

"So—" It was a surprised hiss.

"Yes, you see? I'll bet my eyeteeth on it."

"But how—"

They were interrupted by a low rumbling sound. Corcail Sendijen turned around quickly, his fighting-claws opening and closing spasmodically. "The ore wagon," he whispered. The rumbling grew louder, then began to fade away to the right. "For the outer wall they're headed, probably for the main castle gates; they must outside be going. Wondering am I—"

Jaeger grinned. "Want proof of my theory? If we could get up on the top of the outer wall, we should be able to see . . ."

Corcail Sendijen grunted, turned, and scurried away, Jaeger following. They melted from shadow to shadow, angling toward the outer wall. They reached the wall. Jaeger looked up along it, one hand resting against the cold stone; it took warmth greedily from his hand. The wall was almost as smooth as glass; no handholds or footholds. Silently, Corcail Sendijen wrapped two large tentacles around Jaeger, leaped, and then flowed up the wall effortlessly. Jaeger dangled behind like the tail of a kite. Corcail Sendijen reached the top of the wall and deposited Jaeger on his feet. They crouched low to avoid silhouetting themselves against the sky. Jaeger beckoned, and crawled to the outer edge of the wall and looked down. "Look," he whispered. "After the way you got us here, I was beginning to think I wasn't going to be good for anything."

Almost directly below, the ore wagon gleamed toy-tiny in the pale moonlight. It had come to rest outside the main gate on a narrow concrete quay that protruded out into the gently ruffled lake. A group of about ten Aensamen squatted by the sides of the ore wagon, panting from their recent exertion. Two aristocratic Aensalords stood at the end of the quay, looking patiently out over the lake. Jaeger squinted. He was amazed to see that they were accompanied by two humans. The group on the quay was as motionless as a sculptured tableau. The only sound was the steady lapping of miniature waves against stone.

Corcail Sendijen wriggled down next to Jaeger, edged his

eyes over the lip of the wall. His feeding-mandibles writhed. "What are they doing? I—"

"Watch!"

Jaeger became aware of a soft, rhythmic pounding, and a labored wheezing, gasping, and sucking noise, like a gigantic monster with a respiratory illness. It seemed to come from somewhere out across the lake. They both leaned forward, straining to see. The waters of the lake were beginning to pucker and quiver, rippling as though stirred by invisible oars. Now there was another noise, the rushing, cackling sound water makes as it flows through pipes. A bubble formed in the middle of the lake, and burst with a great watery belch. A small whirlpool grew where the bubble had been, rapidly increasing in size. The monster's panting became louder, more strained. The water was dancing now, speckled with tiny whitecaps. There was a lusty gurgling sound that seemed to fall away from Jaeger and Corcail Sendijen's position. The whirlpool grew more violent.

"It looks like," said Corcail Sendijen, groping for words. "It looks like—"

"Like water going down a drain," said Jaeger, nodding. "That's just what it is."

The water-level in the lake was dropping visibly. The dominant noise was the rapid rush of the water through the drain. With one last, long, rattling gurgle, the lake was dry.

"You see?" Jaeger whispered. "You see?"

The dry lake bottom was covered with thousands of basketball-sized plastic spheres, all interconnected by an intricate system of plastic pipes and camouflaged to blend with the color of the lake water. One pipe, larger than the others, ran down the center of the dry lake bed. Protruding from the central pipe were the bulky mass of the drain apparatus and a swan-necked faucet with a spigot. All were expertly camouflaged.

Corcail Sendijen's tentacles squirmed like panicked worms. "They've borrowed a trick," said Jaeger. "An old trick of the Luftwaffe during World War II. During the day they pump water into that artificial lake of theirs and fill it up.

Then if someone should chance to fly over, or if an orbiting spy satellite should happen to peek that way, there'll be nothing to see but water. Then at night they drain the lake again, and they're in business. The Luftwaffe used the same gimmick to hide their airfields from Allied bombers when things got tough; drain the field at night, bring up the planes from an underground hangar on a camouflaged elevator, and no one was any the wiser. It's an effective stunt." Jaeger's eyes glinted. "Who would ever suspect that there was an airfield—or a drug factory, for that matter—at the bottom of a lake?" Jaeger smiled. Corcail Sendijen gave a soft hoot and waved a tentacle respectfully.

Below, one of the Aensalords snapped a curt gesture. The Aensamen sprang up, seized the ore wagon, and began to push. The ore-wagon rumbled down a gently sloping ramp that had been concealed by the water-line, rolled ponderously across the lake bed, making squelching noises in the wet silt. The Aensalords and the two humans followed closely behind. The ore wagon drew level with the swan-necked faucet and stopped. One of the Aensalords knelt near the base of the faucet and operated its simple mechanism. The faucet swung gracefully, stopped directly above the ore wagon. Rising, the Aensalord twisted the spigot. The spigot sputtered momentarily, and then a steady stream of bright blue liquid was pouring from the faucet into the ore wagon.

"My God," Jaeger whispered. "As simple as that. As easy as tapping maple trees in Vermont for sap." He watched, fascinated, as the ore wagon filled. There was something strangley beautiful about the gleaming, deadly liquid as it fell in a twisted spurt from the spigot, its remote jewel-glow flickering in the muted light. The humans and the Aensalords watched greedily as it flowed—

Something dropped from the sky.

Just before hell broke loose, Jaeger noticed that it was a Terran helijet. For a moment, he thought it was his helijet returned; but this one was much larger, the sort used by IC peace patrols. But this couldn't be an IC craft. There were no identification markings on the sides. Corcail Sendijen stared at the helijet, one tentacle wrapped in a crushing grip on

Jaeger's arm. The two allies could do nothing but watch in silent amazement.

The helijet swooped low over the ore wagon; coaxial machine guns in the nose stitched death across the dry lake bottom. The Aensamen were cut down in rows by the ceaseless fire. One of the Aensalords gave a terrible howl, clutched at his head, and toppled backward. The remaining Aensalord and the two humans dove behind the ore wagon. Bullets screamed and whined from the ore wagon's heavy metal body, leaving rough pockmarks. The helijet hovered. Men appeared in the open bay of the helijet; Jaeger heard the crackle of small arms fire, the tiny pops of needle guns. The Aensamen still alive ran in aimless, terrified circles until they were shot down. A plastic needle gun gleamed in the hand of one of the humans as he crouched behind the ore wagon; its flat explosions rose above the whine of the twin coaxials. One of the men in the helijet jerked and fell, kicking and clutching his red-stained belly. Little slivers of metal were being slowly chipped from the ore wagon. There was a noise like a giant stick being run along a picket fence.

The gunman's companion went berserk, screamed, and ran out into the open. The coaxial machineguns swiveled to follow him, and rattled. The stream of bullets caught the running man, picked him up, shook him in the air like a scrap of paper in a gale wind and blew him apart. The man's corpse fell and lay motionless. The helijet touched down a few yards from the ore wagon; its engines continued to roar.

Before the helijet's landing struts had fairly hit the ground, men had leaped from the open bay and were dashing toward the ore wagon, firing their weapons. Jaeger watched a man in a wine-red suede jacket leading the attack. The blond giant! He had a heavy automatic slug rifle; it fired almost soundlessly, the only sign of its operation evident to Jaeger was the bucking recoil of the man's arms. Aensamen fell like tenpins, their bodies kicked about the lake bed by the force of the slugs.

The Aensalord produced a hand weapon and was firing, although there was no noise or muzzle-flash. His aim was deadly. One, two, then three men staggered, fell, and writhed briefly before slipping into death. The attacking party overran the ore wagon. Three lances of fire pierced the Aensalord from different directions; there were three muffled pops as three bolts from needle guns pulled the Aensalord in a drunken, circular dance. At last he crumpled face-first into the black silt. Bullets continued to smack into the Aensalord's corpse after he fell, and needle guns tore the body to pieces.

A familiar figure leaped down from the helijet. Jaeger's breath whistled from between his teeth. Schiller! Schiller ran toward the ore wagon, dragging something behind him. It was a rubber hose, connected to a bulky tank on the underbelly of the helijet. Jaeger's jaw muscles tightened. They were going to try to siphon the drug out of the ore wagon. It was a hijack. Schiller had almost reached the ore wagon when—

When death flowed like a tide across the dry lake bed.

The Dktar! Snapping, slashing, snarling, slaughtering, the Aensahounds rolled unstoppably forward like dark death, swirling over and around the ore wagon, leaving mangled corpses in their wake. Flashing jaws that dripped cold fire closed with a snap on the head of the blond giant, flung him high in the air; the body fell and disappeared beneath a wave of clawing multiple legs. In a moment, the attacking.party from the helijet was gone without a trace. Jaeger found himself sobbing uncontrollably. In spite of everything, in spite of their greed and weakness, they had been men, they had been *men*—

Schiller, a few seconds ahead of the Dktar pack, flung himself into the helijet, screaming in unbearable horror. The helijet leaped into the air, clawed its way crazily into the sky; the Dktar flowed beneath it, milling in frustration. They turned their glowing, dripping maws hopefully up toward the heavens. Jaeger prayed that the helijet wouldn't fall back, not into that. God! Not into that! The helijet climbed higher; now it was well above the level of the Aensa fortress—

A streak of blue-white fire lashed from the keep's ramparts, searing the eyes of every living creature within the keep. For a few moments, all Jaeger could see were swirls of colored fire and madly dancing lights, and the lingering image of the blue-white bolt. When his vision finally cleared, the helijet had disintegrated into a cloud of fine gray ash that was slowly settling back down to the corpse-strewn lake bottom below.

Jaeger lay sprawled face-down on top of the wall, nauseated, and tried to keep his mind from screaming into insanity. No man should have to see what he had just seen. The fangs and the black flowing horror and the screams, the screams—they would haunt his dreams for the rest of his life. When at last he could gain control of his shattered nerves, the Dktar had been herded away to their pen, and a new squad of Aensamen was pushing the ore wagon, still full of bright blue liquid, up from the lake bed. Jaeger glanced at his companion. Corcail Sendijen seemed just as shaken as he was; the creature's tentacles quivered jerkily and there seemed to be an ashen tint to his skin now. Jaeger and Corcail Sendijen stared at each other for long seconds, each hesitant to speak. The rumbling of the ore wagon reached their ears; it was passing through the inner courtyard. Jaeger fought down memory and a hot rising surge of nausea. "Well," he said, "I suppose we should do something." His voice was a sad croak. He tried to keep his tone normal. He failed. His eyelid twitched in a nervous tic.

Corcail Sendijen nodded slowly. Somehow, unbelievably, Jaeger forced a tight grin; it took all of his will power. "We've found the source," he said, "but it's no good trying to destroy it. It would take more explosives than we could carry. What do we do now?"

"With our plan proceed," said Corcail Sendijen, his voice unnaturally thick and slurred. "Except that if the source we can't now destroy, we should I think try instead to destroy their stockpile of the narcotic. Incredible amounts of it they must by now have stored, and disastrous it would be if any of it should manage before help arrives to be shipped out. And we know how the stockpile to reach." Corcail Sendijen gave Jaeger directions for finding the ventilator grill that served as his secret pathway to the lower levels. "Very rough walls the shaft has and is narrow; even a human wouldn't any trouble have down climbing. You'll have to hurry if you want to the railhead before the ore wagon to get, yes? I will the black gang into rioting stir; simple for any Adept, their minds low-grade are. This a diversion will create. Under this cover easy it should be for me the communications center to take. We will at the keep building later meet after everything all over is, yes, more than no?"

Jaeger looked at him levelly, straining his self-control to the utmost to keep from breaking down. Every portion of his personality argued against going down there, going anywhere near the Dktar. He didn't care if the world ended, he didn't care if everyone died; just so long as he didn't have to die *that* way. Somehow, Jaeger managed to nod agreement.

Corcail Sendijen grunted. "Good," he said. A tentacle weaved an elaborate pattern in the air. The golden eyes stared into Jaeger's briefly; then Corcail Sendijen whirled and scuttled noiselessly away. In a moment, he had disappeared into the deep shadows.

Jaeger looked for a few seconds toward the stars and the bright sliver of a moon; the rumble of the ore wagon was fainter now. Reluctantly, he forced his eyes away from the stars and down into the black depths of the inner courtyard. He shuddered and began to crawl along the top of the wall, searching. A ladder meant for use by the Aensamen appeared ahead; Jaeger touched the ladder and hesitated, trembling.

Scowling, Jaeger gathered his courage together, grasped the ladder, and forced his body to swing out and over the edge, his foot searching for the first rung.

Chapter Ten

The ore wagon arrived some time later than Karl Jaeger expected. He peered at it from the shadows near the bottleneck tunnel that led to the railroad. His mind churned. How the hell was he going to get close to it? The ore wagon was being pushed by about a dozen frightened Aensamen, directed by one tense, angry Aensalord; the Aensalord's hand rested constantly on the butt of his holstered pistol, and there was something reminiscent of an angry jungle beast in his tense stride and his wary, flashing eyes. He looked like a big cat ready to spring; a bundle of maniacal rage, energy, and tension badly contained within a humanoid form, a tornado in a paper bag. The incident in the dry lake had stirred the Aensalords into a red fury, like a dozing snake jabbed with a pointed stick.

Jaeger watched them roll by; he chewed his lip and thought. He couldn't afford to be seen until he was very close, if at all; the weapon made the odds too great in the Aensalord's favor at close range. Of course, Jaeger still had his blindcoat—

The Aensalord entered the bottleneck tunnel, the wagon rumbling close behind. Jaeger rose to his feet. This might be his best opportunity; the Aensalord was blocked from view by the bulk of the ore wagon. Cautiously, Jaeger entered the tunnel and approached the ore wagon until the pungent reek of the Aensamen's sweat was strong in his nostrils. Jaeger walked more slowly to avoid bumping against the bowed, straining bodies of the Aensamen. The walls of the tunnel closed in black and tight around them. Suddenly the air felt stuffy and the tons of stone above seemed to be pressing down upon Jaeger with an almost physical force. The only sounds were the rumble of the wheels, the squeak of the brake, and the labored, gasping breath of the Aensamen, all horribly loud as the sounds reverberated in the narrow tunnel. At least Jaeger wouldn't have to worry about making some suspicious noise.

The walls of the tunnel opened up into a square chamber. The ore wagon bumped gently against the railhead and was still. The Aensamen collapsed, gasping. Jaeger saw his chance. He slipped silently forward, picked his way cautiously among the exhausted Aensamen, placed a foot on one of the wheel spokes, and climbed slowly atop the ore wagon, moving his body carefully in order not to tip the thing. He hooked an arm over the edge of the wagon's body and waited. Nothing happened. Jaeger frowned and looked up. What could have gone wrong? According to Corcail Sendijen's account, the metal hose should have appeared immediately to suck up the narcotic. The Aensamen were muttering to themselves now; this was not part of the established routine. The Aensalord stared at the ceiling in puzzlement. There was no sign of the hose. Jaeger grimaced. If something had gone wrong with the pipeline system, his plan was ruined.

Loud footsteps clattered along the tunnel toward them. All eyes turned in that direction. Jaeger crouched on the top of the ore wagon like a watchful mouse, waiting. Now what? He smelled trouble.

The Aensamaster stepped from the tunnel. With a rustle of fur and fabric, the Aensamen snapped to rigid attention; the supervising Aensalord saluted, his other hand still resting on his pistol butt. The Aensamaster stood in the entrance to the tunnel, grim eyes raking the chamber, and then moved slowly forward.

The Aensamaster walked slowly into the center of the chamber, every step precise and controlled as a ballet, perfectly self-assured. Jaeger stared at him with grudging wonder, which took priority even over the animal fear that made his skin crawl and tighten.

The Aensamaster was beautiful; Jaeger had to admit that, in spite of the instinctive, unreasoning hatred that made his heart slam in his chest. The Aensamaster, Jaeger thought, while everyone in the subterranean room waited for the next development, was beautiful the way a cobra reared to strike might be beautiful, the way a volcanic eruption or a forest fire or a nuclear blast might be beautiful. The way the sea is beautiful during a hurricane, when it shrieks and tears, rips and claws the shore. The Aensamaster was beautiful, graceful the way all cold and deadly, powerful and wild things could be, with a beauty that is dangerous and untouchable, because it is a beauty that eats away the eye of the beholder.

And as the Aensamaster stood there, his eyes squinted against even the dim light of the cavern, his nostrils flaring and his savage mouth open, his fangs glowing, shining wetly, Jaeger realized that he did not, could not, understand the Aensa, and that knowledge was a sighing regret and an ache in his mind. Even if the Aensamaster should kill Jaeger later, he could do nothing to the human that would be more painful than Jaeger's own certainty that he could not understand.

The Aensamaster's eyes began a long sweep of the room, and those whom his flashing gaze touched did not move or appear to breathe. Jaeger studied him with a deadly intensity. Strange, so strange. Jaeger's human brain refused to accept the strangeness for a moment, whispering that it was not real, that it was a dream; but it wasn't a dream because the Aensamaster was now moving slowly forward again and he, Jaeger, had to watch like a charmed bird.

What did Jaeger really know about this creature's race? Corcail Sendijen had tentacles and claws, and an absurd comic-opera accent that he didn't even know he had, while the Aensamaster was an oxygen-breathing, humanoid mammal who spoke perfect Terran. Nevertheless, Jaeger was a great deal closer to understanding Corcail Sendijen than he'd ever be to understanding this frightening being. The difference here was not merely in the alien form; it was the fleshy patterns locked within his skull, the coded secrets tattooed on his genes, stretching back through a billion lives. These were the reasons the Aensamaster was whatever the hell he was today. Corcail Sendijen—Jaeger's lips twisted into something that might have been a smile if it hadn't been so horribly bitter. Had he been about to begin on the same terrible fallacy that had motivated and mocked the human race since the beginning of its time? Divide the universe up into two camps, the Good Aliens and the Bad Aliens, with the status of every species dependent on whether or not it happened to be working at cross-purposes with humanity at the time? "The only good alien is a dead alien, kid." Was it going to be that all over again? What was the sense in going to the stars at all if you were going to drag all that medieval garbage right along with you? Corcail Sendijen could and would make a deadly enemy, if the circumstances were different; technically speaking, there was no reason to trust him any more than Jaeger trusted the Aensamaster. Other than the fact that such a rule followed religiously enough tended to make a man pretty damn lonely, and why did the light have to gleam from the Aensamaster's fangs in just that particularly nasty way when he opened his demon's mouth just then?

The Aensamaster closed his mouth, turned around slightly, and slowly answered the other Aensalord's salute. The skill and killing passion of the hunter flowed in his every movement, and cruel intelligence blazed nakedly from the pupil-less eyes set in the arrogant face. Jaeger chewed his lip. Could the human race—the good old doddering, fallible human race—ever hope to compete successfully with the kind of creature the Aensa represented? Human beings had better be able to. It was just going to be too bad if they couldn't. It was going to be a real shame.

The Aensamaster waved his arm in a neat, economical gesture, without looking back. Behind him, two figures appeared at the entrance to the tunnel and moved forward slowly—two human figures. Jaeger stiffened on his perch. One was a burly red-head. The other human was—Healey! Jaeger pursed his lips and whistled silently. Healey! The unpleasant, pompous IC representative who, along with Huston and Teresky, had come to hire Jaeger in the first place. Suddenly everything tumbled into place; the last missing piece of the puzzle had been found.

He smiled slowly. An ambitious politician—or an addicted tool himself? It made little difference—plus a war within the human part of the drug pipeline. Yes. Healey conspiring against the government he served, and Schiller secretly conspiring against Healey to take over the tremendously profitable traffic the politician had created. Wheels within wheels, and all of them crooked. This explained the contradictory attempts on his life that had taken place in Nürnberg. Considered as the efforts of a single man, the conflicting motivations of the incidents were irreconcilable; but if there had been two plans working toward mutually exclusive ends—

Schiller had hired Jaeger to spy on Healey's operations at the Aensa keep, using the excuse of a magazine photo story. When Schiller received word through his spy networks that Jaeger was to do some secret work for Healey as well—the politician whom he trusted no more than Jaeger trusted—Schiller had coldly decided to wring the story from Jaeger. The publisher suspected a double-cross, and sent the Turk and the blond, armed with the Aensa truth serum and a bomb to erase his trail.

Of the two men, Healey was apparently the coolest, and he had come off the best. This was somewhat of a surprise to Jaeger; he hadn't given Healey enough credit at their only meeting. Schiller had panicked, forcing a test of strength before his men and strategy were ready. The attack and attempted hijack on the lake bed had been crude and poorly planned. Schiller had stampeded, and Healey had retained his composure. Today Schiller was dead, and Healey stood calmly beside the Aensalord in the heart of the alien keep.

The redhead grasped something that looked like a small cart with three wheels and a plastic tank. There was a flexible siphon hose attached; it was evident that the human accomplices were going to be paid their share. He rolled the cart closer to the ore wagon. The Aensamaster looked down at the wheelbarrow, glanced at the man in mild distaste, and then spoke to the other Aensalord in a sibilant, snarling buzz.

"Speak Terran," said Healey sharply. "I don't see why I should trust you. You could be telling your friend anything. I want to hear what's going on."

The Aensamaster glared down from his imposing height; his eyes burned like dry ice. A snarl rumbled deep in the silver-furred throat. "Do not press me," he said, speaking very softly. Still, there was the weight of death behind his voice, the imprint of the billion red-black jungle nights that had passed since his race first began climbing toward dominance.

Healey wavered visibly, then shrugged and tilted his head at a defiant angle. His fat face flowed into lines of hard greed and stubborn shrewdness. He looked like a domesticated bookkeeper or public accountant, but his eyes were hard and cold as stone, and there was a mad glint in their mild color. "Why should I trust you?" Healey said in a reasonable, wheedling tone. "I know you've got close-knit clans, and that usually means some kind of vendetta system. Your men are probably still in an uproar about what that idiot Schiller did, and you could easily use me to work off their aggressions. Maybe you're planning some elaborate revenge, eh? How can I be sure?" A note of insolence crept into his voice. "This shipment has cost me a fortune. I've a right to see that everything goes smoothly."

The Aensamaster looked at Healey the way a human would look at a bug crawling across a bathroom wall. The Aensa's expression changed only slightly, but it became clear that the Aensamaster was thinking of stepping on the bug. "You have no rights," said the Aensamaster, hissing, after a terrible pause. The sibilant whisper splintered the air like a blow from a cracking whip. The Aensamaster's lips drew back to expose his glistening fangs, and the killing fury blazed up and out of him as if a furnace door had been suddenly swung open somewhere deep inside. Healey cringed and took an involuntary, staggering step backward; his face paled to a bloodless white. Slightly pleased by the human's reaction, the Aensamaster relaxed a bit and began to smooth his fur. He spitted Healey with his gaze, holding him as helpless and squirming as the man would be on the end of a rapier.

Another stern terrible silence grew while Healey twitched and turned even more ashen beneath the alien's fiery, implacable eyes. "Remember," the Aensamaster whispered, the words rolling out slowly from between the needle-teeth, with all the finality and consequence of a divine revelation, "I am Aensamaster here—no other." His eyes held Healey for another few seconds, then cast him contemptuously aside. Healey glared, but remained silent.

The Aensamaster grunted and turned away regally; nevertheless, when he spoke to the other Aensalord, it was in Terran. "The black gangs are rioting. Heavy fighting has broken out in certain sections, and some of the power lines are interrupted. Use the manual control to activate the conveyor system." He glanced at Healey. "The entire system is backed by a series of alternate procedures in case of just this sort of emergency." The Aensamaster allowed himself a bored yawn, and turned to watch the other Aensalord. Healey muttered something under his breath, but said nothing aloud. The Aensalord walked stiffly to the far wall and did something at a bank of controls.

There was a humming in the ceiling. Jaeger tensed. The metal hose poked its snout from the ceiling, snaked down toward the ore wagon. This was the crisis. The metal hose touched the bright blue liquid, began to drink noisily. Jaeger plucked a small transparent plastic tube from his pocket, the same one he had smuggled in within his walking stick. He broke the seal with his thumbnail and began to drip the greenish paste the tube contained into the ore wagon. The greenish paste mixed with the blue drug, swirled briefly, and then liquid and paste were sucked up by the metal hose. The ore wagon slowly emptied until only enough of the drug was left on the bottom to fill the small cart of the blond man. The Aensamaster gestured; the metal hose retracted into the ceiling.

Jaeger grimaced. The greenish paste had been a chemical explosive, prepared by Herr Stahl, inert until exposed to air; after it was removed from the tube, it exploded within eight minutes, give or take a few seconds. "Give or take a few seconds." The banal words echoed through Jaeger's mind.

Even in his desperate, perilous situation, he could laugh to himself nervously, still on the knife-edge of panic. Eight minutes should give the narcotic, carrying its freight of explosive, plenty of time to reach the underground storage tanks. The problem was, how near were the storage tanks? It was possible that he was now within the danger zone of the explosion. He had to get clear. Which way? How far?

Jaeger gripped the edge of the ore wagon's body, preparing to lower himself to the floor. His sweating hands slipped a fraction of an inch; his knees cracked into the metal side of the wagon with a horrifying clunk. The Aensamaster started, then made a curt, chopping gesture. A line of Aensamen sprang to block the entrance to the tunnel. The Aensalord shouted, and snatched his weapon from its holster. Jaeger's stomach twisted into a sick knot. The Aensalord was swinging his weapon up into firing position, his eyes blazing. Desperately, Jaeger swung himself up, placed a foot on the edge of the wagon's body, and jumped. His blindcoat caught on the sharp corner of the ore wagon, and came loose with a shriek of ripping fabric. A great shout went up as Jaeger appeared suddenly in mid-air, at the apex of his leap. For a moment, Jaeger seemed to hang suspended over the muzzle of the Aensalord's weapon; then his knees slammed solidly against the black-cloaked body and they went down in a struggling tangle.

Jaeger rolled and came up on top. Crackling, phosphorescent eyes were inches from his, he could feel a hot blast of fetid breath from between the needle-like teeth; beneath him, the silver-furred body twisted and bucked like a berserk tiger. Jaeger knew that he couldn't hold onto the creature for much longer. He grabbed a double handful of black cowl and slammed the Aensalord's head solidly against the floor. The phosphorescent eyes became unfocused, rolling up under the lids. Jaeger dropped the evil head.

He rolled backward, twisting and scrambling to his feet. A bolt from a needle gun exploded by his ear at very close range, deafening him momentarily and stinging his cheek with hot fragments of chipped stone. Jaeger's shoulder smacked heavily into something solid. He lashed out blindly with a knotted fist and felt something give slightly; he kicked the burly redhead fiercely in the head as the man fell. The Aensamaster and Healey would have had Jaeger then, but the Aensamen washed suddenly over him in a howling fury, trying to rip apart the creature who had dared to assault an Aensalord. Everyone was shouting, and the whole world seemed a mass of leaping bodies and confusion. Jaeger staggered under the shock of a hundred flailing blows. His body was lacerated and aching. He couldn't fight them all; he had to get free. The Aensamaster had his weapon out and was shooting in spite of the danger to the mob of Aensamen wrestling around Jaeger. The black weapon in the Aensamaster's hand fired; one of the Aensamen who was pummeling Jaeger jerked and collapsed, blood seeping from a gaping wound in his side. Jaeger snarled; the Aensamaster's aim was casual, but at this short range it was only a matter of time. Jaeger put his head down, bulled, shoved, and kicked his way through the Aensamen; the inferior Aensamen were much weaker physically than the aristocratic, better nourished Aensalords. Now Healey also was shooting at Jaeger, with a small automatic pistol; Jaeger heard another poor Aensaman's death cry, just inches away.

Jaeger tore himself free of the mob and dashed into the tunnel. How much time before the explosion? It couldn't be too much longer, now. "Give or take a few seconds." Grimacing, he ran, racing out of the tunnel and along the underground corridor. Corcail Sendijen's ventilator shaft was his only chance for escape. Healey was jogging ponderously behind Jaeger now, firing as he ran, but his aim hadn't seemed to improve; only in stereop shows can you shoot accurately while running. Bullets skipped around Jaeger; something burning hot screamed by his ear like the devil's breath. Pain sliced across his shoulder blade, scorching his flesh as if it had been touched by a molten finger; he felt a slow trickle of blood, dampening and matting his shirt. Jaeger cursed; he reached the small plastic spheroid from his pocket and turned.

Healey's strained, gaping face loomed before him, about eight feet away and closing; the politician was swinging his pistol up for another shot. Jaeger squeezed the spheroid; a jet of clear liquid hissed from the needle-spray nozzle and splattered against Healey's eyes and nose. This was a potent chemical extract, prepared ingeniously by Herr Stahl for Jaeger's use, in case the big man had to make another forced run across the blasted landscape of the Aensa realm. The chemical was much more concentrated and more effective than the photographic fixative had been; a much worse effect on the Dktar could be achieved with a single drop of the new preparation. It had not been intended for use against human beings—Jaeger had not foreseen meeting any on his mission. He wondered briefly whether it would have any effect. Healey's face contorted, the eyes screwing shut and the lips riding back sharply from the teeth. Healey screamed and bellowed, clawing at his face, but Jaeger had already turned and was sprinting toward the ventilator shaft; the screams reached him faintly as he ran. Evidently the chemical *did* work.

Corcail Sendijen slipped through the dark hallways of the Aensa fortress, moving easily and familiarly down toward the kennel-like quarters of the black gangs. Few Aensa were about on the lower levels; after the helijet attack in the courtyard, most of the Aensalords had begun marshaling the Aensamen into fighting squads; thc whole Aensa keep was on a battle-ready alert.

There was a long corridor, damp and dark, through which Corcail Sendijen had to travel before he arrived at the sleeping chamber of the black gang. His senses detected a high-grade consciousness ahead, between him and his goal. He stopped and waited, listening quietly, smelling the dank air, picking up the nervous emotions of the Aensalord. The creature was afraid, a state that was relatively rare in the masterful race of the Aensa. The attack of Schiller's men, the battle, and the subsequent need for unusual haste in the preparation of the drug shipment had punctured the Aensa's customary self-assurance. Corcail Sendijen was glad of that; it could only work in his favor. Still, he had to get around the guard. Being caught away from the black gang's sleeping room could only mean death, the death of a spy.

Corcail Sendijen rippled a tentacle in a shrug. Well, he thought, that was only fair. He *was* a spy, after all. But they'd have to catch him first.

The thoughts of the Aensalord were easy to read; the creature had no idea that there was a reason to mask them. The minds of the other slaves in the black gang were no puzzle to Corcail Sendijen, just as they would present no difficulty to any Aensalord who wanted to probe their meager depths. The Aensalords themselves could be listened to only with their permission or, as in this case, their carelessness. When an Aensalord wanted to mask his thoughts, not even such talents as Corcail Sendijen's could break through the shield. That was what had made his investigation so troublesome; in the early stages of planning, Corcail Sendijen believed that he could easily obtain the information he needed from the minds of the Aensalords around him or, at least, from the inferior Aensamen. But the Aensalords were impervious to his mental searching, and the Aensamen employed in dragging the ore wagon filled with the blue drug were kept in a walking-dead state of unconsciousness. Their minds retained no record of their midnight labors. Corcail Sendijen's chief weapon in his mission had been rendered useless.

Now, though, with the help of Karl Jaeger, a human whose mind was not as developed as even the lowest member of the black gang, at least as far as telepathic communication was concerned, that aspect of the task was over. The source of the drug had been located and, hopefully, the stored quantities could now be destroyed. Corcail Sendijen's mental adeptness would have to work well from now on, though, if he and Karl Jaeger were to get out of the Aensa hold alive.

The Aensalord who stood guard over the slumbering members of the black gang began to pace along the catwalk above the sleeping chamber. Corcail Sendijen heard the sound of his steps and caught the impressions of the creature's mind. He sent a quiet suggestion of alarm to the Aensalord; not a loud, heavy thought,one that would make the Aensalord suspicious, but a vague notion of unease.

Corcail Sendijen heard the Aensalord stop his pacing, then begin again, in the opposite direction. The sound of the black, boot-shod feet descending metal stairs echoed in Corcail Sendijen's corridor. The Aensalord was coming to investigate. Corcail Sendijen tensed his fighting-claws in readiness. He raised two of his longer, outer tentacles.

The Aensalord walked slowly around the outer perimeter of the black gang's dormitory room, picking his way with some distaste among the varied collection of species represented among the slaves. He came to the dark entrance to the exit corridor and peered into the blackness. Corcail Sendijen tried to flatten himself into invisibility against the wall; he knew that he wouldn't succeed.

The Aensalord saw him; the black figure's eyes glowed, unblinking and golden. A weapon was pointed at Corcail Sendijen's chest. The Aensalord was almost invisible himself, black against the drak black background; only the golden eyes and the creature's golden aura gleamed in the mouth of the corridor. A crisp stream of thought speech filled Corcail Sendijen's mind. "—you—not—sleeping—here—why?—you—answer—" asked the Aensalord.

Corcail Sendijen did not bother to reply. One tentacle crashed down, breaking the Aensalord's grip on the weapon, sending the gun rattling along the stone floor of the hall. At the same time, the other tentacle smashed with equal force against the side of the black-cowled head. The golden aura faded and died. The Aensalord lay twisted at Corcail Sendijen's feet. The whole episode had taken not more than five seconds. The Aensalord, not expecting to meet anything more than a somnambulant slave, had not been prepared for a battle and had not sent any kind of mental alarm to his fellows. The slaves in the sleeping chamber had not even awakened. Corcail Sendijen traced a quick figure in the air (the Forty-fourth Gesture of the Rites: Desire for a speedy conclusion) and walked to the middle of the black gang's room.

"—all—awake— now—awake—" he ordered. Around him, heads began to raise, roused from the night's sleep. "—stand—follow—awake—anger—stand—all—you—

time—now—anger—hate—follow—follow—follow—hate—follow—black—lords—hate—hate—hate—"

He kept broadcasting that same message of hatred for the Aensalords until the last member of the black gang was on its feet. Corcail Sendijen could feel that assembled, collective hatred in the slaves growing and building. He fed the emotion. He urged them into a rage, but one which he could still manage and direct. He compelled them to follow him and to destroy every Aensalord in their path, along with whatever emblem of their mastery he pointed out. They cried and screamed in the multifarious voices. They shook fists or beat wings or jiggled loose protoplasm in an obscene dance of wrath. Corcail Sendijen led them out of the chamber, upward through the levels, toward the communications center. He did not have much time, and he knew well the tasks he had yet to perform.

They walked as quickly as they could, while still keeping together in some kind of disciplined squad. Corcail Sendijen made certain that none of the slower members of the black gang were left behind; he did not want his fighting force dispersed behind him the length of the distance between the sleeping chamber and the communications room. Stragglers would weaken his diversion and bring him too quickly to the attention of the Aensalords. Corcail Sendijen kept his followers in a mood of intense hatred, but held them back from racing ahead out of control. At last, though, they reached the communications center; it was guarded as usual by four Aensalords, each armed with the strange, silent hand weapons of awesome power. Corcail Sendijen released his small army; they rushed forward, many dying immediately in the startled reaction of the Aensa. Black gang members dropped in the front ranks, but Corcail Sendijen kept the slaves in the rear pressing on. He himself waded through the battle, his empathic sense tortured by the dying cries of the minds around him; he felt a horrible responsibility for the poor slaves he had sent to destruction, but he repressed the emotion. He had to ignore those twinges. Decisions had to be made, actions had to be taken. These slaves were not dying for him, and they were not dying for the comparatively senseless people of Earth. They were dying in a greater battle than they knew, one against the entire vast empire that the Aensa had stolen from the massed peoples of the galaxy at large. Corcail Sendijen heard the shouts of the black gang as members of many species perished; one by one the Aensa were overpowered. Corcail Sendijen himself struck down one of the guards and squeezed through the mob into the communications room. He locked the door from the inside and pushed a heavy computer console against it. He would not be disturbed, either by the Aensalords or by his own fellows in the black gang.

The floor moved, rippling forward like a long sea swell. Jaeger staggered and managed to stay erect on the dancing concrete; he lurched forward and jarred his spine every time the floor dropped away below his feet or leaped up to meet them with a knee-buckling smack. The roar of the explosion sounded like a tiny muffled cough, far away and below.

The echoes of the explosion died away, but the floor continued to heave and surge, and now there was a grinding growl that was growing steadily louder. The first detonation had set off some series of reactions; there were going to be more explosions. Powdered concrete showered down on him from the ceiling like gray rain. Jaeger threw himself flat along the boiling corridor floor, barely in time to miss a massive chunk of rock and mortar that fell from the cracking wall above his head.

Ahead was the ventilator shaft. He ran toward it, being knocked repeatedly to his knees by sudden underground shocks, then picking himself up again and careening forward across the quaking floor. He wondered whether the shaft was still usable; he had nothing else to hope for.

The incessant, jarring impacts had not done his sore ankle any good; fire lanced through it with every step, seeking to join the throbbing ache in his head and the stabbing pain from the wound in his back. Around him, the deep-throated roar of the crumbling fortress became a scream. The corridor shivered with vibration; huge yawning cracks were opening in the floor, criss-crossing the paving stones with fissures.

God, the whole place was coming down! Jaeger's section of floor was tilting heavily at a forty-five-degree angle. He climbed painfully forward.

Finally, he managed to haul himself into the ventilator shaft and jammed his bleeding back against one wall. He braced his legs against the other and began to climb slowly. Ignoring the rough stone that tore at his hands and back, he wormed and humped his way desperately upward. Impact struck the shaft wall like an iron fist; he slid down two of the feet he had so arduously won, and then he braced himself enough to stop. The shaft seemed to sway drunkenly. A gigantic crack moved slowly across the stone in front of his eyes. Powder sifted first onto his face, then bits of stone, then pebble-sized debris, then rocks. Jaeger screamed. This was it! This was it—

A blazing red mist seemed to consume the air around him; it filled the shaft, and then it swallowed him whole.

Beyond the orbit of the moon, a communications teleprinter buzzed and typed its message silently. Colonel John Robert Devaney looked at the paper as if it were a large venomous insect. He turned pale and reached to tear off the thin strip of tape as it emerged from the teleprinter. He flattened the small scrap on his desk with the slow, exaggerated motions of a man who was sternly repressing hysteria. He forced his eyes to read the words.

Colonel Devaney interpreted the coded message, his wide, unblinking eyes straining with unnecessary effort. He read the tape again. Anger began to seep into him, replacing the sick fear and the visions of burning, dying cities. He crumpled the paper in a spasm of fury. Colonel Devaney uttered a short, precise word. He said several more. The fools! The only chance was obviously a surprise attack, with every weapon in the arsenal. And here the idiots were, ordering him to close with the Aensa ships and attempt to board, not to fire unless fired upon. It was suicide. With the Aensa, any fair fight was suicide. His were interplanetary ships, fitted out for ferry duty between Earth and the small stations on the moon and the nearer planets and satellites. The Aensa vessels were interstellar craft, with all that implied. Devaney's eyes glinted. Well, what the IC command didn't know wouldn't hurt them. After all, he was in control here . . .

Slowly, Colonel Devaney relaxed. He seemed to sink into himself. He looked suddenly very, very tired. What difference did it make what he did? Either way, once an attack had begun, Earth's life expectancy could almost certainly be measured in minutes. Had he ever suspected as a boy that his would be the hand that would bring the age-old struggle to an end, would send the dreams of mankind crashing down in flaming ruin? No, he couldn't have, for then he might well have killed himself, and he was plainly here in this damn cold, stark chamber, all alone. Well, then, he would play it their way. He had never disobeyed a direct order in his entire career, and it was not fitting that his final act in this life should foul that record. He would follow the directive. He would attack by the book, attempting to board. You three damn black monsters, he thought. He laughed. It was an ugly sound in the narrow confines of his quarters.

Colonel Devaney hesitated for a moment, trying to fix an image of his boyhood home, with its crooked streets and painted lobster-boats, the lingering fiery sunsets, the wheeling seagulls. He saw it all, trying to capture it one last time; then he turned to his command board. His fingers pressed the button that sounded General Quarters.

Karl Jaeger decided that he didn't like being dead. It was dark and hot and it hurt. He coughed and strangled; something was choking him, trickling and sifting down his throat like a tide of gritty feathers. He spat, blowing up a plume of gray ashes, and then he vomited. A faint spark of irrational anger stirred to life in the back of his mind. You'd think that one could do without such unpleasantries after death. His feet slipped; instinctively, he stopped his slide by bracing his back and stiffening his legs. The stone was hot; it burned his shoulders and the soles of his feet. There was a definite, acrid reek of smoke. That explained the situation to Jaeger. He obviously was in Hell. Well, of course, he'd never really had much hope that he'd end up anywhere else. At least there were bound to be quite a few of his friends about somewhere. He had a large number of acquaintances he ought to look up as soon as he was settled in . . .

Jaeger winced at the pain in his ankle and in his head and in everything in-between. It seemed somehow unfair that you should have to feel physical pain when you were dead; agony was supposed to be the exclusive domain of the living. Could this be the start of the famous torment of the damned he had heard so much about when he was a boy? He'd always thought that would be a bit more metaphysical, a little more sophisticated. Where were the fiendish tantalizing punishments? After all, Hell had an image to keep up. Jaeger wondered in his foggy mind about his particular torment. What would it be? The only organized torture he'd experienced while alive was in a suburban car pool. The pain was too generalized to keep him awake. He slowly sank beneath a quiet, gray lake and drowned in his own fatigue.

Agony jerked him awake. He screamed. There was no telling how long he had been unconscious. It was getting hotter, much hotter. Unbearably skin-scorching hot. He gasped, sweating. He had a brief, insane thought: if you could sweat when you were dead, could you do other things? Could you . . . Without thinking, he began to shove with his legs, inching his back up the wall. Agony was a moving red flood, but he ignored that, too. He kept inching and jerking and twisting his way up until the heat became slightly less and his bones stopped feeling like they were melting. He rested there a while, panting, but the heat came again and broiled his legs. He grunted. This, then, was his torment. To crawl forever up this cramped shaft (what could it be? Satan's own throat?) followed and prodded and goaded by the fires of Hell, never resting, never escaping. Grimacing, he began to squirm upward again.

His head crunched against something solid. The way was blocked; he couldn't go any further. The heat licked greedily after him. He would be burned, killed again. How could he be killed, when he was dead already? This wasn't in the plan at all. He lunged upward; the obstacle buckled slightly. Groaning, he thrust with all his waning strength. One clawing hand broke through the mass, into the open. He shoved his way up through the crumbling stuff, which seemed to be a layer of shattered concrete; his head emerged into the cool air. He lifted both arms out, then gave one last giant heave and rolled free of the shaft, into the courtyard.

Cold air kicked him in the face, dissolving his mental cobwebs. Suddenly he knew where he was and why, and that he was genuinely alive.

And he looked up from the dust of the courtyard and saw the peace patrol helijets drifting down from the shoulder of Hohenstaufen, toward the deserted ramparts of the keep. For the second time that night, he wept.

Chapter 11

When Karl Jaeger arrived home at last, he knew that he must have presented a strange picture to the old woman who lived across the hall. He saw her door open a bit, and he caught a quick glimpse of her bright eyes watching. Jaeger wondered what she might be thinking. Certainly, his return was not as loud or as agitating as the battle with the Turk and the blond man had been; with a smile, Jaeger realized that the woman ought now, to be properly mystified. Jaeger was nearly naked, under a borrowed IC coat, his clothing almost completely burned off in the blast at the Aensa keep and during his laborious and painful climb up the ventilator shaft. His body was decorated with broad swaths of bandage, which seemed even whiter against his smoke-blackened skin.

Jaeger was accompanied by two trim, neatly uniformed IC armed forces officers. They said nothing while he opened the door to his apartment; he wondered if the old woman would suppose that he was their prisoner. The door swung open, and Jaeger turned to face his escort. The two officers saluted respectfully, turned, and walked briskly to the elevator. Jaeger stared after them; he had been about to offer them a drink. He shrugged, walking into his apartment and closing the door behind him. He was home. Everything was finished, and he had time to feel satisfied with himself. He didn't, not now, not yet, not at the moment. All he felt now was amazingly tired. He made a mental note to feel proud, sometime in the distant future.

He flung himself down on a couch; he felt as though he didn't have strength enough even to lift his feet from the floor. He rested like that for several moments, staring at the familiar ceiling. There were cracks up there, but they were a pattern that reassured him, proved to him that he was truly home. Those cracks wouldn't widen and split while he watched; the wood and steel and plastic and concrete around him would stay put, in one piece, and not come tumbling down on his head. Not, he said to himself ruefully, until some crazy client or some vengeful enemy sent a gang of thugs to plant another bomb. Jaeger closed his eyes, listening to the familiar humming noises from the kitchen, feeling the steady background pain in every part of his body. He had nothing to do until morning, when he ought to go to the office and fake some reports for the official records. No one would likely ever know exactly how he had spent the last day, but that didn't bother him. Jaeger wasn't concerned with glory. After the faked reports, he would play bridge with Marga Geier and Hans and Herr Stahl. He might play bridge for a long time.

Herr Stahl had really saved Jaeger's neck; the big investigator wondered if thetech man guessed what the mission had been about. Probably so; Stahl loved puzzles and mysteries, and it didn't take a genius to figure that Jaeger was making another raid into the Aensa keep. But Stahl never knew about the blue drug. Hans Weissmann never knew, either, and the same was true for the large majority of people on Earth. They would never believe how close they had come to utter hopelessness or destruction. And, naturally, they would never find out. Naturally, Jaeger had to go along with the cover-up. He had his duty. Hell. He was tired.

Huston and Teresky had met him, soon after the peace patrol soldiers had rescued him from the collapsing courtyard. Jaeger had been lifted onto a stretcher, and the medics had done their best to ease his pain. Huston had demanded that the IC representatives be allowed to talk with Jaeger; Teresky had gravely and speechlessly shaken Jaeger's hand, and Huston himself permitted slow tears to glisten on his hard face. They had learned about Healey's treachery, but too late. Healey had not kept the appointment to meet his colleagues, could not be traced; Teresky had guessed the truth. After a brief meeting with Jaeger, Huston and Teresky departed again; a promise had been made for a substantial transfer of IC Security Bureau funds to the JAEGER, INC. account, enough so that Jaeger wouldn't have to accept more mundane employment for a while. He was going to play a lot of bridge. And he'd even let old Herr Stahl win once in a while.

Corcail Sendijen had said farewell, while the medics were still tending to Jaeger's wounds. Of the entire affair, next to the death of Nati, the leave-taking of the tentacled alien was the most painful episode. Jaeger had formed an intense feeling of comradeship with Corcail Sendijen, oddly so, because they had been acquainted only a matter of hours. But Jaeger felt a rare sense of warmth and honor exuding from the being; he regretted that Corcail Sendijen had to go. But Huston explained the situation; according to the standards of the galactic government, whatever form it took, a new planet such as Earth could not be opened by an individual or a private commercial concern. Jaeger could see the fearful reactions of the soldiers who caught sight of Corcail Sendijen; that kind of feeling could not be permitted on a worldwide scale. It might eclipse the terror of the Thirty-Day Riots, after the Aensa were first contacted; after all, the Aensalords were more human-looking than Corcail Sendijen ever could be. So Corcail Sendijen would be returned to his brothers by an IC shuttle ship; the brothers now controlled the three Aensa warships. The Aensalords themselves were held captive in their own immobilizing devices; Corcail Sendijen and his brothers would navigate the ships back to the galactic center, turn the Aensa over to their authorities, and report Earth to the proper department. In time, a formal contact team would be sent, and Earth would be educated and groomed toward membership in the family of worlds. Jaeger tried to express his thanks to Corcail Sendijen, but the alien only waved a tentacle in one of his odd gestures. Jaeger didn't interpret the sign explicitly, but he felt an overwhelming glow of brotherhood, kinship, and respect pass over him. Then Corcail Sendijen was led aboard one of the helijets, and Jaeger was alone with his thoughts.

Remembering these things, which already seemed to Jaeger to have occurred days ago, weeks ago, rather than only a matter of two or three hours, he decided that what he needed most now was a complete break with the entire situation. He would ignore his aching body, and he would immerse himself in a flood of human triviality. He was saddened to think that there was no one whom he could call and complain to; this Aensa thing would have to stay locked inside him forever, to heal or fester as it would. But Jaeger could try to cover over the raw facts of the affair with flashy living. He didn't expect that would work, either, but he couldn't think of anything else to do.

First, though, he sat down and wrote a rough draft of the falsified report he would file in his office and with the SEPG, explaining such loose ends as the deaths of the Turk and Nati, Schiller's disappearance, and his own activities. He left all mention of the Aensa out of this report; he tried to make it seem that the upheaval at the Aensa keep was an independent, accidental occurrence. While sifting through the material on his desk in his apartment, Jaeger came across another copy of the Central Data fiche concerning Connor Coffey. There was a loose end, for sure. Jaeger thought for a moment, then smiled. He went to the telephone and called the message service. "Hello," he said, when a pretty but tired-looking young woman appeared on the screen, "I'd like to send a special delivery message, please."

"Certanly, sir," said the young woman. "Can I have the name and address of the party?"

"Mr. Connor Coffey," said Jaeger, adding Coffey's address.

"Your name and telephone number, please."

Jaeger complied. "The message is as follows: A last chance. Jaeger. Tonight." The woman repeated the brief message and Jaeger checked it. "Oh," he said, "enclose five hundred eurodollars with that, and charge it to my phone bill."

"Certainly," said the young woman, and Jaeger broke the connection. Then he made himself a drink and sat down to wait. He put some music on the omni set—at first, he had started to slip in the old Scott Joplin rags, but he caught himself. That music belonged with Nati. He could still hear her playing, in his mind; that was the only way he'd ever hear her play again. Rather than disturb that memory, Jaeger tossed the Joplin recordings into his wastebasket. In their place he put on a French woman whom the critics believed to sing very much like Edith Piaf. No one had ever heard Piaf, of course, and no records remained to compare; but, judging from the emotion and pathos of the songs themselves, Piaf must have been overwhelming. The new versions played softly in the dimly lit apartment. Jaeger wished that he could experience something that wasn't just an attempt to recreate something that had died a hundred years ago. His own profession was just that; he himself was an anachronism, no better than the unauthentic singers and musicians. And, he realized bitterly, it just might be that from now on, every woman he met would be just an unauthentic Nati. Nati, who had died a hundred years ago.

Jaeger was awakened by the sounds of someone trying to force his way into the apartment. Calmly, smiling, Jaeger went to the door. He stood behind it and unlocked it, so that when Coffey flung the door open, it would hide Jaeger from view. Coffey kicked the door and started firing. There were the coughing pops as the weapon spat holes into the wall opposite the door. "Coffey," said Jaeger softly, "you're an idiot. I sent you that letter."

Coffey stepped into the room, cautious and wary. He pointed the gun at Jaeger. "You sent it?"

"I signed it, didn't I?"

Coffey took the letter from his jacket pocket. The five hundred eurodollars fell to the carpet; Coffey didn't seem to notice. Jaeger covered the money with his foot. "It just says Jaeger here. I thought that meant that they were sending me after you again."

"No," said Jaeger. "I sent it. You can check with the telephone company." He led the bearded youth to the phone, dialed the message service, and spoke to the same young woman. She verified the matter to Coffey's satisfaction.

"All right," said Coffey, putting his gun away, "what do you want? I'm taking a chance being here, you know.

Especially if they didn't send me here. I think they're after me. I know they still are."

"No," said Jaeger, yawning, "no, they're not. That's why I wanted to see you. You hired me, remember? I just wanted to show you that your money wasn't wasted."

Coffey stared in disbelief. He was remembering how he had turned Jaeger over to the Turk and the blond giant. He wondered if Jaeger could really have fixed things with Coffey's employers. The thoughts were so easy to read in the youth's expressions, which changed moment by moment, as more strands in the tangled web claimed his attention. "You sure?" was all that he could say.

"I'm sure," said Jaeger. "You don't have anything to worry about. You were part of Schiller's machinery, or maybe Healey's. It doesn't make any difference. They're both dead."

Coffey relaxed a little. "Look—" he started to say, but Jaeger raised a hand.

"I know," said the big man, "you want to say that you're sorry for all the trouble you caused me. Don't think about it. You had a job to do. I had a job to do. Sometimes we just get unpleasant jobs, that's all."

"I'm glad you understand. Is there anything I can do to—"

"Just stand there," said Jaeger. He dropped one shoulder low, then swung up, his fist starting almost at knee level, moving in a perfect arc, a wonderfully clean, completely satisfying blow right on the very point of the youth's jaw. Coffey staggered back, then doubled over as Jaeger hit him again, in the gut. Jaeger allowed himself one last, final punch, again to Coffey's jaw; this time there was a faint but unmistakable cracking of bone. Coffey flew backward, through the door, into the hallway. He lay there, not moving. Jaeger slammed the door shut and walked to where the five hundred eurodollars lay. He considered tossing the money onto Coffey's inert body; instead, he just put it in his own pocket. Then he made himself another drink and sat down in Dark Lightning. He clicked the machine on and was instantly asleep.

It was late at night. Jaeger was blind. He was old, poor, and completely without vision. All there was about him was blackness. In the dream, Jaeger felt helpless. He felt old, but he couldn't even see his hands to verify that.

He had been staying at the home of a friend, and it was now time to depart. The friend came to him and said, "How will you find your way home? It is well past midnight, and there is no moonlight to guide you."

Jaeger laughed. "I am blind, my friend, remember? All the moonlight in the world would not aid me. Still, please, may I take a lantern with me?"

The friend was puzzled. "Why, Karl?" he asked. "As you say, you will not see any better with it."

"No," said Jaeger, "of course not. But other travelers will see me coming and will not run me down or trample me. I cannot avoid them, and if they cannot see me, they can't help but hurt me on these narrow rural lanes."

"Ah," said the friend respectfully, "that is very wise." And the friend gave Jaeger a lantern made of rice paper and bamboo strips, with a candle inside.

Jaeger set off in the direction of his poor hut. He had not walked more than a mile when suddenly he was struck painfully by someone walking in the opposite direction. Jaeger grew outraged. "What's the matter?" he shouted, very angry. "Are you blind, too? Can't you see this lantern I'm carrying?"

The other person laughed softly. "You forgot to light the candle," he said.

Jaeger awoke. He sat in the padded chair for a moment, blinking. He thought about the dream Dark Lighting had given him. He had been so sure of himself; he had thrashed Coffey, he had tied up all the loose ends, not to mention saving the world. But now he had been told off by a machine. Jaeger stared at his glass of scotch. He snorted. Then he laughed. Dark Lightning was always right. He sat in the black vinyl seat and laughed until the pain in his chest brought tears into his eyes.